Stan Lee PRESENTS

UNTOLD TALES OF SPIDER-MAN

A COLLECTION of ALL-NEW ADVENTURES SET in the EARLIEST DAYS of the WONDROUS WEB-SLINGER'S CAREER!

KURT BUSIEK
WRITER

PAT OLLIFFE
PENCILER

AL VEY
PAM EKLUND
AL MILGROM
INKERS

RICHARD STARKINGS
AND **COMICRAFT'S**
JOHN G. ROSHELL
LETTERING & DESIGN

STEVE MATTSSON
COLORIST

INTERIM MATERIAL BY
STAN LEE AND **STEVE DITKO**

GLENN GREENBERG
ASSISTANT EDITOR

TOM BREVOORT
EDITOR

BOB HARRAS
EDITOR IN CHIEF

UNTOLD TALES OF SPIDER-MAN® Originally published in magazine form as UNTOLD TALES OF SPIDER-MAN #'s 1 8. Published by MARVEL COMICS; 387 PARK AVENUE SOUTH, NEW YORK, N.Y. 10016. Printed in the U.S.A. First Printing, January, 1997. ISBN #0-7851-0263-9. GST #R127032852.

10 9 8 7 6 5 4 3 2 1

WHAT HAS COME BEFORE:
PETER PARKER WAS A SHY, UNASSUMING HONOR STUDENT AT MIDTOWN HIGH.
SALLY, I, EH, WAS WONDERING IF YOU'RE BUSY TONIGHT...?
PETER, FOR THE UMPTEENTH TIME, YOU'RE JUST NOT MY TYPE...
...NOT WHEN DREAM BOATS LIKE FLASH THOMPSON ARE AROUND!
I ADMIRE YOUR GOOD TASTE, DOLL! GET LOST, BOOKWORM!
OW!
WHILE ATTENDING A SCIENTIFIC DEMONSTRATION, PETER WAS BITTEN BY A SPIDER WHICH HAD ABSORBED A MASSIVE AMOUNT OF RADIATION.
REALIZING THAT HE HAD SOMEHOW GAINED THE SPIDER'S ABILITIES, PETER ADOPTED THE GUISE OF SPIDER-MAN, AND SET OUT TO MAKE HIS FORTUNE IN SHOW BUSINESS.
DRUNK ON HIS OWN SUCCESS, PETER ALLOWED AN ESCAPING THIEF TO GET PAST HIM, RATHER THAN TAKING THE EFFORT TO HALT HIS FLIGHT.
STOP! THIEF! STOP HIM! IF HE MAKES IT TO THE ELEVATOR, HE'LL GET AWAY!
SEVERAL DAYS LATER, AFTER RETURNING HOME FROM A PERFORMANCE, PETER WAS SHOCKED TO LEARN THAT HIS BELOVED UNCLE BEN HAD BEEN KILLED BY A BURGLAR.
BAD NEWS, SON--YOUR UNCLE HAS BEEN SHOT-- MURDERED!
UNCLE BEN --DEAD! NO, NO, IT CAN'T BE!
SPIDER-MAN TRACKED THE BURGLAR DOWN TO AN ABANDONED WAREHOUSE AND CAPTURED HIM --
-- ONLY TO DISCOVER THAT IT WAS THE SAME MAN HE'D ALLOWED TO ESCAPE AT THE TELEVISION STUDIO!
HAVING LEARNED THAT WITH GREAT POWER, THERE MUST ALSO COME GREAT RESPONSIBILITY, PETER SWORE THAT NO INNOCENT PERSON WOULD AGAIN COME TO HARM BECAUSE SPIDER-MAN FAILED TO ACT.

AS SPIDER-MAN'S CRIMEFIGHTING CAREER BEGAN, HE FOUND HE HAD A DETRACTOR IN J. JONAH JAMESON, CRUSADING PUBLISHER OF THE DAILY BUGLE.
WE CANNOT ALLOW THAT MASKED MENACE TO TAKE THE LAW INTO HIS OWN HANDS! HE IS A BAD INFLUENCE ON OUR YOUNGSTERS!
TELL ME, PARKER, ARE YOU A MAGICIAN? HOW DOES A TEEN-AGER LIKE YOU MANAGE TO GET PICTURES THAT OUR BEST STAFF PHOTOGS WOULD GIVE THEIR EYE TEETH FOR?
REMEMBER OUR DEAL, MR. JAMESON THAT'S MY SECRET! NOW IF YOU DON'T WAN THE PIX--
TURNING ADVERSITY INTO ADVANTAGE, PETE BEGAN TAKING PHOTOS OF HIS EXPLOITS AS SPIDER-MAN, AND THEN SELLING THEM TO JAMESON.
PETER ALSO FOUND HIMSELF BECOMING ATTRACTED TO JAMESON'S SECRETARY, BETTY BRANT.
I THINK PARKER IS RIGHT, SIR! I'VE HEARD SOME OF OUR READERS MENTION THAT THEY THINK YOU'RE JEALOUS OF SPIDER-MAN FOR SOME REASON!
WELL, WELL! I NEVER KNEW I HAD AN ALLY IN J.J.'S SECRETARY! AND I NEVER REALIZED HOW PRETTY BETTY BRANT WAS, EITHER.. TILL NOW!
THAT'S ENOUGH! I'M STILL THE PUBLISHER HERE, AND I'LL DECIDE OUR EDITORIAL POLICY!
MEANWHILE, SPIDER-MAN CONTINUED TO RACK UP VICTORY AFTER VICTORY AGAINST THE CITY'S MOST NOTORIOUS CRIMINALS, INCLUDING THE CHAMELEON, THE VULTURE, DR. OCTOPUS, THE SANDMAN, DR. DOOM, AND THE LIZARD.

UNTOLD TALES OF
SPIDER-MAN
1st ISSUE
SEPT • 1
MARVEL
SPIDER-MAN GROUP
DIRECT EDITION
00111 >
7 59606 04255 5

Bitten by a radioactive spider, high school student **Peter Parker** gained the spider's powers, and soon became the costumed crimefighter the entire world would one day come to know as **Spider-Man!** In the early days of his career, when his amazing powers were still new to him, the teenaged Spider-Man struggled to learn about himself and his abilities, while trying to lead a **normal life!** It would **not** be easy...

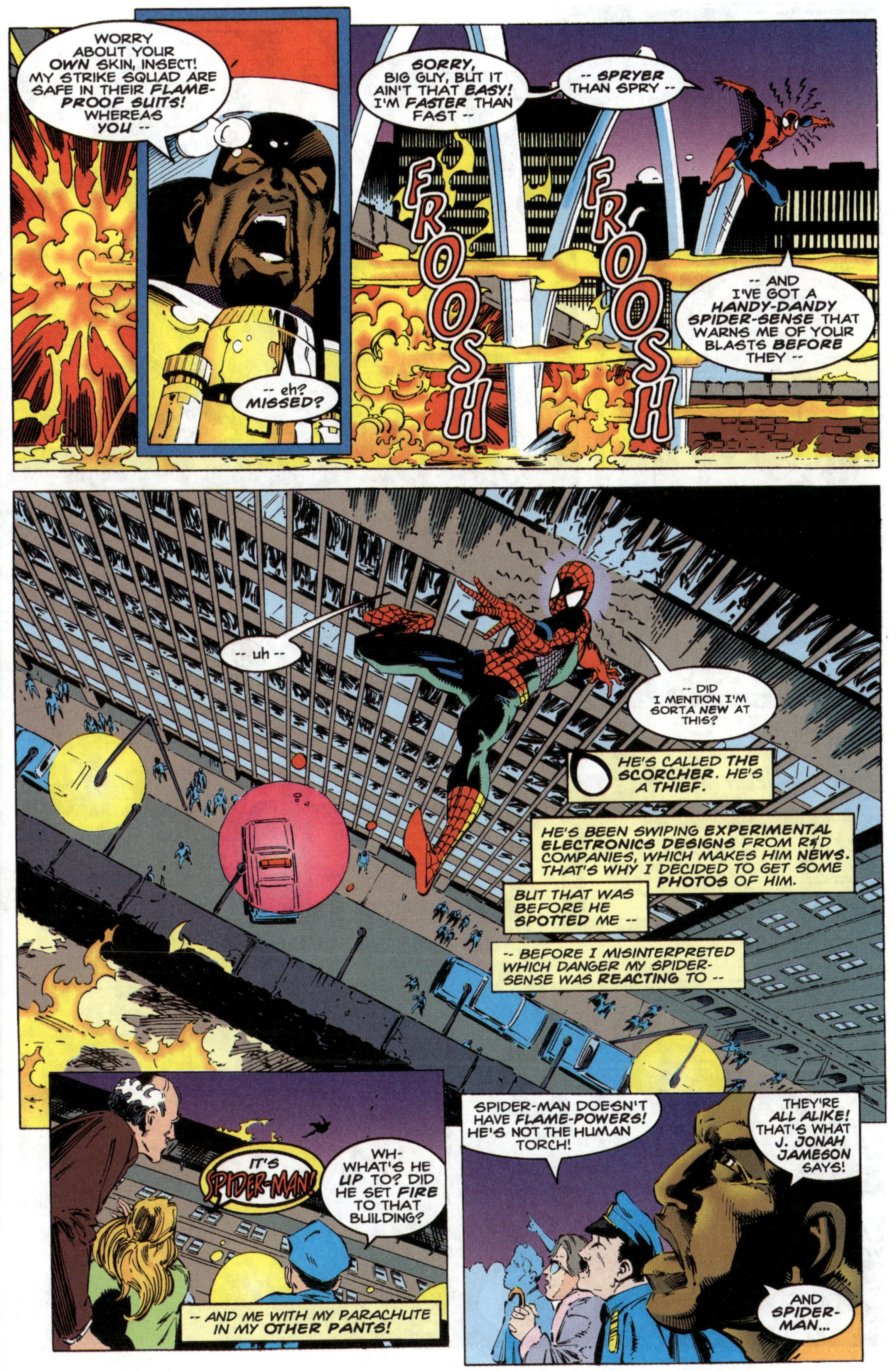
WORRY ABOUT YOUR OWN SKIN, INSECT! MY STRIKE SQUAD ARE SAFE IN THEIR FLAME-PROOF SUITS! WHEREAS YOU --
-- eh? MISSED?
SORRY, BIG GUY, BUT IT AIN'T THAT EASY! I'M FASTER THAN FAST --
-- SPRYER THAN SPRY --
FROOSH
FROOSH
-- AND I'VE GOT A HANDY-DANDY SPIDER-SENSE THAT WARNS ME OF YOUR BLASTS BEFORE THEY --
-- uh --
-- DID I MENTION I'M SORTA NEW AT THIS?
HE'S CALLED THE SCORCHER. HE'S A THIEF.
HE'S BEEN SWIPING EXPERIMENTAL ELECTRONICS DESIGNS FROM R&D COMPANIES, WHICH MAKES HIM NEWS. THAT'S WHY I DECIDED TO GET SOME PHOTOS OF HIM.
BUT THAT WAS BEFORE HE SPOTTED ME --
-- BEFORE I MISINTERPRETED WHICH DANGER MY SPIDER-SENSE WAS REACTING TO --
IT'S SPIDER-MAN!
WH-WHAT'S HE UP TO? DID HE SET FIRE TO THAT BUILDING?
-- AND ME WITH MY PARACHUTE IN MY OTHER PANTS!
SPIDER-MAN DOESN'T HAVE FLAME-POWERS! HE'S NOT THE HUMAN TORCH!
THEY'RE ALL ALIKE! THAT'S WHAT J. JONAH JAMESON SAYS!
AND SPIDER-MAN...

"-- HE'S THE WORST OF THE LOT!"
READ THE SPIDER-MAN MENACE IN THE DAILY BUGLE NEW YORK'S PICTURE NEWSPA
THWIP
WEB-SHOOTERS -- I LOVE YOU!
IT'S A THRILL TO BE ABLE TO SWING ALONG ABOVE THE CITY STREETS, BUT I'M STILL NOT 100 PERCENT WITH THESE THINGS --
-- AND IT GIVES ME BUTTERFLIES TO THINK ABOUT WHAT MIGHT HAPPEN IF I MISSED ONE OF THOSE FLAPPIN' FLAGPOLES!
BUT NOW --
HEY, SCORCHER! LET'S HAVE A GET-TOGETHER! MY FISTS -- YOUR FACE! WHADDYA SAY?
GO AWAY, SPIDER-MAN...
" -- YOU'RE STARTING TO ANNOY ME!"
FROOSH
AWP!
WASN'T PREPARED -- OFF-BALANCE --
-- NO TIME TO SNAG ANOTHER FLAGPOLE -- JUST GOTTA TWIST SO I CAN FIRE A WEB DOWNWARD -- AND --
THWIPIPIP
H-HE'S AFTER US!
BOOF
YEAH? LET'S SEE HIM TRY SOMETHING!

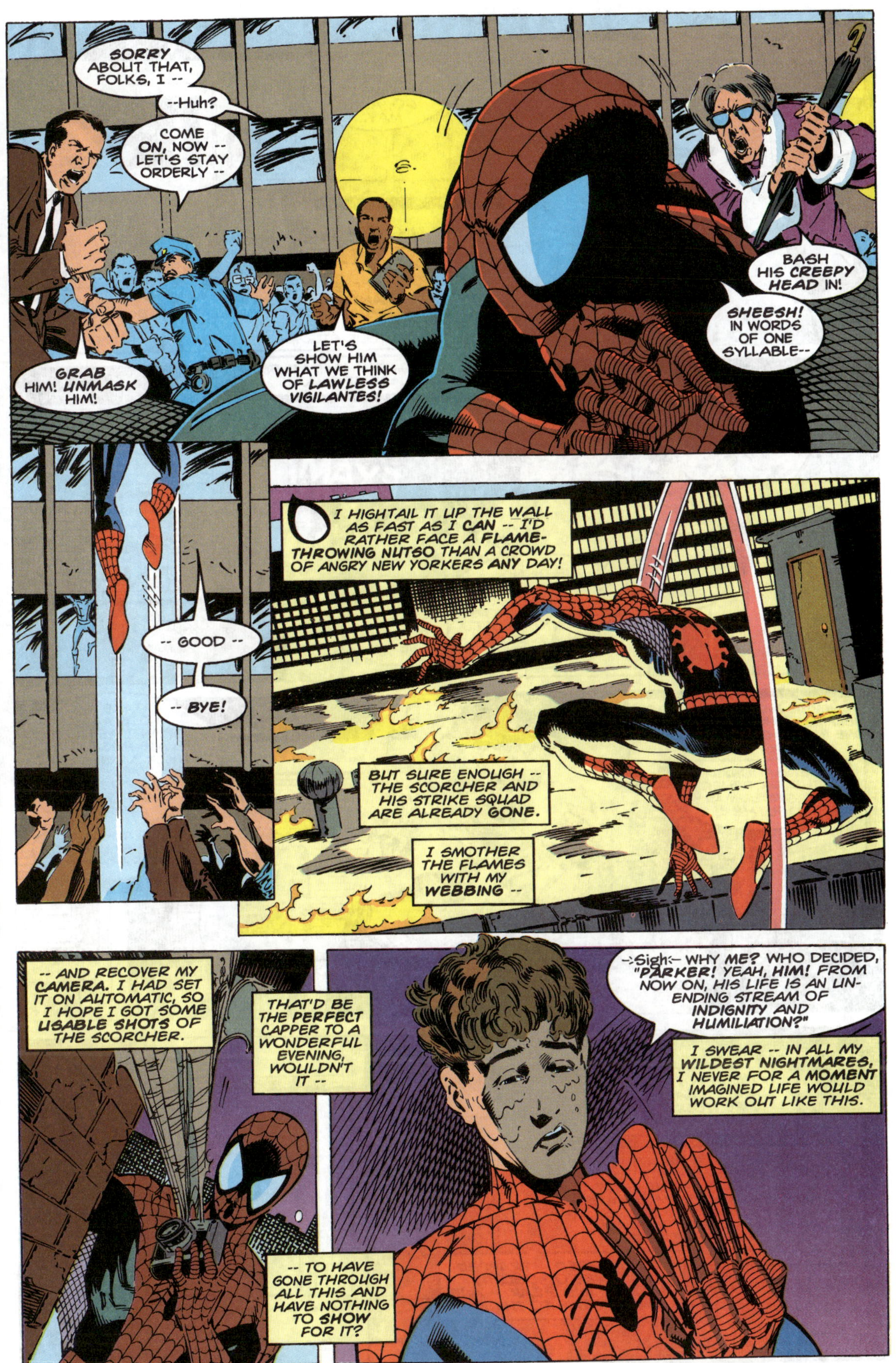
SORRY ABOUT THAT, FOLKS, I --
--Huh?
COME ON, NOW -- LET'S STAY ORDERLY --
BASH HIS CREEPY HEAD IN!
SHEESH! IN WORDS OF ONE SYLLABLE--
LET'S SHOW HIM WHAT WE THINK OF LAWLESS VIGILANTES!
GRAB HIM! UNMASK HIM!
-- GOOD --
-- BYE!
I HIGHTAIL IT UP THE WALL AS FAST AS I CAN -- I'D RATHER FACE A FLAME-THROWING NUTSO THAN A CROWD OF ANGRY NEW YORKERS ANY DAY!
BUT SURE ENOUGH -- THE SCORCHER AND HIS STRIKE SQUAD ARE ALREADY GONE.
I SMOTHER THE FLAMES WITH MY WEBBING --
-- AND RECOVER MY CAMERA. I HAD SET IT ON AUTOMATIC, SO I HOPE I GOT SOME USABLE SHOTS OF THE SCORCHER.
THAT'D BE THE PERFECT CAPPER TO A WONDERFUL EVENING, WOULDN'T IT --
-- TO HAVE GONE THROUGH ALL THIS AND HAVE NOTHING TO SHOW FOR IT?
-Sigh- WHY ME? WHO DECIDED, "PARKER! YEAH, HIM! FROM NOW ON, HIS LIFE IS AN UN-ENDING STREAM OF INDIGNITY AND HUMILIATION?"
I SWEAR -- IN ALL MY WILDEST NIGHTMARES, I NEVER FOR A MOMENT IMAGINED LIFE WOULD WORK OUT LIKE THIS.

I NEVER IMAGINED MY AUNT WOULD HAVE TO SCRIMP AND PINCH JUST TO KEEP A ROOF OVER OUR HEADS --
IF THERE'S ANYTHING I CAN DO, AUNT MAY...
NO, PETER -- THAT PART-TIME JOB OF YOURS AT THE DAILY BUGLE TAKES TOO MUCH TIME AWAY FROM YOUR STUDIES AS IT IS.
BUT DON'T WORRY. WE'LL MANAGE -- SOMEHOW...
-- NEVER IMAGINED THAT I'D BE A TOTAL OUTCAST AT SCHOOL --
EXAM
DID YOU HEAR THE ONE ABOUT PARKER?
HE DIDN'T HAVE A DATE FOR SATURDAY NIGHT 'CAUSE HIS FAVORITE TEST TUBE ELOPED WITH A BUNSEN BURNER!
OH, JASON -- YOU'RE SO MEAN!
-- NEVER IMAGINED I'D BE HELPING MAKE SURE EVERY-ONE IN THE CITY DISTRUSTS AND DESPISES ME --
SENSATIONAL! THE SCORCHER AND SPIDER-MAN -- TOGETHER!
TAKE A NOTE, MISS BRANT! WE'LL RE-PLATE PAGE ONE, WITH A BANNER HEAD-LINE -- "THE SCORCHER AND SPIDER-MAN: PARTNERS IN CRIME?"
WHAT, YOU STILL HERE, PARKER?
I GUESS I JUST NEVER IMAGINED LIFE WOULD BE THIS HARD.
I HAVE THESE AMAZING SUPER-POWERS -- STRENGTH, SPEED, AGILITY -- BUT WHAT DOES IT GET ME? I'M ALWAYS HIDING, ALWAYS KEEPING SECRETS -- LYING TO MY AUNT EVERY TIME I PRETEND I'M A NORMAL KID!
I'M TRAPPED -- TRAPPED IN A WEB OF DECEIT, HATRED AND FEAR -- AND I'M STARTING TO THINK --
-- THAT I ALWAYS WILL BE!

IT WASN'T ALWAYS LIKE THIS --
I COOKED YOUR FAVORITE BREAKFAST, PETEY -- WHEAT-CAKES!
DON'T FATTEN HIM UP TOO MUCH, DEAR! I CAN HARDLY OUT-WRESTLE HIM NOW!
-- I USED TO BE A NORMAL, EVERY-DAY KID -- UNTIL THAT SCIENCE EXHIBIT --
-- UNTIL I GOT BITTEN BY THAT RADIOACTIVE SPIDER -- AND SOME-HOW GAINED ITS BIZARRE ABILITIES!
I WANTED TO CASH IN ON MY POWERS, SO I DESIGNED A COSTUME -- BECAME A TV CELEBRITY --
-- BUT I WAS TOO SELFISH, TOO BUSY THINKING ABOUT MY-SELF TO HELP A COP STOP A BURGLAR --
STOP! THIEF! STOP HIM!
-- AND MY UNCLE BEN PAID FOR THAT MISTAKE -- WITH HIS LIFE!.
I CAUGHT HIS MURDERER -- BUT IF I'D ONLY ACTED EARLIER, UNCLE BEN WOULD STILL BE ALIVE!
SINCE THEN, I'VE TRIED TO LIVE UP TO THE RESPONSIBILITIES THAT GO WITH POWERS LIKE MINE, AND IT'S LED TO SOME PRETTY WILD ADVENTURES --

-- BUT IT'S SO HARD TO BE AN OUTCAST, AS BOTH PETER PARKER AND SPIDER-MAN.
AND JONAH JAMESON DOESN'T MAKE IT ANY EASIER, WITH HIS ONE-MAN CRUSADE AGAINST SPIDEY, SMEARING ME EVERY CHANCE HE GETS --
PETER? PETER! I BROUGHT YOUR CHECK...
Huh?
HONESTLY, YOU'VE BEEN STARING OUT THAT WINDOW FOR TEN MINUTES! ARE YOU ALL RIGHT?
Oh, uh, SURE, BETTY -- I WAS JUST, UH, WOOL-GATHERING. UM, LISTEN, BETTY -- THERE'S SOMETHING I'VE BEEN MEANING TO ASK YOU --
YES, PETER?
WOULD YOU -- I MEAN, DO YOU THINK WE COULD --
EUREKA!
I WANT ALL THE PHOTOS PARKER'S TAKEN TO DATE! I'LL PRINT A GALLERY -- SHOWING THAT BLASTED WALL-CRAWLER CONSORTING WITH KNOWN CRIMINALS!
HE MUST BE IN CAHOOTS WITH THEM -- AFTER ALL, IF SPIDER-MAN ISN'T A CROOK, WHY WOULD THE POLICE HAVE WARRANTS OUT ON HIM?
THAT'S CRACKERS! THE ONLY REASON THERE ARE WARRANTS ON ME IS BECAUSE JAMESON BULLIED THE COPS AND THE F.B.I. INTO IT!
MOST OF THE POLICE DON'T THINK I'M A MENACE -- THEY THINK I'M A HELP TO THEM! THEY --
HEY! THAT'S IT!
SORRY, BETTY -- GOTTA RUN! I'LL CATCH YOU LATER!
WELL, MISS BRANT? DON'T JUST STAND THERE LIKE AN EMPTY-HEADED TEENAGER!
THIS IS AN OFFICE, NOT A MALT SHOPPE!

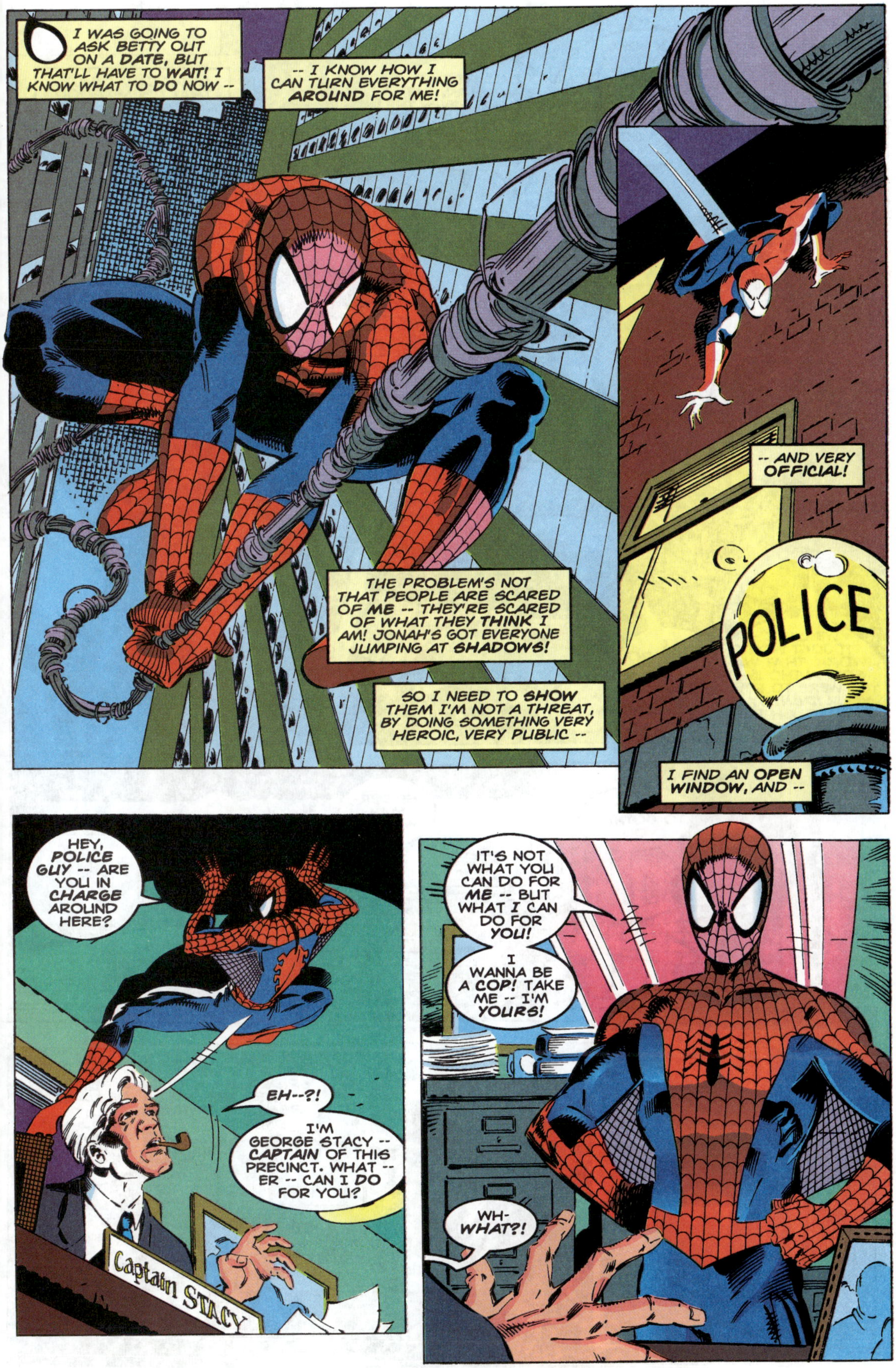

I WAS GOING TO ASK BETTY OUT ON A *DATE*, BUT THAT'LL HAVE TO *WAIT!* I KNOW WHAT TO *DO* NOW --

-- I KNOW HOW I CAN TURN EVERYTHING *AROUND* FOR ME!

THE PROBLEM'S NOT THAT PEOPLE ARE SCARED OF *ME* -- THEY'RE SCARED OF WHAT THEY *THINK* I AM! JONAH'S GOT EVERYONE JUMPING AT *SHADOWS!*

SO I NEED TO *SHOW* THEM I'M NOT A THREAT, BY DOING SOMETHING VERY HEROIC, VERY PUBLIC --

-- AND VERY *OFFICIAL!*

POLICE

I FIND AN *OPEN WINDOW*, AND --

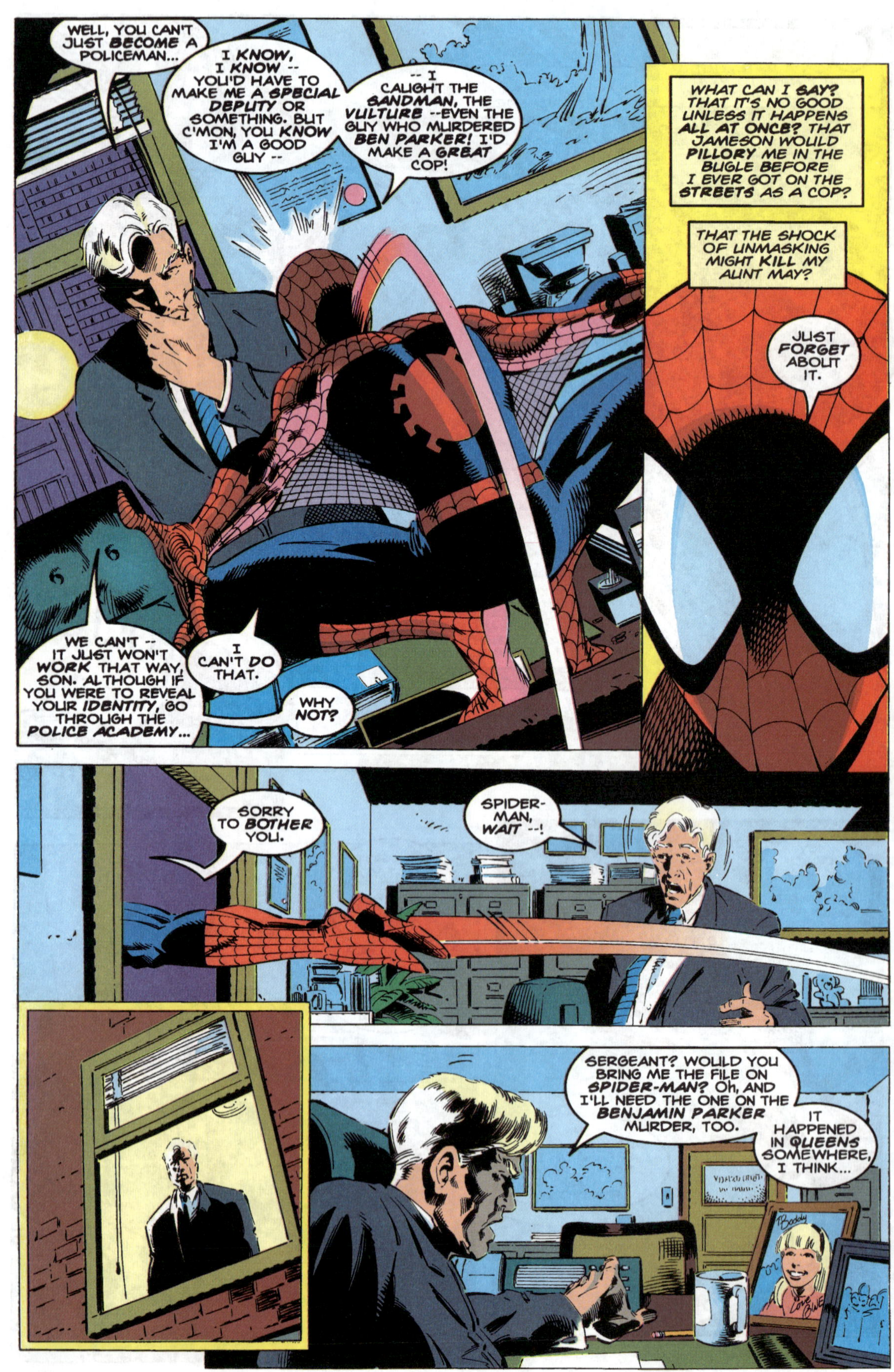
WELL, YOU CAN'T JUST BECOME A POLICEMAN...
I KNOW, I KNOW -- YOU'D HAVE TO MAKE ME A SPECIAL DEPUTY OR SOMETHING. BUT C'MON, YOU KNOW I'M A GOOD GUY --
-- I CAUGHT THE SANDMAN, THE VULTURE --EVEN THE GUY WHO MURDERED BEN PARKER! I'D MAKE A GREAT COP!
WE CAN'T -- IT JUST WON'T WORK THAT WAY, SON. ALTHOUGH IF YOU WERE TO REVEAL YOUR IDENTITY, GO THROUGH THE POLICE ACADEMY...
I CAN'T DO THAT.
WHY NOT?
WHAT CAN I SAY? THAT IT'S NO GOOD UNLESS IT HAPPENS ALL AT ONCE? THAT JAMESON WOULD PILLORY ME IN THE BUGLE BEFORE I EVER GOT ON THE STREETS AS A COP?
THAT THE SHOCK OF UNMASKING MIGHT KILL MY AUNT MAY?
JUST FORGET ABOUT IT.
SORRY TO BOTHER YOU.
SPIDER-MAN, WAIT --!
SERGEANT? WOULD YOU BRING ME THE FILE ON SPIDER-MAN? Oh, AND I'LL NEED THE ONE ON THE BENJAMIN PARKER MURDER, TOO.
IT HAPPENED IN QUEENS SOMEWHERE, I THINK...

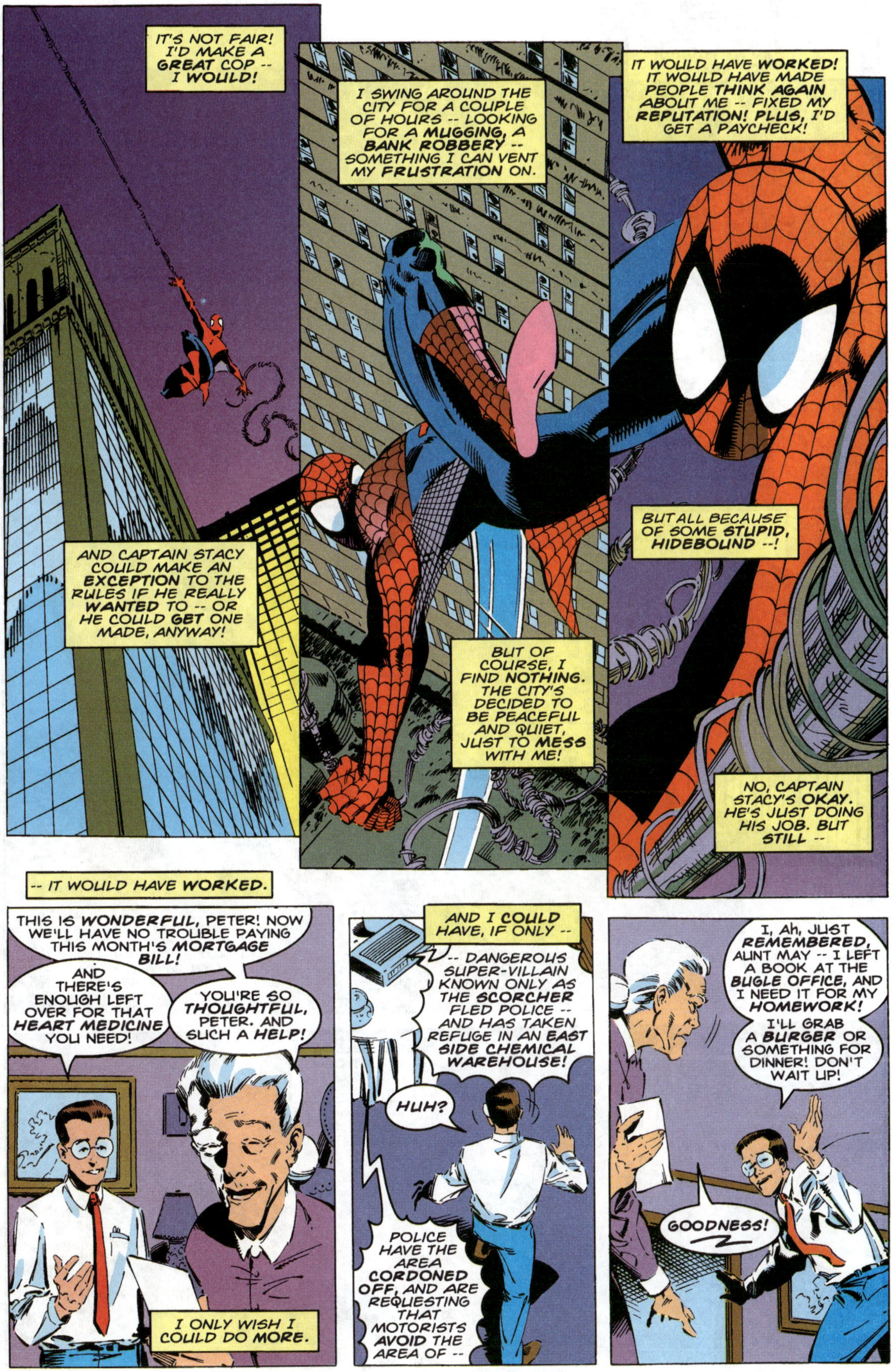

IT'S NOT FAIR! I'D MAKE A **GREAT** COP -- I **WOULD!**

AND CAPTAIN STACY COULD MAKE AN **EXCEPTION** TO THE RULES IF HE REALLY **WANTED** TO -- OR HE COULD **GET** ONE MADE, ANYWAY!

I SWING AROUND THE CITY FOR A COUPLE OF HOURS -- LOOKING FOR A **MUGGING**, A **BANK ROBBERY** -- SOMETHING I CAN VENT MY **FRUSTRATION** ON.

BUT OF COURSE, I FIND **NOTHING**. THE CITY'S DECIDED TO BE PEACEFUL AND QUIET, JUST TO **MESS** WITH ME!

IT WOULD HAVE **WORKED!** IT WOULD HAVE MADE PEOPLE **THINK AGAIN** ABOUT ME -- FIXED MY **REPUTATION! PLUS**, I'D GET A PAYCHECK!

BUT ALL BECAUSE OF SOME **STUPID, HIDEBOUND** --!

NO, CAPTAIN STACY'S **OKAY**. HE'S JUST DOING HIS JOB. BUT **STILL** --

-- IT WOULD HAVE **WORKED**.

I'M GOING TO PROVE TO THE POLICE THAT I CAN BE USEFUL TO THEM --
-- GET CAPTAIN STACY TO MAKE THAT EXCEPTION --
-- BY BRINGING IN THE SCORCHER FOR THEM!
THEY'VE GOT THE PLANT SURROUNDED PRETTY WELL --
-- EXCEPT FOR ONE AREA AT THE NORTH END! THE SCORCHER AND HIS MEN COULD SLIP OUT THIS WAY, AND THE COPS WOULD NEVER SPOT THEM!
IT'S NOT OBVIOUS FROM THE GROUND, BUT IT JUMPS RIGHT OUT AT YOU FROM THE AIR.
JUST ONE MORE LITTLE REASON --
POLICE DEPARTMENT

-- THEY NEED SOMEONE LIKE ME!
I-I DON'T LIKE THIS, SCORCHER! THERE'S COPS ALL OVER THE PLACE -- HOW'RE WE GONNA GET OUT?
MARC, MARC, MARC! YOU'VE GOT TO LEARN TO RELAX!
WE'VE COMPLETED ALL OUR ROBBERIES, AND WE'RE READY TO HAND OVER THE SCHEMATICS AND CASH IN! DON'T WORRY --
-- EVERYTHING'S GOING ACCORDING TO PLAN!
Oh, REALLY?
AM I PART OF YOUR PLAN? HOW ABOUT SURRENDER -- IS THAT PART OF YOUR SCHEME?
WHAKK
GHUH!
SPIDER-MAN! HE GOT CARL!
FROOSH FROOSH FROOSH
DIDN'T THINK SO!
WELL, THERE'S BEEN A CHANGE OF PLANS, BIG GUY --

-- YOU'RE UNDER ARREST!
YOU'RE JOKING, SPIDER-MAN!
FROOSH FROOSH
YOU MAY BE ABLE TO DODGE MY FLAME-BLASTS FOR A MINUTE OR TWO -- BUT I ONLY NEED TO HIT YOU ONCE!
HE HAS A POINT -- THIS ISN'T LIKE THE ROOFTOP LAST NIGHT! IN AN ENCLOSED SPACE LIKE THIS, IT'S HARDER TO DODGE -- AND THE HEAT --
-- IT'S TURNING INTO AN OVEN HERE!
-- MAYBE THIS WASN'T AS GOOD AN IDEA AS I THOUGHT...
GRAB HIM! HOLD HIM DOWN -- SO THE BOSS CAN FINISH HIM OFF!
HEY, WHAT IS THIS? I HAVE TO STAY OUT OF THE WAY OF THE FLAMES, BUT YOUR FIREPROOF SUITS LET YOU COME AT ME FROM ANY DIRECTION?
AND YOU CALL THAT FAIR?
I'LL SHUT YOUR YAPPING MOUTH, SMART GUY!
YOU WILL? HOW -- LIKE THIS?
WRAK
I'VE GOT HIM! I'VE -- Huh?
WELL, AT LEAST THERE'S ONE THING I DON'T HAVE TO WORRY ABOUT --
-- THE EVIDENCE!
IN THAT FLAME-PROOF BRIEF-CASE, IT'S PERFECTLY SAFE UNTIL THE BATTLE'S OVER!
CORDON TO DISPATCH -- GET CAPTAIN STACY ON THE HORN, WILLYA?
WE'VE GOT A LITTLE PROBLEM HERE...

I CAN'T TELL WHERE ANYTHING IS. THE FLAMES, THROWING GIANT, SHIFTING SHADOWS -- THE SMOKE OVER EVERYTHING --
-- IT'S LIKE BEING IN SOME HELLISH FUNHOUSE, AND IT GETS TO ME -- I FIND MYSELF PANICKING, LASHING OUT AT NOTHING --
-- UNTIL I FORCE MYSELF TO RELAX -- TO TRUST MY SPIDER-SENSE -- TO STOP DODGING AND START CONNECTING --
KRAKTHUDD
-- AND SOON --
WELL, WHADDYA KNOW?
EVERY-ONE'S -KOFF- DOWN FOR THE COUNT!
I TRY TO TAKE A BREATH -- GET SOME AIR -- BUT IT'S SO HOT -- SEARING --
KOFF KOFF
I'VE GOT TO END THIS --
-- BEFORE I CAN'T BREATHE AT ALL!
IT'S JUST YOU AND ME! COME ON, THEN!
COME ON!

HOLD YOUR -koff- HORSES, SCORCH!
OR ARE YOU IN A -koff- HURRY TO GET YOUR HEAD HANDED TO YOU?
HE'S ALMOST TOO HOT TO APPROACH -- AND WAY TOO HOT TO TOUCH--
-- SO I MAKE DO!
KWHAM
IS THAT THE BEST YOU CAN MANAGE, SPIDER-MAN? GO AHEAD -- TRY AGAIN.
KRAMM
BRAKK
KOFF
KLUDD
KOFF KOFF
KOFF KOFF
IT'S NO GOOD --
-- THE HEAT'S TOO INTENSE -- PUSHING ME BACK -- INCINERATING MY WEBBING -- SMOKE INHALATION GETTING TO ME --

YOU'RE AN IDIOT, SPIDER-MAN!
EVERY-THING YOU'VE DONE HAS PLAYED RIGHT INTO MY HANDS. I CAN KILL YOU, AND THEN JUST WALTZ OUT OF HERE --
-- WHILE THE COPS HAVE TO DEAL WITH THE BURNING BUILDING!
HE'S RIGHT --
THE POLICE WON'T BE ABLE TO CHASE HIM -- THEY'LL HAVE TO BE MAKING SURE RESIDENTS EVACUATE THE AREA!
OTHERWISE, ONCE THE FLAMES REACH THE CHEMICAL STORAGE TANKS ON THE LOWER FLOORS --
-- THOUSANDS COULD DIE!
KOFF! KOFF!
KOFF!
THE FIRE'S ALREADY BURNED THROUGH THE ROOF --
-- AND IT'S SPREADING FAST --
SO.
WHAT'LL IT BE? FLAME-BROILED -- OR SLOW-ROASTED?

FROOSH
TARTARE, THANKS!
YOU'VE ALREADY -Koff- LIGHTLY SEARED THE OUTSIDE -- AND I PREFER MY INSIDES -Koff- RAW!
CAN BARELY MOVE --
-- BUT IF THOSE TANKS BLOW -- IF INNOCENT PEOPLE DIE --
-- IT'LL BE PARTLY MY FAULT, FOR STARTING THIS FIGHT --
LIE DOWN AND DIE, SPIDER-MAN!
THWIP
THWIP
NO --
-- I CAN'T LET THAT HAPPEN!
THAPP
I PULL WITH ALL MY MIGHT -- BUT MY STRENGTH'S ALMOST GONE --
-- I'M PRAYING THE FLAMES WEAKENED THE TOWER'S SUPPORTS --

-- AND THEY HAVE --
KRAKAKKKK
SHLOOOSH
SSSSSSSS
TONS OF WATER SLAM DOWN, HITTING US LIKE A SLEDGEHAMMER. I DUCK THE WORST OF IT, BUT IT STILL BATTERS ME NEARLY SENSELESS.
THE SCORCHER GETS IT WORSE, THOUGH. THE SUDDEN COLD SHATTERS HIS HELMET, CRACKS HIS ARMOR --

-- AND ONCE IT'S ALL OVER --
HEY, ANYBODY HERE LOOKING FOR A SLIGHTLY DRENCHED SUPER-VILLAIN? ALL PART OF THE SPIDEY SERVICE!
I ALSO PUT OUT FIRES!
THERE YOU ARE --
-- YOU BONEHEAD! YOU INCOMPETENT! DO YOU REALIZE WHAT YOU'VE DONE?
Er, CAPTURED A DANGEROUS CRIMINAL AND HIS GANG AFTER YOU COULDN'T HANDLE THEM?
EASY, PIETRANTONIO. I'LL HANDLE THIS.
I'M AFRAID YOU'VE DISRUPTED A VERY CAREFULLY PLANNED OPERATION, SPIDER-MAN.
WHAT? I CAUGHT THE GUY! WHAT'S WRONG WITH THAT?!
THE SCORCHER WAS SUPPOSED TO ESCAPE. HE WAS WORKING FOR SOMEONE, BUT WE DIDN'T KNOW WHO --
-- SO WE DELIBERATELY LEFT A HOLE IN OUR CORDON, HOPING HE'D "ESCAPE" AND LEAD US TO THE REAL MASTERMIND.
NOW --
OSBORN Chemical INC
-- WE HAVE NO IDEA WHO WANTED THOSE ELECTRONICS PLANS --
-- OR FOR WHAT...

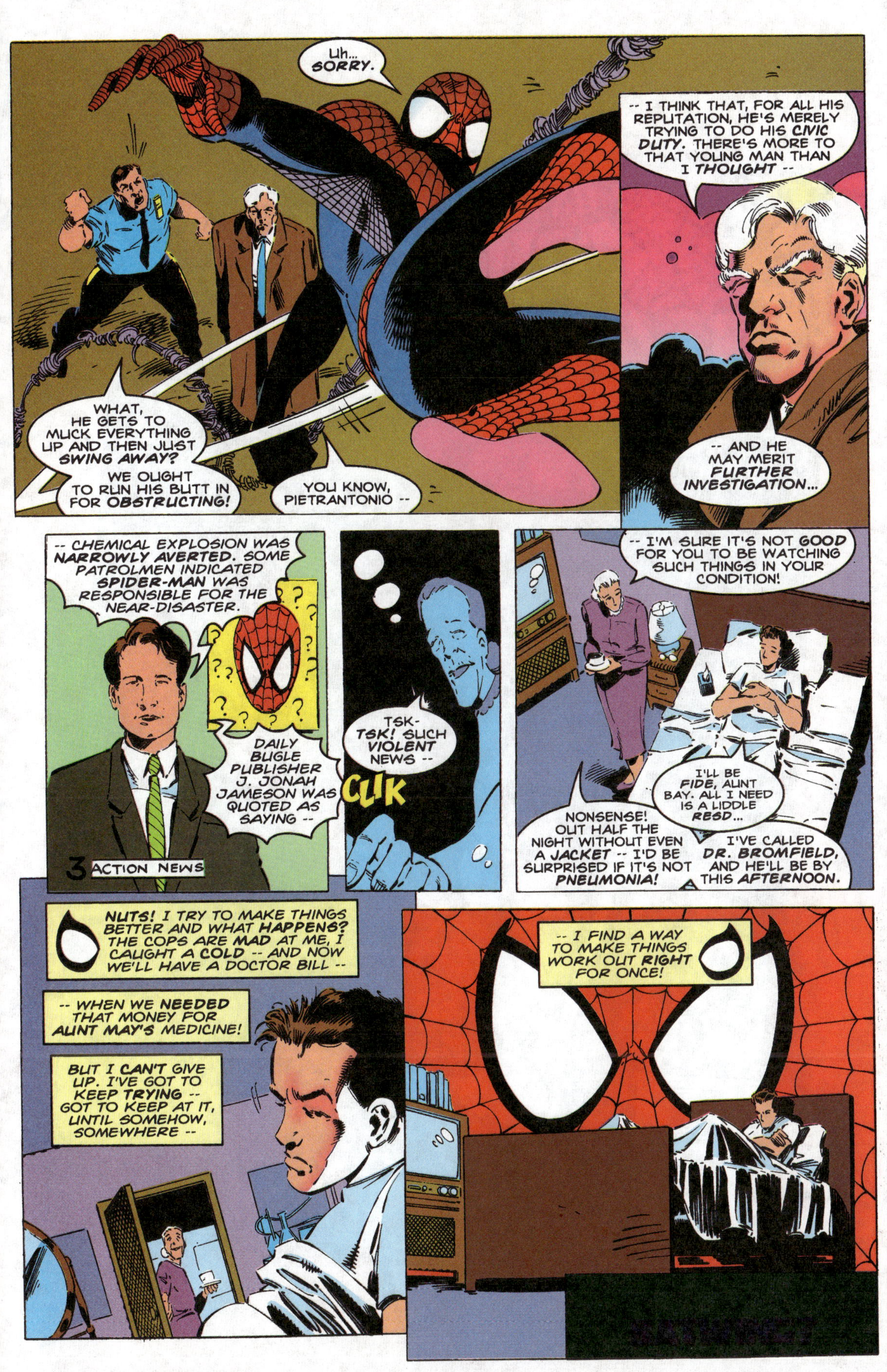

UH... SORRY.
WHAT, HE GETS TO MUCK EVERYTHING UP AND THEN JUST SWING AWAY?
WE OUGHT TO RUN HIS BUTT IN FOR OBSTRUCTING!
YOU KNOW, PIETRANTONIO --
-- I THINK THAT, FOR ALL HIS REPUTATION, HE'S MERELY TRYING TO DO HIS CIVIC DUTY. THERE'S MORE TO THAT YOUNG MAN THAN I THOUGHT --
-- AND HE MAY MERIT FURTHER INVESTIGATION...
-- CHEMICAL EXPLOSION WAS NARROWLY AVERTED. SOME PATROLMEN INDICATED SPIDER-MAN WAS RESPONSIBLE FOR THE NEAR-DISASTER.
DAILY BUGLE PUBLISHER J. JONAH JAMESON WAS QUOTED AS SAYING --
3 ACTION NEWS
TSK-TSK! SUCH VIOLENT NEWS --
CLIK
-- I'M SURE IT'S NOT GOOD FOR YOU TO BE WATCHING SUCH THINGS IN YOUR CONDITION!
I'LL BE FIDE, AUNT BAY. ALL I NEED IS A LIDDLE RESD...
NONSENSE! OUT HALF THE NIGHT WITHOUT EVEN A JACKET -- I'D BE SURPRISED IF IT'S NOT PNEUMONIA!
I'VE CALLED DR. BROMFIELD, AND HE'LL BE BY THIS AFTERNOON.
NUTS! I TRY TO MAKE THINGS BETTER AND WHAT HAPPENS? THE COPS ARE MAD AT ME, I CAUGHT A COLD -- AND NOW WE'LL HAVE A DOCTOR BILL --
-- WHEN WE NEEDED THAT MONEY FOR AUNT MAY'S MEDICINE!
BUT I CAN'T GIVE UP. I'VE GOT TO KEEP TRYING -- GOT TO KEEP AT IT, UNTIL SOMEHOW, SOMEWHERE --
-- I FIND A WAY TO MAKE THINGS WORK OUT RIGHT FOR ONCE!

UNTOLD TALES OF
SPIDER-MAN
ONLY 99¢
$1.35 CAN
OCT • 2
MARVEL
SPIDER-MAN GROUP
DIRECT EDITION
IT STALKS BY NIGHT!

CASTLES IN THE AIR
Ah, A FULL MOON -- A MIDNIGHT SNACK -- A BOTTLE OR TWO OF DOM PERIGNON --
-- AND YOU, MY DEAR! WHAT COULD BE MORE PERFECT?
Oh, RANDOLPH -- YOU'RE SO ROMANTIC!
The creature moves silently on the night wind.
Its approach is swift, sure and undetected --
TERROR STALKS THE CITY SKIES THANKS TO
KURT BUSIEK WRITER
PAT OLLIFFE PENCILER
AL VEY W/PAM EKLUND INKERS
RICHARD STARKINGS AND COMICRAFT LETTERING
STEVE MATTSSON COLORS
TOM BREVOORT EDITOR
BOB BUDIANSKY EDITOR IN CHIEF

-- until --
SHRIIIIIIIIIIIIIIIIIII
Ah --?
WH-WHAT?
N-NO! PLEASE!
I'M A CITY COUNCILMAN! I'M WEALTHY! I CAN PAY YOU!
TAKE THE GIRL! NOT ME! NOT ME!
RANDOLPH!
RANDOLPH!
-- the creature strikes --
-- and is gone.
P-PLEASE..
R-RANDOLPH?
C'MON C'MON C'MON C'MON C'MON C'MON!
GOTTA POUR ON THE SPEED --
-- ONLY MINUTES TO GO -- MAYBE LESS --

Dressing quickly, Peter Parker stifles a **yawn**. He was up **too late** the night before --
-- BEFORE *SCHOOL* STARTS!

-- searching for the **winged creature** the whole city's **abuzz** about.
Somebody's got to catch it before it **hurts** someone --

-- and if he gets some **news photos** to sell to the Daily Bugle along the way, that'd be **good**, too.
HEY, HERE'S *"PUNY" PARKER!* MAN, HE'S *MOVIN'* --
And **hey** --
-- that **reward** sure wouldn't hurt, **either!**
-- WE COULD USE A *WIDE RECEIVER* THAT FAST ON THE FOOTBALL TEAM!
PARKER? HE PROBABLY JUST CAN'T WAIT FOR *CHEM CLASS* -- IT'S GOT HIM ALL A-*TINGLE!* HERE, WATCH ME *TRIP* --
DAILY BUGLE
WINGED MENACE ATTACKS COUNCILMAN
Cherryh Offers $25,000 Reward
-- *HUH?* *SIDE-STEPPED?* BUT HE WASN'T EVEN --
ONE *SIDE,* IONELLO --
-- LET A *PRO* SHOW YOU HOW IT'S *DONE!*
OOF!
WHUMP
FLASH THOMPSON -- YOU ARE *REALLY* TOO MUCH -- !

Y'KNOW, PARKER, YOU REALLY OUGHT TO **WATCH** WHERE YOU'RE GOING.

IMAGINE IF THAT WAS AN **IRON LAMPPOST**, INSTEAD OF SOFT, CUDDLY **ME!**

YOU **DELIBERATELY** STEPPED IN FRONT OF ME, FLASH!

HEY! TAKE A LOOK AT **THIS**, GANG!

PARKER WAS SIMPLY **ABSORBED** BY THE NEWS OF THE DAY! GONNA GO FOR THE **REWARD**, PARKER? MAYBE BECOME A **BIG-GAME HUNTER?**

I CAN SEE IT **NOW** -- PETER PARKER, THE NEXT **SERGEI KRAVINOV!**

VERY **FUNNY**, JASON.

AW, **EASE UP**, PETER -- THEY'RE ONLY HAVING A LITTLE FUN. SCHOOL'S BORING **ENOUGH** -- WE'VE GOT TO FIND SOME EXCITEMENT **SOMEWHERE!**

HAPPY TO BE A CLOWN FOR YOUR **AMUSEMENT**, SALLY.

HEY, TINY, **THANKS!**

THANKS, **NOTHIN'** -- THESE ARE **MINE**. YOU KNOCKED 'EM OUTTA MY HANDS WHEN YOU FELL.

WHAT?! THOSE ARE **MY** MATH NOTES, TINY --

-- **GIVE 'EM BACK!**

I SAID THEY'RE **MINE**, PARKER. NOW GO TO CLASS AND **SHUT UP** -- OR I'LL REARRANGE YOUR **FACE!**

CLANGCLANG

He could put Tiny McKeever through a **window** if he wanted -- a **fourth-story** window. But he can't --

-- not without exposing his **secret identity**. He hears the girls giggle as he walks off -- maybe he **will** get that reward, he thinks.

CLANGCLAN LAN

And maybe he'll **use** it to move himself and Aunt May to another part of the **city** --

-- where kids aren't such **jerks!**

COME OUT, COME OUT, WHEREVER YOU ARE!
After school, he looks around some more.
He stops two muggings and a purse-snatching, but sees no sign of the creature.

Oh, YOO-HOO --
-- LITTLE LEATHER-SKINNED TERROR OF THE SKIES --
It sure would be nice.
Not to have to worry about money -- to feel secure, instead of constantly juggling...

-- PAPA NEEDS NEW SHOES!
AND A HOUSE.
...desperately afraid that this month it'll all fall apart.
AND A YACHT.
It sure would be nice.

OH, PETER--I DIDN'T SEE YOU COME IN. YOU STAY OUT SO LATE THESE DAYS--NEGLECT YOUR SLEEP...
YOU KNOW, AUNT MAY, IF THEY EVER GAVE OUT MEDALS FOR WORRYING -- YOU'D TAKE THE BLUE RIBBON, EASY!
BUT IT'S OKAY -- I'M TURNING IN RIGHT NOW.
WELL, YOU HAVE SWEET DREAMS, THEN -- BUT DON'T DENY AN OLD WOMAN HER LITTLE PLEASURES. IF I CAN'T WORRY ABOUT MY FAVORITE NEPHEW --
-- WHO CAN I WORRY ABOUT?
And what about Aunt May, huh?
She works so hard -- struggles to keep a roof over their heads --

-- doesn't she deserve a break, too?
DAILY BUGLE
TELL ME IT'S NOT TRUE, SOMEBODY --
-- TELL ME THAT THING THEY'RE CALLING BATWING DIDN'T STRIKE AGAIN LAST NIGHT, PANICKING LATE-NIGHT DINERS AT THE ROOFTOP RESTAURANT --
-- AND NOT A SINGLE PAPER IN TOWN HAD A PHOTOGRAPHER PRESENT!
WE'RE LOOKING LIKE LAUGHINGSTOCKS, PEOPLE! WE'RE LOOKING LIKE --
-- WAS WONDERING, BETTY -- IF YOU'RE NOT DOING ANYTHING SPECIAL THIS FRIDAY, uh --
YES, PETER?
PARKER!
-Ulp- I WAS KINDA HOPING HE WOULDN'T SEE ME...
GOT ANY PHOTOS FOR ME TODAY, PARKER? ANY ACTION SHOTS OF A CERTAIN AERIAL HORROR? ANY CANDID SNAPS FOR FRONT-PAGE CONSUMPTION?
Er, NO SIR. I WAS, eh, JUST TALKING TO MISS BRANT HERE ABOUT SEEING THE BATWING FILE -- MAYBE FIGURING OUT WHERE HE'LL STRIKE NEXT...
YOU DO THAT, PARKER -- BUT TALK TO SHUTT -- HE'S THE MAN ON THE STORY. AND IN THE MEANTIME --
-- IF YOU WANT TO MAKE TIME WITH MY SECRETARY, DO IT AFTER WORK!
Uh, YESSIR.
PETER?
BLASTED TEENAGERS! THINK THE WORLD'S RUN FOR THEIR EXCLUSIVE BENEFIT!
I'LL, uh, TALK TO YOU LATER, BETTY...
She must think I'm a total wimp, caving in like that, he thinks. But if I had that reward...

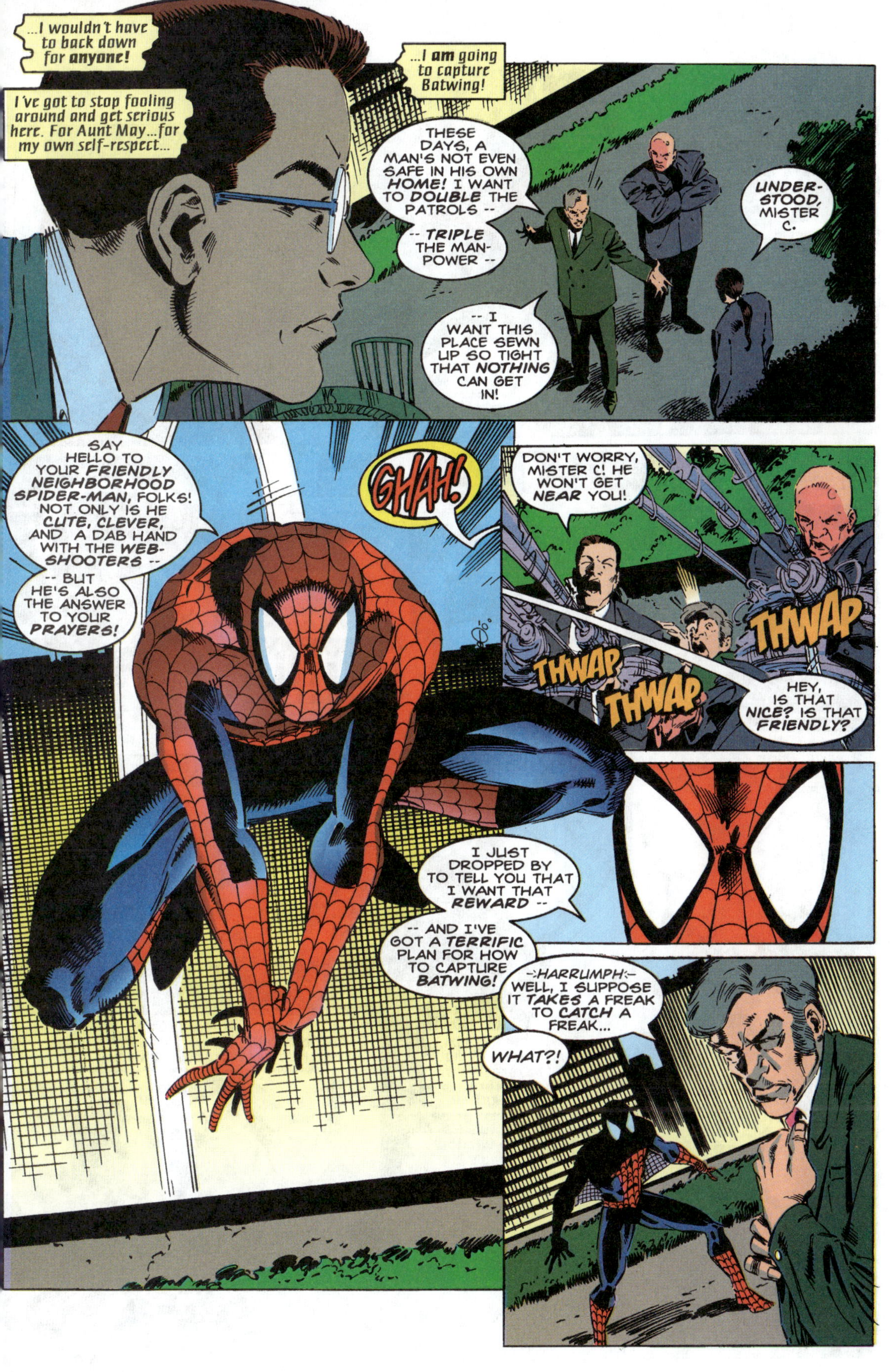
...I wouldn't have to back down for anyone!
I've got to stop fooling around and get serious here. For Aunt May...for my own self-respect...
...I am going to capture Batwing!
THESE DAYS, A MAN'S NOT EVEN SAFE IN HIS OWN HOME! I WANT TO DOUBLE THE PATROLS --
-- TRIPLE THE MAN-POWER --
-- I WANT THIS PLACE SEWN UP SO TIGHT THAT NOTHING CAN GET IN!
UNDER-STOOD, MISTER C.
SAY HELLO TO YOUR FRIENDLY NEIGHBORHOOD SPIDER-MAN, FOLKS! NOT ONLY IS HE CUTE, CLEVER, AND A DAB HAND WITH THE WEB-SHOOTERS --
-- BUT HE'S ALSO THE ANSWER TO YOUR PRAYERS!
GHAH!
DON'T WORRY, MISTER C! HE WON'T GET NEAR YOU!
THWAP
THWAP
THWAP
HEY, IS THAT NICE? IS THAT FRIENDLY?
I JUST DROPPED BY TO TELL YOU THAT I WANT THAT REWARD --
-- AND I'VE GOT A TERRIFIC PLAN FOR HOW TO CAPTURE BATWING!
-HARRUMPH- WELL, I SUPPOSE IT TAKES A FREAK TO CATCH A FREAK...
WHAT?!

-- YOU'RE AN OUTLAW, AND I WOULDN'T ORDINARILY COUNTENANCE YOU.
BUT I'LL USE ANY WEAPON I CAN AGAINST THAT UNDESIRABLE ELEMENT WHO'D THREATEN THE NATURAL SOCIAL ORDER --
-- WHO'D THREATEN THE HARD-WON SECURITY OF THOSE WHO'VE EARNED THEIR PRIVILEGES --
YEAH, WELL, SKIP THE CAMPAIGN SPEECH, COUNCILMAN.
US RIFF-RAFF DON'T CARE ABOUT THE "NATURAL SOCIAL ORDER" -- BUT AS LONG AS THE MONEY'S GOOD, I'M ON THE TEAM.
NOW HERE'S WHAT I WAS THINKING WE COULD DO...
He should just walk up there, he tells himself.
Cherryh's setting things up for tonight and he's got time to kill --
-- so he should just walk up and knock on the McKeevers' door and demand his math notes back.
But no, that would cause trouble.
Still, he can't let him keep the notes -- that would be cheating, or helping him cheat, or something like that.
There's a window open, and a big patch of shadow. If that's Tiny's room --
-- hey, it is, and there are the notes! Doesn't even look like he's opened them!
THAPP
GOT 'EM!
Funny, how Spider-Man can go toe-to-toe with Dr. Doom, but as Peter Parker, he can't face down a single --
HUH?
BUT, DAD --!

DON'T YOU "BUT" ME, BOY!
I GOT A LETTER FROM YOUR SCHOOL, TELLING ME MY SON'S A MORON, AN IDIOT --
-- TOO STUPID TO EVEN PLAY FOOTBALL!
I'VE STILL GOT A CHANCE, DAD --
-- IF I CAN GET MY GRADES UP --
Oh, YEAH! GET YOUR GRADES UP!
A LOSER LIKE YOU'S GONNA TURN INTO EINSTEIN OVERNIGHT, huh?
WELL, MAYBE I AIN'T TOO SMART MYSELF --
-- AND LORD KNOWS I CAN'T BE, TO HAVE A MORON SON WHO GETS HIMSELF KICKED OFF THE FOOTBALL TEAM --
-- BUT I GOT A THOUGHT IN MY HEAD RIGHT NOW, BOY --
-- ABOUT HOW A KID TOO STUPID TO EVEN PLAY FOOTBALL MUST NOT BE WORTH A WHOLE LOT, huh?
OR IS THERE SOMETHING WRONG WITH MY THINKING, GENIUS? Huh? Huh? ANSWER ME!
Peter Parker winces, and pulls away from the window.
This isn't his problem," he tells himself.
He hears a thump, and a crash. Maybe Tiny's Dad is just slamming a table for emphasis. Maybe that's it.
And Tiny's a bully. A bully and a cheat and a thief. He deserves what he gets, doesn't he?
He must...

TOO DIVINE --!
-- PERFECT NIGHT.
NORMAN OSBORN! WHY, I HAVEN'T SEEN YOU IN A --
-- CALLED ME AT ABSOLUTELY THE LAST MINUTE, YOU KNOW --
-- WOULDN'T HAVE COME MYSELF, BUT --
-- AN ADVENTURE -- LURING THAT HORRIBLE BAT-CREATURE OUT OF HIDING --
-- HIRED "EXTRA SECURITY" FOR THE NIGHT --
SHELLY!
-- WOULDN'T BELIEVE WHO IT IS --
-- SO THRILLING -- PRACTICALLY AN UNDERCOVER MISSION --
-- MONSTER COULD BE WATCHING US RIGHT NOW --
-- PRACTICALLY GOT GOOSE-BUMPS!
-- PATÉ IS SIMPLY DELICIOUS --
-- NO, NOT IRON MAN -- EVEN MORE AUDACIOUS --
-- HAS ALWAYS BEEN SUCH AN ORIGINAL THINKER --
-- MAYOR SOMEDAY -- OR EVEN MORE --
-- USED TO CALL HIM RAND-O AT SCHOOL --
-- NOT HALF AS LOVELY AS YOU, DEAR --
The music wafts up into the night air, delicate and peaceful --
-- and above, Spider-Man listens and watches and waits. Gone are thoughts of Tiny McKeever, of school, of money worries.
He could get used to this, he thinks.
Yeah, he could get used to this real easily --!

HAMPTONS
EUROPE
GSTAAD
DEBUSSY
-- GOT TO MEET MY ACCOUNTANT --
Eh?
THAT -- WHISTLING --
-- IT'S NOT WHISTLING --
IT'S --
Oh, LORD
HO-LEE CATS --
INSANE
MONSTROUS
HORRIBLE
"-- HERE IT COMES!"
SHRIIIIIIIIIIIIIIIIIIIIII
It swoops low and fast, screaming to make the people flee, to make them panic and run.
And most of them do. Most of them --
KILL IT! KILL IT! YOU HEAR ME?
BLOW IT OUT OF THE SKY!
-- but not all of them.
For a moment, it hangs in the air, a perfect target.

But...
THAP
WHA --?
THAP
THWUPP
Huh?
WHAT ARE YOU, CRAZY? WE DON'T KNOW WHAT IT WANTS -- HECK, WE DON'T KNOW WHAT IT IS!
YOU CAN'T JUST EXECUTE IT!
A MAN HAS A PERFECT RIGHT TO DEFEND HIS HOME FROM INTRUDERS!
THAT THING'S A MONSTER, SPIDER-MAN --
-- AND IF YOU WANT THAT REWARD, YOU'LL DO AS YOU'RE BLASTED WELL TOLD!
YES SIR, MISTER CHERRYH! RIGHT AWAY, MISTER CHERRYH!
THERE'S JUST ONE PROBLEM. I DON'T DO WINDOWS, AND I DON'T DO MURDER -- SO I'LL CATCH YOU YOUR LITTLE BAT-MONSTER --
-- BUT I'LL BRING HIM BACK ALIVE!!
CONTACT THE CHOPPER. I WANT THEM AIRBORNE TWO MINUTES AGO.
WE'RE NOT LEAVING THIS IN THE HANDS OF SOME SCOFFLAW VIGILANTE. WE'RE GOING TO MAKE SURE THAT SPIDER-MAN'S JOB GETS DONE --
-- AND GETS DONE RIGHT.

Spider-Man reflexively sets his automatic belt-camera to take pictures as he gives chase.
He won't need the money once he gets that reward, he tells himself -- but, in the meantime --
HEY THERE! GOING DOWNTOWN?
WELL, SO AM I -- MIND IF I HITCH A RIDE?
-- why not give Jameson one last thrill?
LISTEN, LET ME KNOW WHEN WE GET TO 34th -- THAT'S MY ST --
WHOA!
SHKKK
PUBLIC TRANSPORTATION'S REALLY HIT THE SKIDS IN THIS TOWN!
BUT YOU WON'T --
-- GET AWAY --
-- FROM ME --
-- THAT EASILY!
SHRRTTT
UHH!
DOUBLED BACK --!

The aerial combat rages on --
-- both sides too fast, too agile, for the other to get an advantage.
Spider-Man presses the chase --
-- and Batwing tries to lose him in the concrete canyons of Manhattan.
But Spider-Man matches every twist every turn --
-- until --
LOOK, FELLA, IT'S NOTHING PERSONAL --
-- BUT YOU'RE COMING WITH ME!
WRAK
With a howl, Batwing tears free --

-- and flees, no longer dodging, no longer trying to evade Spider-Man, but flying flat-out as if in full retreat.
No point in trying to catch him, figures the wall-crawler. Better just to follow --
-- find out where he's running to.
THE PIERS, huh?
NOT A BAD CHOICE. THERE'S ROOM TO HIDE -- NOT A LOT OF COMPETITION FOR THE SPACE EXCEPT RATS AND BARNACLES --
-- KINDA SOGGY, THOUGH...
PLEASE... PLEASE...
Huh?
ONLY... TOOK FOOD!
TRIED... SCARE PEOPLE... SO DIDN'T HAVE... HURT ANYONE!
DON'T... KILL! PLEASE!
His voice is tortured and shrill, like chalk on a blackboard.
And his face --
Y-YOU'RE JUST --
-- A LITTLE KID?

YOU'RE NO MORE THAN TWELVE OR THIRTEEN -- EVEN YOUNGER THAN I AM!
BUT -- WHAT HAPPENED? HOW DID YOU COME TO BE LIKE THIS, TO LIVE LIKE THIS?
HURTS THROAT... TALK! BUT... I SHOW!
A DIARY --!
DIARY
The diary tells a story --
-- about a boy who went with his father on a business trip, investigating possible illegal chemical dumping in Carlsbad Caverns.
Maybe the father should have known better -- or maybe he didn't realize the danger --
-- because he fell (or was there a gunshot? the diary isn't clear) --
DAD!
J-JIMMY
-- and the boy was stranded.
The boy survived -- eating and drinking what he could find -- even filthy, phosphorescent water that tasted like metal --
-- and in time, he was rescued --
-- but something had happened.
MERCIFUL SAVIOR!
His mother called him a demon, and he ran away -- all the way to New York, where he could find food and places to hide --

GEEZ, I DIDN'T DREAM --
-- IT'S GOING TO BE OKAY, KID. I WON'T HURT YOU. WE'LL GET YOU SOMEWHERE SAFE -- SOMEWHERE THEY CAN HELP YOU --
NO!
YOU FOUND... HIDEOUT! NOT SAFE...
NOT GOING... GET CUT UP BY SCIENTISTS...
...LIKE MOM SAID!
KID, WAIT --
WHA -- ?!
CRIPES, IT'S THE CREATURE!
SHRACK
HEY WAIT -- IT'S NOT WHAT YOU THINK!
-- SO MUCH AS TWITCH A WING, AND I'LL SPLATTER YOUR BRAINS ALL OVER --
Ah, SPIDER-MAN!
YOU'VE EXCEEDED MY EXPECTATIONS!

YOU LED US RIGHT TO HIM -- AND DELIVERED UP WITHOUT INJURY, AS YOU SAID!
I'M QUITE IMPRESSED. THE REWARD IS YOURS -- AND PERHAPS WE SHOULD TALK ABOUT MORE REGULAR EMPLOYMENT...
AND WHAT ABOUT THE KID?
THE... CREATURE?
NO NEED TO WORRY, SPIDER-MAN. WE'LL SEE THAT IT DOESN'T BOTHER ANYONE EVER AGAIN, AND YOUR HANDS ARE CLEAN...
LIAR!
YOU SAID... NOT HURT! BUT... JUST WANT MONEY... LET MEN KILL ME!
Eh -- ?!
NO!
NO ONE'S KILLING ANYBODY, KID -- NOT WHILE I'M AROUND!
THWIP
HEY -- WAIT! I MEANT WHAT I SAID ABOUT HELPING YOU!
THERE ARE SCIENTISTS -- GOOD GUYS, LIKE REED RICHARDS AND HENRY PYM --
NO!
EVEYBODY... HATE ME! WANT... HURT ME!
FIND NEW PLACE... NEW PLACE TO HIDE!
And like that, he's gone -- and Spider-Man watches him go --

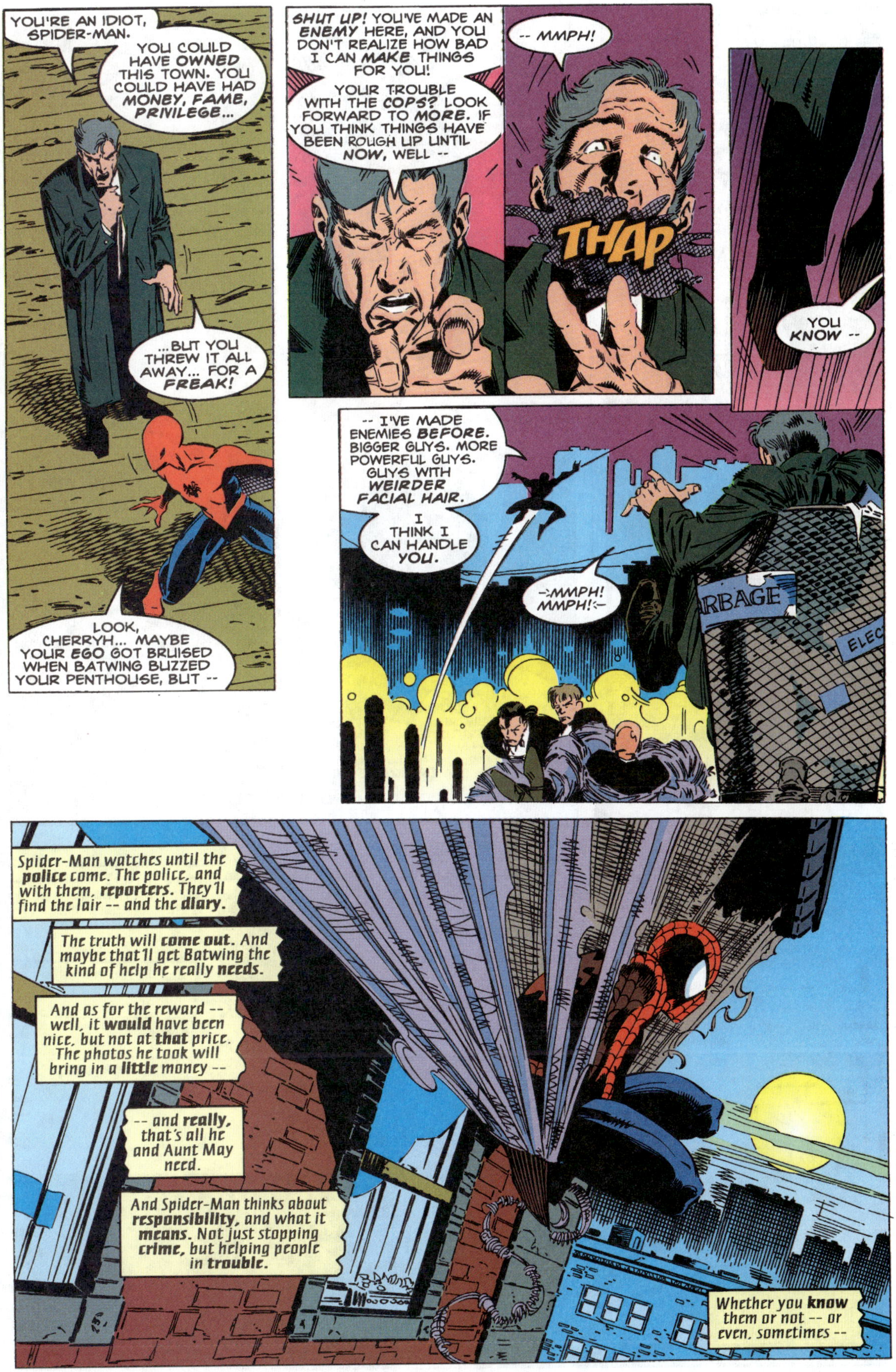

YOU'RE AN IDIOT, SPIDER-MAN.
YOU COULD HAVE **OWNED** THIS TOWN. YOU COULD HAVE HAD **MONEY, FAME, PRIVILEGE...**
...BUT YOU THREW IT ALL AWAY... FOR A **FREAK!**
LOOK, CHERRYH... MAYBE YOUR **EGO** GOT BRUISED WHEN BATWING BUZZED YOUR PENTHOUSE, BUT --

SHUT UP! YOU'VE MADE AN **ENEMY** HERE, AND YOU DON'T REALIZE HOW BAD I CAN **MAKE** THINGS FOR YOU!
YOUR TROUBLE WITH THE **COPS?** LOOK FORWARD TO **MORE.** IF YOU THINK THINGS HAVE BEEN ROUGH UP UNTIL **NOW,** WELL --
-- MMPH!
THAP
YOU **KNOW** --
-- I'VE MADE ENEMIES **BEFORE.** BIGGER GUYS. MORE POWERFUL GUYS. GUYS WITH **WEIRDER FACIAL HAIR.**
I THINK I CAN HANDLE **YOU.**
-MMPH! MMPH!-
ARBAGE
ELEC

Spider-Man watches until the **police** come. The police, and with them, **reporters**. They'll find the lair -- and the **diary**.

The truth will **come out**. And maybe that'll get Batwing the kind of help he really **needs**.

And as for the reward -- well, it **would** have been nice, but not at **that** price. The photos he took will bring in a **little** money --

-- and **really**, that's all he and Aunt May need.

And Spider-Man thinks about **responsibility**, and what it **means**. Not just stopping **crime**, but helping people in **trouble**.

Whether you **know** them or not -- or even, sometimes --

-- whether you like them or not.
NOK NOK
HOLD ON A SEC! I'LL BE THERE IN A --

-- PARKER? "PUNY" PARKER? WHAT ARE YOU DOING HERE?
WOW -- THAT'S SOME SHINER, TINY...
I SLIPPED DURING FOOTBALL PRACTICE, OKAY? GOT AN ELBOW IN THE EYE. WHAT DO YOU WANT, ANYWAY?
WELL, I... KINDA SWIPED MY MATH NOTES BACK DURING FIFTH PERIOD STUDY HALL. BUT I THOUGHT --
-- WELL, IF YOU'RE REALLY HAVING TROUBLE WITH IT, MAYBE I COULD GIVE YOU A FEW POINTERS.

YOU? COACH ME IN MATH? WHY WOULD YOU --
-- aw, NEVER MIND. YOU WANNA HELP, I'M NOT COMPLAININ'. COME ON IN.

Soon...
FOUR TIMES PI TIMES THE RADIUS... aw, YOU'RE WASTIN' YOUR TIME, PARKER. I'M NOT WORTH IT -- I'M NEVER GONNA GET IT.
DON'T SAY THAT, TINY. EVERYBODY'S WORTH IT. EVERYBODY.
Maybe he can't help here, Peter thinks. Maybe even if Tiny gets back on the football team, it won't fix things.
But all you can do is try, right? Just keep trying --
-- and see what life throws at you next...
ISTORY
AMERICA

SHORTLY THEREAFTER:
HAVING ESCAPED FROM PRISON, THE VULTURE RESUMED HIS CRIMINAL CAREER.
YOU NEVER SUSPECTED I HAD IMPROVED MY WINGS SO THAT THEY COULD CHANGE MAGNETIC POLES INSTANTLY, NULLIFYING YOUR USELESS INVERTER!
SO THAT'S WHY... OOOF--!
ENGAGING THE VULTURE IN THE SKIES ABOVE MANHATTAN, SPIDER-MAN WAS SOUNDLY DEFEATED BY THE HIGH-FLYING VILLAIN...
SPIDER-MAN IS FINISHED! MY REVENGE IS COMPLETE! NOW THE VULTURE IS SUPREME!
...AND WAS BADLY INJURED IN THE BATTLE.
OHH! MY ARM! MUST HAVE LANDED ON IT!
FEELS LIKE IT'S BROKEN!
I DON'T WANT TO DIE! SAVE ME! SOS-DO SOMETHING! PLEASE--PLEASE! SAVE ME!
I CAN'T! I'M TOO BUSY ADMIRING YOUR TIGHT-LIPPED COURAGE!
DESPITE THE HANDICAP OF HIS INJURED ARM, SPIDER-MAN CAME BACK TO DEFEAT THE VULTURE AFTER THE SUPER-POWERED MALEFACTOR ATTEMPTED TO LOOT THE DAILY BUGLE'S PAYROLL.
HI, BETTY! WHAT ARE YOU DOING BEHIND THAT DESK?
IT'S THE ONLY SAFE PLACE, PETER! THIS OFFICE WAS A MADHOUSE A FEW MINUTES AGO!
MIND IF I JOIN YOU?
BE MY GUEST!
AND, IN THE AFTERMATH OF THE STRUGGLE, PETER PARKER AND BETTY BRANT CONNECTED WITH ONE ANOTHER.

SANDBAGGED!
UNTOLD TALES OF
SPIDER-MAN
ONLY 99¢ US
$1.35 CAN
NOV • 3
MARVEL
SPIDER-MAN GROUP
DIRECT EDITION

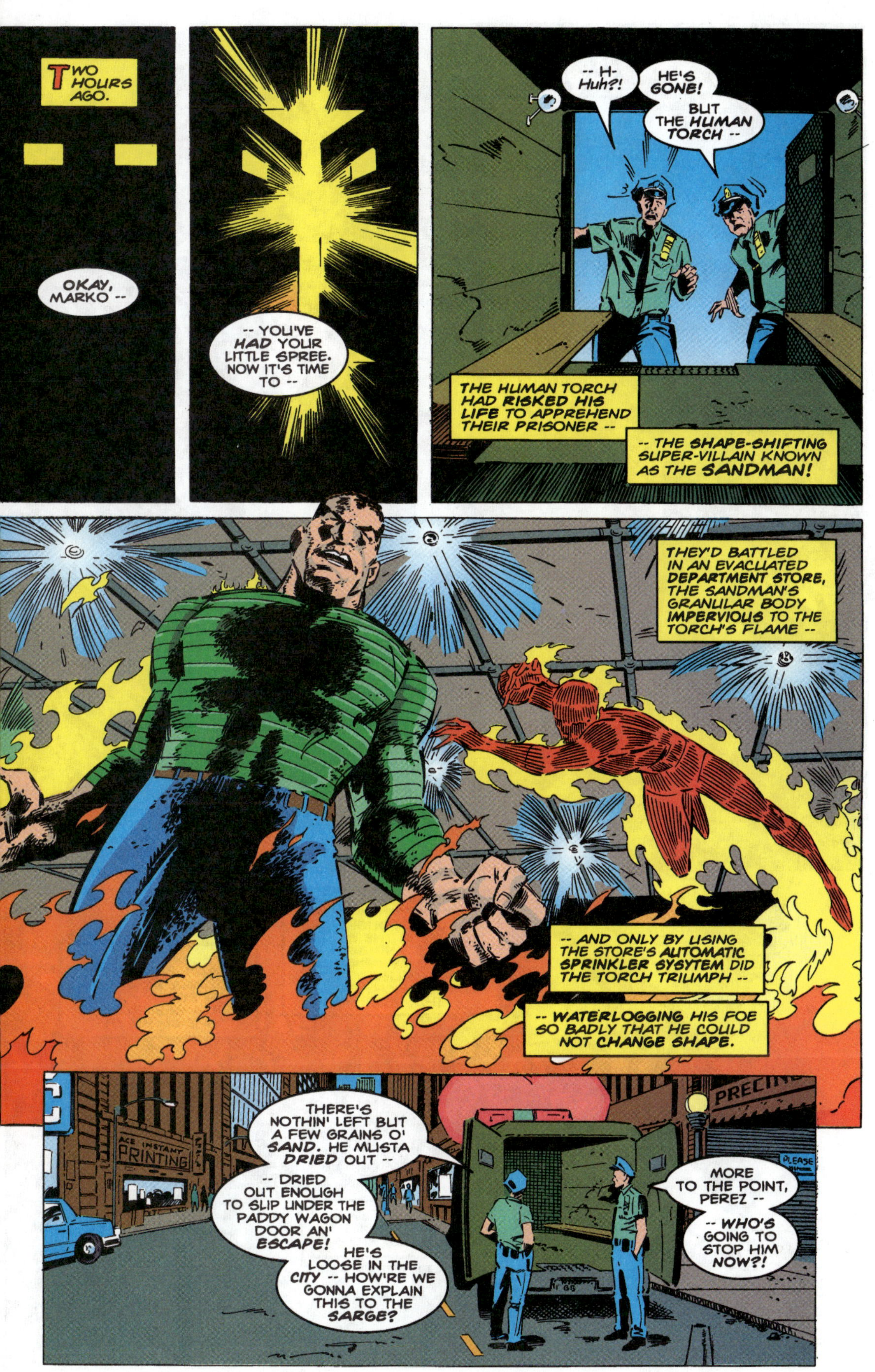
TWO HOURS AGO.
OKAY, MARKO --
-- YOU'VE HAD YOUR LITTLE SPREE. NOW IT'S TIME TO --
-- H-Huh?!
HE'S GONE!
BUT THE HUMAN TORCH --
THE HUMAN TORCH HAD RISKED HIS LIFE TO APPREHEND THEIR PRISONER --
-- THE SHAPE-SHIFTING SUPER-VILLAIN KNOWN AS THE SANDMAN!
THEY'D BATTLED IN AN EVACUATED DEPARTMENT STORE, THE SANDMAN'S GRANULAR BODY IMPERVIOUS TO THE TORCH'S FLAME --
-- AND ONLY BY USING THE STORE'S AUTOMATIC SPRINKLER SYSYTEM DID THE TORCH TRIUMPH --
-- WATERLOGGING HIS FOE SO BADLY THAT HE COULD NOT CHANGE SHAPE.
THERE'S NOTHIN' LEFT BUT A FEW GRAINS O' SAND. HE MUSTA DRIED OUT --
-- DRIED OUT ENOUGH TO SLIP UNDER THE PADDY WAGON DOOR AN' ESCAPE!
HE'S LOOSE IN THE CITY -- HOW'RE WE GONNA EXPLAIN THIS TO THE SARGE?
MORE TO THE POINT, PEREZ --
-- WHO'S GOING TO STOP HIM NOW?!
ACE INSTANT PRINTING
PLEASE

NOW.
WAH-HOOO!
SAND
LOOK OUT, WORLD -- I'M COMIN' THROUGH!
I'M SPIDER-FAST --
-- SPIDER-STRONG --
-- LARGE AS LIFE AND HANDSOME, TOO!
I STILL CAN'T BELIEVE IT!
ME, THE GUY THEY VOTED MOST LIKELY TO SIT HOME ALONE ON SATURDAY NIGHTS -- I'M TAKING BETTY BRANT TO DINNER!
"I'D JUST FOUGHT THE VULTURE IN THE BUGLE OFFICES, AND BEAT HIM DESPITE MY SPRAINED ARM. I MUST'VE STILL BEEN PUNCHY FROM THE FIGHT --
"-- BECAUSE I WAS BRAVE ENOUGH TO ACTUALLY FLIRT WITH BETTY -- AND IT SORTA SEEMED AS IF SHE LIKED IT!
"I FIGURED I'D SAY SOMETHING BEFORE I LOST MY NERVE, SO --
Ah, BETTY. ah -- I WAS THINKING --
YES, PETER?

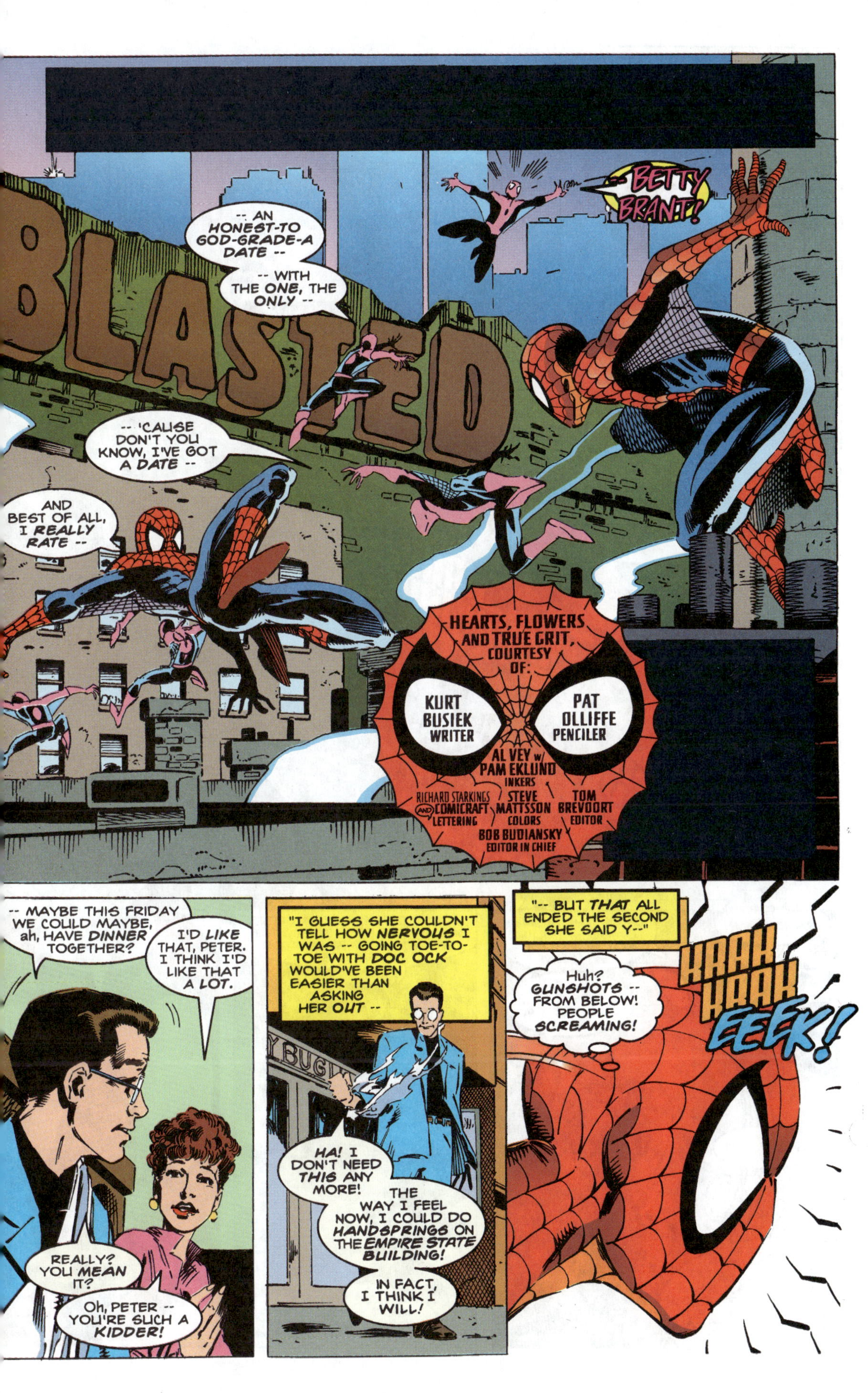
BLASTED
-- AN HONEST-TO GOD-GRADE-A DATE --
-- WITH THE ONE, THE ONLY --
-- BETTY BRANT!
-- 'CAUSE DON'T YOU KNOW, I'VE GOT A DATE --
AND BEST OF ALL, I REALLY RATE --
HEARTS, FLOWERS AND TRUE GRIT, COURTESY OF:
KURT BUSIEK WRITER
PAT OLLIFFE PENCILER
AL VEY w/ PAM EKLUND INKERS
RICHARD STARKINGS AND COMICRAFT LETTERING
STEVE MATTSSON COLORS
TOM BREVOORT EDITOR
BOB BUDIANSKY EDITOR IN CHIEF
-- MAYBE THIS FRIDAY WE COULD MAYBE, ah, HAVE DINNER TOGETHER?
I'D LIKE THAT, PETER. I THINK I'D LIKE THAT A LOT.
REALLY? YOU MEAN IT?
Oh, PETER -- YOU'RE SUCH A KIDDER!
"I GUESS SHE COULDN'T TELL HOW NERVOUS I WAS -- GOING TOE-TO-TOE WITH DOC OCK WOULD'VE BEEN EASIER THAN ASKING HER OUT --
HA! I DON'T NEED THIS ANY MORE!
THE WAY I FEEL NOW, I COULD DO HANDSPRINGS ON THE EMPIRE STATE BUILDING!
IN FACT, I THINK I WILL!
"-- BUT THAT ALL ENDED THE SECOND SHE SAID Y--"
KRAK KRAK EEEK!
Huh? GUNSHOTS -- FROM BELOW! PEOPLE SCREAMING!

Uh-oh! I WAS THINKING THAT MAYBE I COULD GET SOME NEWS PIX TO SELL TO JAMESON, SO I COULD TAKE BETTY SOMEPLACE REALLY SWANKY --
-- BUT THIS IS NO ORDINARY URBAN CRISIS --
-- IT'S THE SANDMAN!
N- NO! STAY AWAY!
KRAK
KRAK KRAK
KRAK
SAPS! YOUR BULLETS DON'T MEAN SQUAT TO A GUY MADE OF SAND --
-- OR HAVEN'T YOU FIGGERED THAT OUT YET?!
SANDMAN!
DROP THE MONEY BAGS -- YOU'RE NOT GOING ANY-WHERE!
HEY, SPIDEY! NICE TO SEE YA, PAL!
WHAT --?!
OKAY, I'LL ADMIT, I USEDTA BE PRETTY MAD AT YOU FER CAPTURIN' ME THAT TIME -- BUT HEY, THEN THE TORCH CAUGHT ME, TOO --
-- AN' I DON'T WANT TA SPEND ALL MY TIME SETTLIN' SCORES WHEN I COULD BE LIVIN' THE LUSH LIFE!
SO I TELL YA WHAT -- YOU DON'T BOTHER ME, I DON'T BOTHER YOU. OKAY?
FORGET IT, SANDMAN! I'M TAKING YOU --

WHOAAH!
FINE! YOU WANNA GET STOMPED INTA THE GROUND, I'LL STOMP YOU INTA THE GROUND!
SHRAKK
BUT DON'T SAY I DIDN'T GIVE YA A CHANCE!
PAT YOURSELF ON THE BACK MUCH, BIG GUY? I MEAN, CORRECT ME IF I'M WRONG --
-- BUT I'M THE GUY WHO BEAT YOU, NOT THE OTHER WAY AROUND!
SHASSSH!
THWIPP
YOU GOT LUCKY, PAL --
THAP
-- JUST LIKE YOU THINK YOU'RE GONNA DO AGAIN, TRYIN' TA WEB ME IN THE EYES LIKE THAT! BUT I'M TOO SMART FOR YA!
C'MERE!
YANKED MY WEB -- WASN'T EXPECTING THAT!
PULLED ME OFF-BALANCE --
SO TELL ME, SPIDEY --
Oh, GREAT! MY SPIDER-SENSE IS HELPFULLY WARNING ME I'M IN DANGER --
-- BUT I'M IN MIDAIR -- NO CHANCE TO DODGE --

FKRM
—WHO'S WINNING NOW?!
OHH!
HIS PUNCH... LIKE HAVING A BUILDING FALL ON ME!
GOTTA GET SOME DISTANCE... CLEAR MY HEAD...
WAK
KRAK
HFF!
FASH
...BUT HE'S NOT...
...GIVING ME A CHANCE...
HLUD
... TO... TO RECOVER...
KRAM

YOU'RE JUST NOT IN MY LEAGUE, SPIDER-MAN.
YOU DARE MESS WITH ME AGAIN, YOU'LL GET WORSE...
...MUCH WORSE!
OOOOHHH...
GOTTA STAY CONSCIOUS... GOTTA GET UP...
...CAN'T PASS OUT IN THE STREET...
FREEZE!
Huh --?
M-MAYBE THE SANDMAN GOT AWAY -- BUT THERE'S A REWARD OUT ON YOU, AND I'M GOING TO COLLECT IT!
I M-MEAN IT -- I'LL SHOOT!
GO AHEAD...IT COULDN'T POSSIBLY HURT ANY MORE THAN I ALREADY DO...
STOP! I MEAN IT!
SORRY, FELLA...
SPLOOSH
Ooh! Owtch! Ow!
MY RIBS ARE ON FIRE, MY WHOLE BODY ACHES, AND I CAN BARELY WALK! ALL I WANT TO DO IS TO GET HOME AND CRAWL INTO BED!
I WONDER... DO THOR AND GIANT-MAN EVER HAVE DAYS LIKE THIS --
--OR IS IT JUST ME?

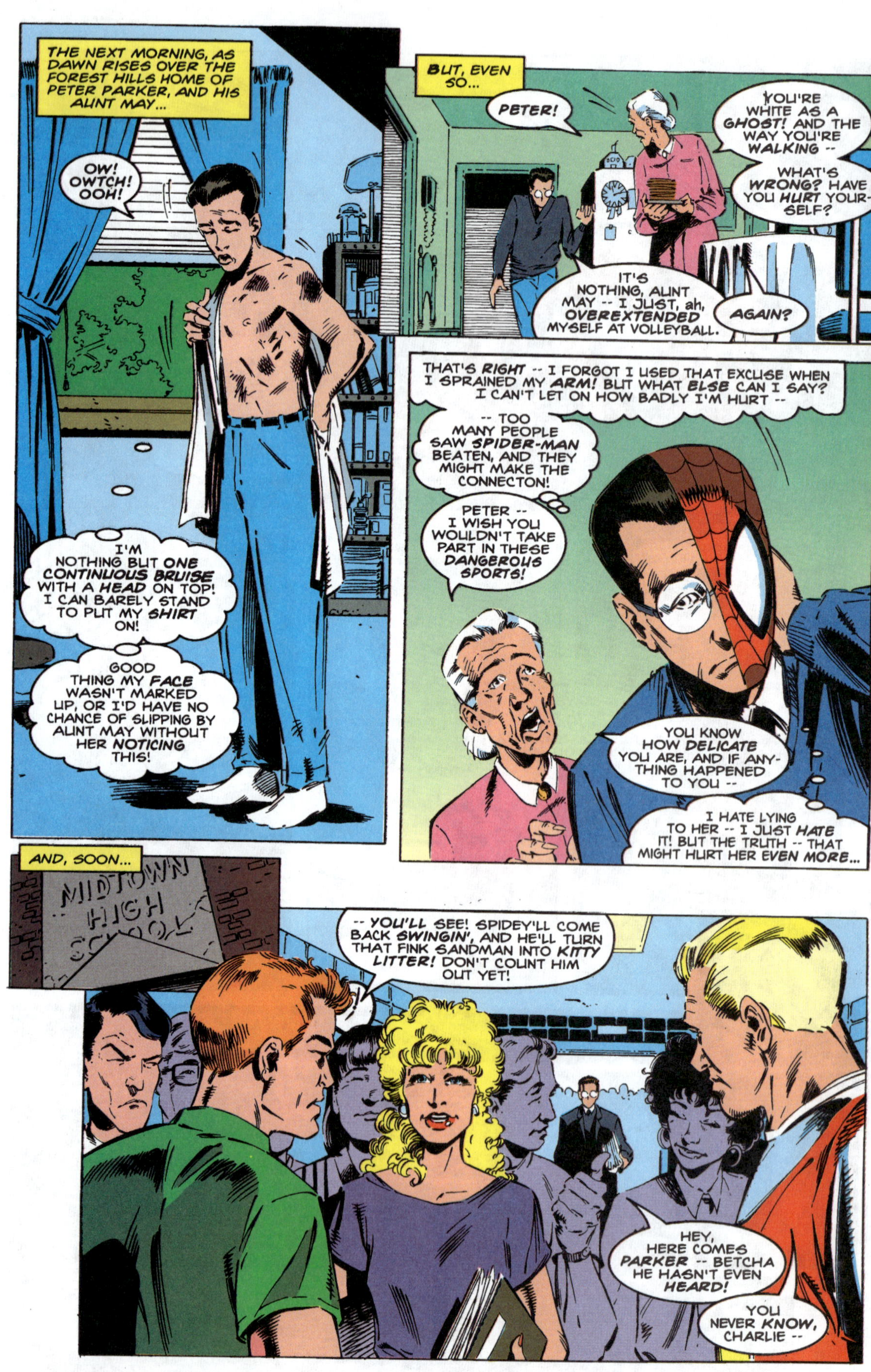
THE NEXT MORNING, AS DAWN RISES OVER THE FOREST HILLS HOME OF PETER PARKER, AND HIS AUNT MAY...
OW! OWTCH! OOH!
I'M NOTHING BUT ONE CONTINUOUS BRUISE WITH A HEAD ON TOP! I CAN BARELY STAND TO PUT MY SHIRT ON!
GOOD THING MY FACE WASN'T MARKED UP, OR I'D HAVE NO CHANCE OF SLIPPING BY AUNT MAY WITHOUT HER NOTICING THIS!
BUT, EVEN SO...
PETER!
YOU'RE WHITE AS A GHOST! AND THE WAY YOU'RE WALKING --
WHAT'S WRONG? HAVE YOU HURT YOURSELF?
IT'S NOTHING, AUNT MAY -- I JUST, ah, OVEREXTENDED MYSELF AT VOLLEYBALL.
AGAIN?
THAT'S RIGHT -- I FORGOT I USED THAT EXCUSE WHEN I SPRAINED MY ARM! BUT WHAT ELSE CAN I SAY? I CAN'T LET ON HOW BADLY I'M HURT --
-- TOO MANY PEOPLE SAW SPIDER-MAN BEATEN, AND THEY MIGHT MAKE THE CONNECTON!
PETER -- I WISH YOU WOULDN'T TAKE PART IN THESE DANGEROUS SPORTS!
YOU KNOW HOW DELICATE YOU ARE, AND IF ANYTHING HAPPENED TO YOU --
I HATE LYING TO HER -- I JUST HATE IT! BUT THE TRUTH -- THAT MIGHT HURT HER EVEN MORE...
AND, SOON...
MIDTOWN HIGH SCHOOL
-- YOU'LL SEE! SPIDEY'LL COME BACK SWINGIN', AND HE'LL TURN THAT FINK SANDMAN INTO KITTY LITTER! DON'T COUNT HIM OUT YET!
HEY, HERE COMES PARKER -- BETCHA HE HASN'T EVEN HEARD!
YOU NEVER KNOW, CHARLIE --

HEY, PETE -- WE WERE JUST TALKIN' ABOUT WHETHER SPIDER-MAN IS WASHED UP, OR IF HE'LL MAKE A COMEBACK AND BEAT THE SANDMAN.
WHAT DO YOU THINK?
GEEZ, TINY, WHEN DID YOU GET SO FRIENDLY WITH PARKER?
HE ISN'T EVEN LISTENING -- HE'S LOST IN A FOG LIKE ALWAYS. BESIDES --
-- PARKER WOULDN'T KNOW ANYTHING ABOUT FIGHTING UNLESS IT WAS WRITTEN IN A BOOK! SEE?
UH? JASON?!
PARKER!
PETER!
HEY!
WHAP
THUD
HE'S OUT COLD!
JASON IONELLO, YOU -- !
WELL, WHADDYA KNOW?
SAVE IT, FLASH -- THIS DOESN'T LOOK GOOD.
PETER?
WHAT? WHAT? I BARELY TOUCHED HIM!
SOON, IN THE SCHOOL NURSE'S OFFICE...
OW, MY HEAD! I HOPE I DON'T HAVE A CONCUSSION OR ANYTHING!
I CAN'T BELIEVE I HUMILIATED MYSELF LIKE THAT! THE KIDS MUST ALL THINK I'M A COMPLETE WIMP --
-- BUT I CAN'T LET ON THE TRUTH, EVEN IF THEY'D BELIEVE IT. "NO, HONEST, GUYS -- I WAS BRUTALLY BEATEN BY THE SANDMAN!"
YEAH, RIGHT.

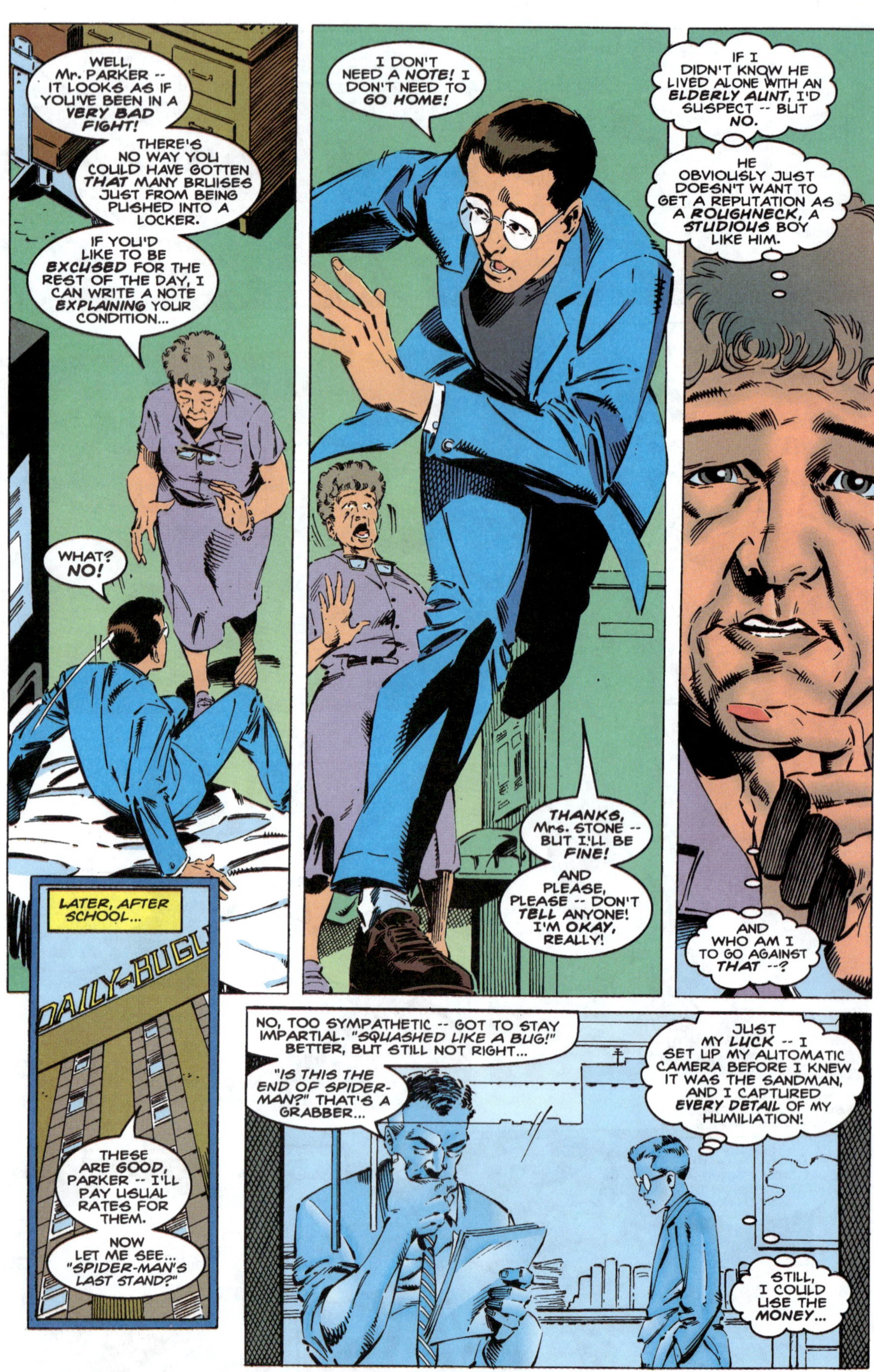
WELL, Mr. PARKER -- IT LOOKS AS IF YOU'VE BEEN IN A VERY BAD FIGHT!
THERE'S NO WAY YOU COULD HAVE GOTTEN THAT MANY BRUISES JUST FROM BEING PUSHED INTO A LOCKER.
IF YOU'D LIKE TO BE EXCUSED FOR THE REST OF THE DAY, I CAN WRITE A NOTE EXPLAINING YOUR CONDITION...
WHAT? NO!
I DON'T NEED A NOTE! I DON'T NEED TO GO HOME!
THANKS, Mrs. STONE -- BUT I'LL BE FINE!
AND PLEASE, PLEASE -- DON'T TELL ANYONE! I'M OKAY, REALLY!
IF I DIDN'T KNOW HE LIVED ALONE WITH AN ELDERLY AUNT, I'D SUSPECT -- BUT NO.
HE OBVIOUSLY JUST DOESN'T WANT TO GET A REPUTATION AS A ROUGHNECK, A STUDIOUS BOY LIKE HIM.
AND WHO AM I TO GO AGAINST THAT --?
LATER, AFTER SCHOOL...
DAILY BUGL
THESE ARE GOOD, PARKER -- I'LL PAY USUAL RATES FOR THEM.
NOW LET ME SEE... "SPIDER-MAN'S LAST STAND?"
NO, TOO SYMPATHETIC -- GOT TO STAY IMPARTIAL. "SQUASHED LIKE A BUG!" BETTER, BUT STILL NOT RIGHT...
"IS THIS THE END OF SPIDER-MAN?" THAT'S A GRABBER...
JUST MY LUCK -- I SET UP MY AUTOMATIC CAMERA BEFORE I KNEW IT WAS THE SANDMAN, AND I CAPTURED EVERY DETAIL OF MY HUMILIATION!
STILL, I COULD USE THE MONEY...

...ESPECIALLY SINCE JONAH MAY BE RIGHT -- THIS REALLY MAY BE THE END OF SPIDER-MAN!
RIGHT NOW, I COULDN'T BECOME SPIDER-MAN IF I HAD TO -- I'M ALMOST TOO WEAK TO WALK, LET ALONE WEB-SLING.
BUT EVEN WHEN I'M RECOVERED...
...CAN I FACE THE SANDMAN AGAIN, KNOWING HOW MUCH HE HURT ME? KNOWING HE PROMISED TO DO WORSE NEXT TIME?
WILL THE FEAR OF BEING HURT AGAIN SLOW ME DOWN -- COST ME THAT EDGE I NEED TO SURVIVE? OR IS IT WORSE THAN THAT?
NOW THAT I'VE BEEN INJURED LIKE THIS, AM I JUST GUN-SHY --
-- HAVE I BECOME A COWARD?
HI, PETER! ARE WE STILL ON FOR FRIDAY NIGHT?
WHY? YOU WANT TO CANCEL OUT?
WHAT? NO -- I'M LOOKING FORWARD TO IT! I WAS JUST MAKING CONVER --
PETER! YOU LOOK TERRIBLE! ARE YOU ALL RIGHT?
I'M JUST DANDY, BETTY!
I DON'T HAVE A CARE IN THE WORLD, I JUST JOINED THE U.S. OLYMPIC TEAM, AND HOLLY-WOOD STUDIOS ARE VYING TO FILM MY BIOGRAPHY!
OKAY?
I -- YOU SEEM SO BITTER, SO DE-PRESSED -- I DON'T KNOW WHY --
-- BUT IF THERE'S ANYTHING I CAN DO --!
THANKS FOR THE OFFER, BETTY -- BUT I DON'T KNOW IF THERE'S ANYTHING ANY-ONE CAN DO.
THIS MAY JUST BE THE ALL-NEW, ALL-DIFFERENT, LIFE-OF-THE-PARTY PETER PARKER, THAT'S ALL...

BUGLE
NEW YORK'S FINEST DAILY NEWSPAPER
SANDMAN STRIKES AGAIN!
VILLAIN ESCAPES POLICE!
IN THE DAYS THAT FOLLOW, IT SEEMS AS IF THE SANDMAN IS EVERYWHERE --
ANTE UP WITH THE PROTECTION MONEY, CHUMPS --
-- OR YOUR BOSS DEVELOPS RESPIRATORY TROUBLE!
-- ROBBING BANKS, BROKERAGE HOUSES, RESTAURANTS --
OUTTA THE WAY, FLATFOOT!
-- AND NO ONE SEEMS TO BE ABLE TO STOP HIM! THE POLICE, THE CITY'S HEROES --
HE WAS HERE A SECOND AGO!
I COULD HAVE SWORN --
WEDWEDWEDWEDWEDWEDWED
-- THEY HUNT HIM EVERYWHERE -- BUT FIND HIM NOWHERE!

AND, AS FOR PETER PARKER...
I CAN'T CONCENTRATE ON THIS ASSIGNMENT... I JUST KEEP SEEING THE SANDMAN'S FACE --
-- TELLING ME I'M NOT IN HIS LEAGUE -- THAT HE'LL HURT ME WORSE NEXT TIME!
ISN'T IT EXCITING, FLASH! THE SANDMAN, HE'S LIKE DILLINGER, OR BONNIE AND CLYDE -- !
AND HE'LL END UP LIKE THEM, TOO, ONCE SPIDEY CATCHES UP WITH HIM! POW! -- HE'LL BE FLATTER THAN SAND-PAPER!
SAFETY DAY
PHYSICS
PSST! HEY GUYS -- WATCH THIS!
JASON! DON'T YOU DARE -- !
WHAT -- PARKER'S OFF-LIMITS, NOW THAT HE'S OFFICIALLY A PANTY-WAIST?
WHAP
THE BRUISES ARE HEALING -- I'M STILL STIFF, BUT A LOT BETTER THAN I WAS!
BUT I MIGHT AS WELL ADMIT IT -- I'M AFRAID! WHEN DOCTOR OCTOPUS BEAT ME THE FIRST TIME WE FOUGHT, I WAS RATTLED --
-- BUT NOW I'M SCARED FOR MY LIFE!
WHAT AM I GONNA DO?

SOON, AT THE ELEGANT AVENUE DINNER CLUB...
EARTH TO PETER PARKER! EARTH TO PETER PARKER! COME IN, PARKER!
Huh? Oh, SORRY, BETTY -- I GUESS I WASN'T PAYING ATTENTION.
I SHOULD HOPE NOT! I'VE BEEN TELLING YOU ALL ABOUT MY ADVENTURES AS A SNAKE HANDLER FOR THE GOVERNMENT DURING THE CIVIL WAR --
-- AND YOU DIDN'T SO MUCH AS BAT AN EYE!
YOU'VE BEEN GLUM AND UNCOMMUNICATIVE FOR DAYS -- AND I WANT TO KNOW WHY!
I'M SORRY TO DISAPPOINT YOU, BETTY, BUT I DON'T KNOW WHAT TO TELL YOU.
MAYBE I'M JUST NOT THE MAN YOU THOUGHT I WAS...
HOLD IT RIGHT THERE, PETER. YOU DON'T HAVE TO TELL ME WHAT'S GOING ON -- BUT MAYBE I CAN HELP ANYWAY.
I... KNEW SOMEONE ONCE WHO WAS FACING A PRETTY TOUGH SITUATION --
-- AND HE GAVE UP ON HIMSELF, BECAUSE HE THOUGHT THAT EVERYONE ELSE HAD -- THAT NOBODY BELIEVED IN HIM.
I DON'T KNOW YOU THAT WELL YET...
-- BUT I DO KNOW THAT YOU'RE STRONGER THAN YOU THINK YOU ARE.
AND MAYBE THE QUESTION YOU SHOULD BE ASKING YOURSELF ISN'T WHETHER YOU'RE THE MAN YOU THINK I THINK YOU ARE --
-- BUT WHETHER YOU'RE THE MAN YOU YOURSELF WANT TO BE.
YOU... YOU'RE RIGHT, BETTY.
I'VE BEEN WALLOWING IN SELF-DOUBT, BUT I'M NOT HELPING ANYONE BY DOING THAT -- LEAST OF ALL MYSELF.
HERE -- THIS SHOULD COVER THE CHECK --
-- I'VE GOT SOMETHING TO DO, BUT I HOPE I'LL BE SEEING YOU AGAIN SOON. AND, BETTY...
...THANK YOU.

MINUTES LATER...
I HOPE BETTY'S NOT TOO MAD AT ME FOR WALKING OUT ON HER LIKE THAT -- BUT IF I'M GOING TO WIN BACK MY SELF-RESPECT, I'VE GOT TO START NOW!
I'LL MAKE IT UP TO HER -- IF I LIVE THAT LONG!
MEANWHILE, THIS IS THE AREA THE SANDMAN'S BEEN SIGHTED IN RECENTLY, HITTING UP BUSINESSES FOR PROTECTION MONEY...
...SO THAT'S WHERE I START LOOKING!
SPIDER-MAN SWINGS OVER THE CITY'S ROOFTOPS, WATCHING AND WAITING --
-- UNTIL --
KRASH
GRABOIS AEROSPACE LABORATORIES
BINGO!
NOW, HE CAN SLIP AWAY FROM ME AS EASILY AS HE'S ESCAPED THE OTHER HEROES WHO'VE GONE AFTER HIM...
-- SO, SCARED OR NOT, I'VE GOT TO MAKE HIM MAD ENOUGH TO FIGHT INSTEAD OF RUN!
HEY, SANDMAN -- NICE NIGHT FOR GOING TO JAIL, DON'T YOU THINK?
WHAT?!
SPIDER-MAN?! I WARNED YOU ONCE TO STAY AWAY FROM ME --
-- I WON'T BE SO EASY ON YOU TWICE!
YOU REALLY THINK I COULD BE WARNED OFF BY A WALKING, TALKING ANT-HILL?!
Oh, THAT WAS A WARNING?
GEE, I'VE BEEN IN BERMUDA ALL WEEK, CATCHING SOME SUN, OR I'D HAVE BEEN BACK ON YOUR BUTT SOONER!

SMASH
OWPP!
ROLLED WITH THE PUNCH TO GET HIM INSIDE, IN AN ENCLOSED SPACE! LOOKS LIKE MY STRATEGY'S WORKING!
NOW ALL I'VE GOT TO DO --
-- IS STAY ALIVE LONG ENOUGH TO FIGURE OUT A WAY TO CAPTURE HIM.
NOBODY MAKES FUN OF ME, YOU HEAR ME?
NOBODY!
WELL, JUST CALL ME NOBODY, GRIT-GUY! BECAUSE EVERY TIME I LOOK AT YOU --
-- ALL I CAN THINK IS, "GOT DRY, ITCHY SKIN?! TRY OUR NEW MOISTURIZING CREME!"
THIS IS REALLY STUPID! HE'S ATTACKING ALL-OUT -- AND I'M ONLY STAYING OUT OF HIS WAY BY INCHES! UNLESS I THINK OF SOMETHING FAST --
WHAM
WHAM
-- I'M DEAD MEAT!

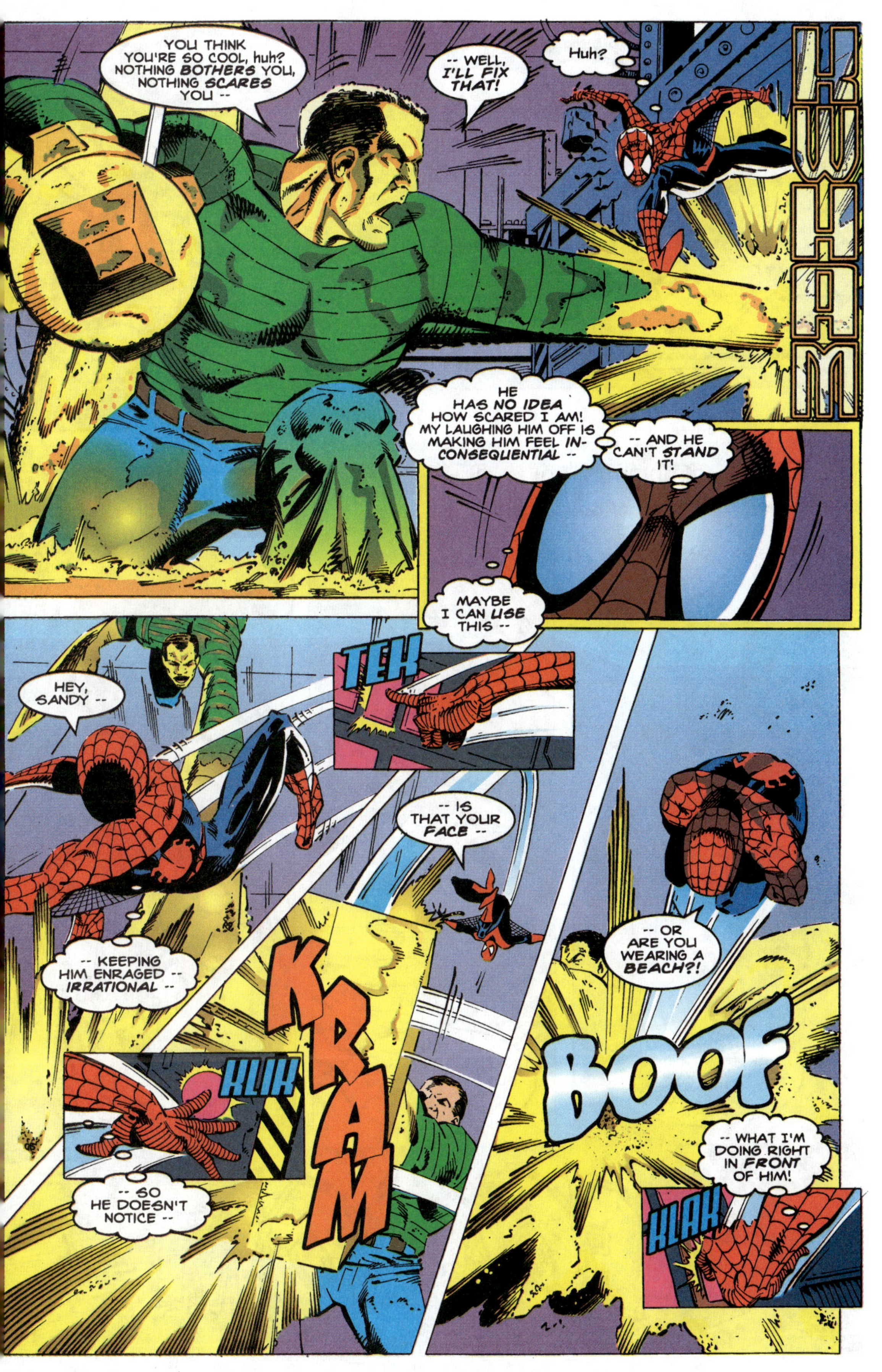
YOU THINK YOU'RE SO COOL, huh? NOTHING BOTHERS YOU, NOTHING SCARES YOU --
-- WELL, I'LL FIX THAT!
Huh?
KWHAM
HE HAS NO IDEA HOW SCARED I AM! MY LAUGHING HIM OFF IS MAKING HIM FEEL IN-CONSEQUENTIAL --
-- AND HE CAN'T STAND IT!
MAYBE I CAN USE THIS --
TEK
HEY, SANDY --
-- IS THAT YOUR FACE --
-- OR ARE YOU WEARING A BEACH?!
-- KEEPING HIM ENRAGED -- IRRATIONAL --
KRAM
BOOF
KLIK
-- SO HE DOESN'T NOTICE --
-- WHAT I'M DOING RIGHT IN FRONT OF HIM!
KLAK

TUNK
THERE!
Huh? WHAT'RE YOU DOING?!
Oh, YOU FINALLY NOTICED, huh? WELL, TOO LATE!
YOU'RE STANDING IN FRONT OF SOME KIND OF EXPERIMENTAL TURBINE, AND I'VE JUST TURNED IT ON --
"-- FULL POWER!
UUUMMMMMMMMMMM
WH -- ? Oh, CRUD!
YOU'RE NOT GETTIN' AWAY WITH THIS, SPIDER-MAN! YOU JUST BOUGHT YOURSELF A WORLD OF HURT!
I WAS WILLIN' TO LET BYGONES BE BYGONES, BUT FROM NOW ON, IT'S PERSONAL, YOU GOT THAT?!
IT'S PERSONALLLL
KFOOOOM

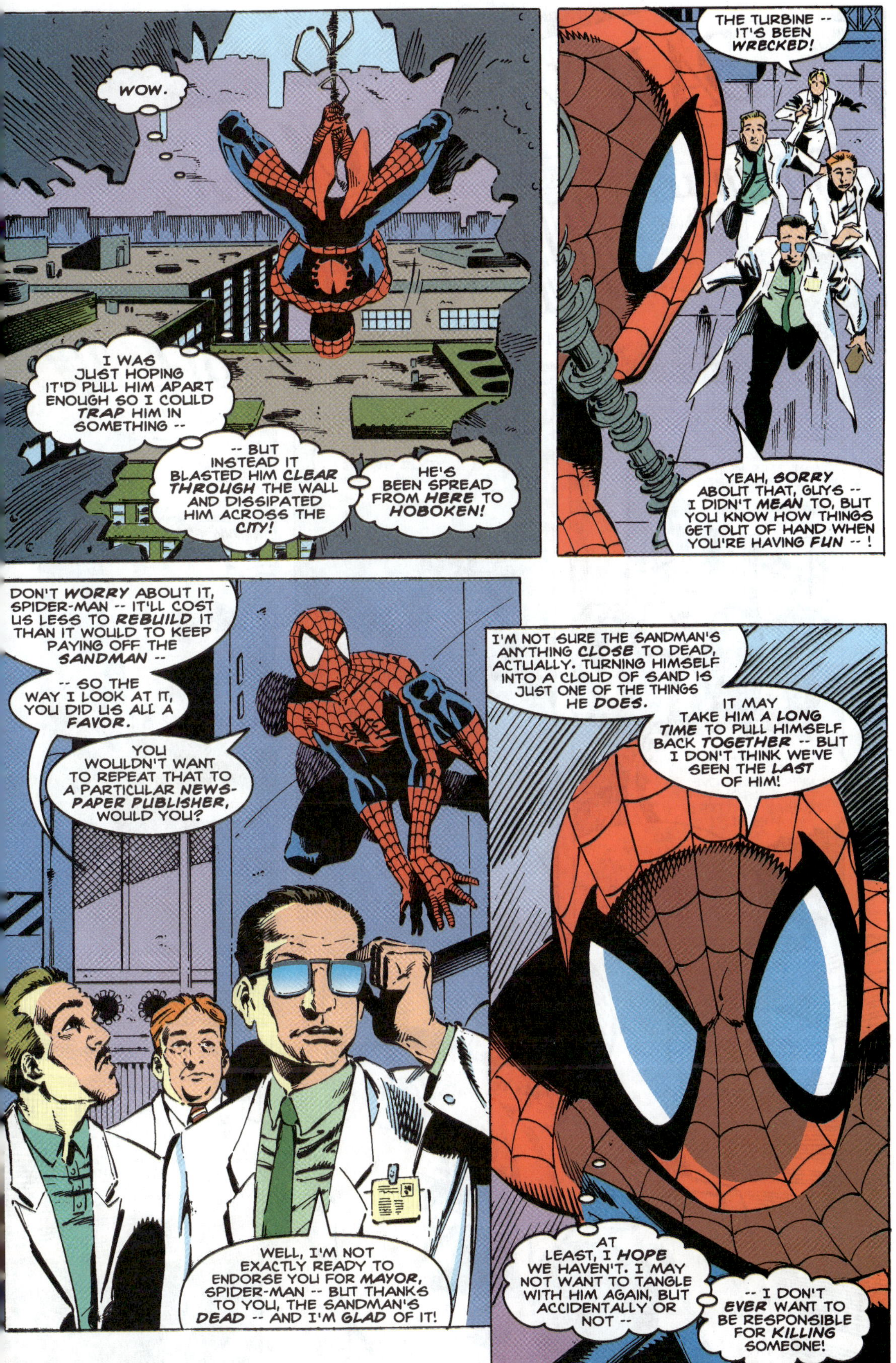
WOW.
I WAS JUST HOPING IT'D PULL HIM APART ENOUGH SO I COULD TRAP HIM IN SOMETHING --
-- BUT INSTEAD IT BLASTED HIM CLEAR THROUGH THE WALL AND DISSIPATED HIM ACROSS THE CITY!
HE'S BEEN SPREAD FROM HERE TO HOBOKEN!
THE TURBINE -- IT'S BEEN WRECKED!
YEAH, SORRY ABOUT THAT, GUYS -- I DIDN'T MEAN TO, BUT YOU KNOW HOW THINGS GET OUT OF HAND WHEN YOU'RE HAVING FUN -- !
DON'T WORRY ABOUT IT, SPIDER-MAN -- IT'LL COST US LESS TO REBUILD IT THAN IT WOULD TO KEEP PAYING OFF THE SANDMAN --
-- SO THE WAY I LOOK AT IT, YOU DID US ALL A FAVOR.
YOU WOULDN'T WANT TO REPEAT THAT TO A PARTICULAR NEWS-PAPER PUBLISHER, WOULD YOU?
WELL, I'M NOT EXACTLY READY TO ENDORSE YOU FOR MAYOR, SPIDER-MAN -- BUT THANKS TO YOU, THE SANDMAN'S DEAD -- AND I'M GLAD OF IT!
I'M NOT SURE THE SANDMAN'S ANYTHING CLOSE TO DEAD, ACTUALLY. TURNING HIMSELF INTO A CLOUD OF SAND IS JUST ONE OF THE THINGS HE DOES.
IT MAY TAKE HIM A LONG TIME TO PULL HIMSELF BACK TOGETHER -- BUT I DON'T THINK WE'VE SEEN THE LAST OF HIM!
AT LEAST, I HOPE WE HAVEN'T. I MAY NOT WANT TO TANGLE WITH HIM AGAIN, BUT ACCIDENTALLY OR NOT --
-- I DON'T EVER WANT TO BE RESPONSIBLE FOR KILLING SOMEONE!

THE NEXT DAY, AT THE DAILY BUGLE...
DAILY BUGLE
NEW YORK'S FINEST DAILY NEWSPAPER
SPIDER-MAN HELPS SANDMAN ESCAPE
PERFECT! THIS PROVES THAT WALL-CRAWLING WEASEL IS THE MENACE I'VE ALWAYS SAID HE IS --
-- AND IT'S SELLING LIKE HOTCAKES ALL OVER THE CITY!
POOR JONAH! THIS IS THE ONLY JOY HE GETS IN LIFE! BUT LET HIM HAVE HIS FUN --
-- I'VE ALREADY PROVED EVERYTHING I NEED TO PROVE TO THE PERSON WHO REALLY MATTERS -- MYSELF!
SO, PRETTY LADY -- CARE TO LET ME MAKE GOOD ON THAT RAIN CHECK I GAVE YOU LAST NIGHT? I'VE GOT TWO TICKETS TO THIS GREAT JAZZ CLUB -- !
I'LL BE WITH YOU IN A SEC, PETER.
Mr. JAMESON -- A CALL FOR YOU. YOUR SON'S HOLDING ON LINE ONE.
NOW THEN, KIND SIR -- YOU WERE SAYING?
I KNOW IT'S SHORT NOTICE, BUT IT IS SATURDAY --
-- SO MAYBE JOLLY JONAH CAN SPARE YOU FOR --
WHAT?!
Hunh?
YOU'RE JOKING! YOU'RE LYING! YOU'RE INSANE!
I'M COMPLETELY SERIOUS, DAD!
I'LL BE UP IN NEW YORK IN A WEEK OR TWO TO START THE BALL ROLLING -- AND I'LL TELL YOU ALL ABOUT IT WHEN I GET THERE!

SHORTLY THEREAFTER:
THE I.C.M. CORPORATION ARRANGED A DEMONSTRATION OF ITS NEW SUPER-COMPUTER -- DUBBED "THE LIVING BRAIN" -- FOR THE SCIENCE CLASS AT MIDTOWN HIGH.
WOW! WHAT A CREEPY-LOOKIN' GIZMO THAT IS!
THAT "GIZMO" HAPPENS TO BE ONE OF THE SCIENTIFIC MARVELS OF THE AGE, LOUDMOUTH!
WELL, WELL! LISTEN TO PETER PARKER, THE DEMON SCIENTIST!
YOU SURE TALK BIG AND BRAVE WHEN THE TEACHER'S AROUND, EH, PUNY PARKER?
LOOK OUT, YOU DUMB CLOWN! MY GLASSES--!!
WHILE WAITING FOR THE DEMONSTRATION TO BEGIN, FLASH THOMPSON ACCIDENTALLY BROKE PETER'S GLASSES WHILE HORSING AROUND.
AS A TEST OF THE LIVING BRAIN'S POWERS, THE CLASS DECIDED TO DEDUCE SPIDER-MAN'S TRUE IDENTITY.
AND SO, THE CLASS CALLS OUT ALL THE FACTS THEY CAN THINK OF ABOUT THE COSTUMED MYSTERY MAN...
HE'S ABOUT FIVE FEET, TEN INCHES TALL!
WEIGHS ABOUT ONE-HUNDRED SIXTY POUNDS!
HE'S BEEN SIGHTED IN THE FOREST HILLS AREA A LOT!
HE'S THE MOST WONDERFUL, HEROIC, GLAMOROUS MAN IN THE WHOLE WORLD!
IF YOU ASK ME, HE'S A NEUROTIC NUT!
WE CAN'T STOP IT! CAN'T GET NEAR IT WHILE ITS ARMS ARE SWINGIN' THAT WAY!
ANYTHING CAN HAPPEN NOW! LET'S GET OUT OF HERE-- WHILE WE CAN!
BUT WHEN TWO TECHNICIANS ATTEMPTED TO STEAL THE BRAIN, THEY ACCIDENTALLY CAUSED A SHORT-CIRCUIT WHICH MADE THE MACHINE RUN WILD!
BECOMING SPIDER-MAN, PETER WAS ABLE TO BRING THE LIVING BRAIN'S RAMPAGE TO A HALT.
HE-- CAUGHT ME! HE CAN MOVE FASTER THAN I SUSPECTED!
I JUST REALIZED, FLASH-- YOU'RE THE ONLY ONE WHO WASN'T AROUND WHILE SPIDER-MAN WAS FIGHTING THE LIVING BRAIN!
AND YOU KNOCKED THESE TWO BURLY GUYS OUT AS EASY AS PIE! AND YOU'RE JUST ABOUT SPIDER-MAN'S SIZE!
SAY! PARKER'S RIGHT FOR ONCE! I NEVER THOUGHT OF THAT!
AND SO, SPIDER-MAN'S SECRET IDENTITY REMAINED A SECRET.

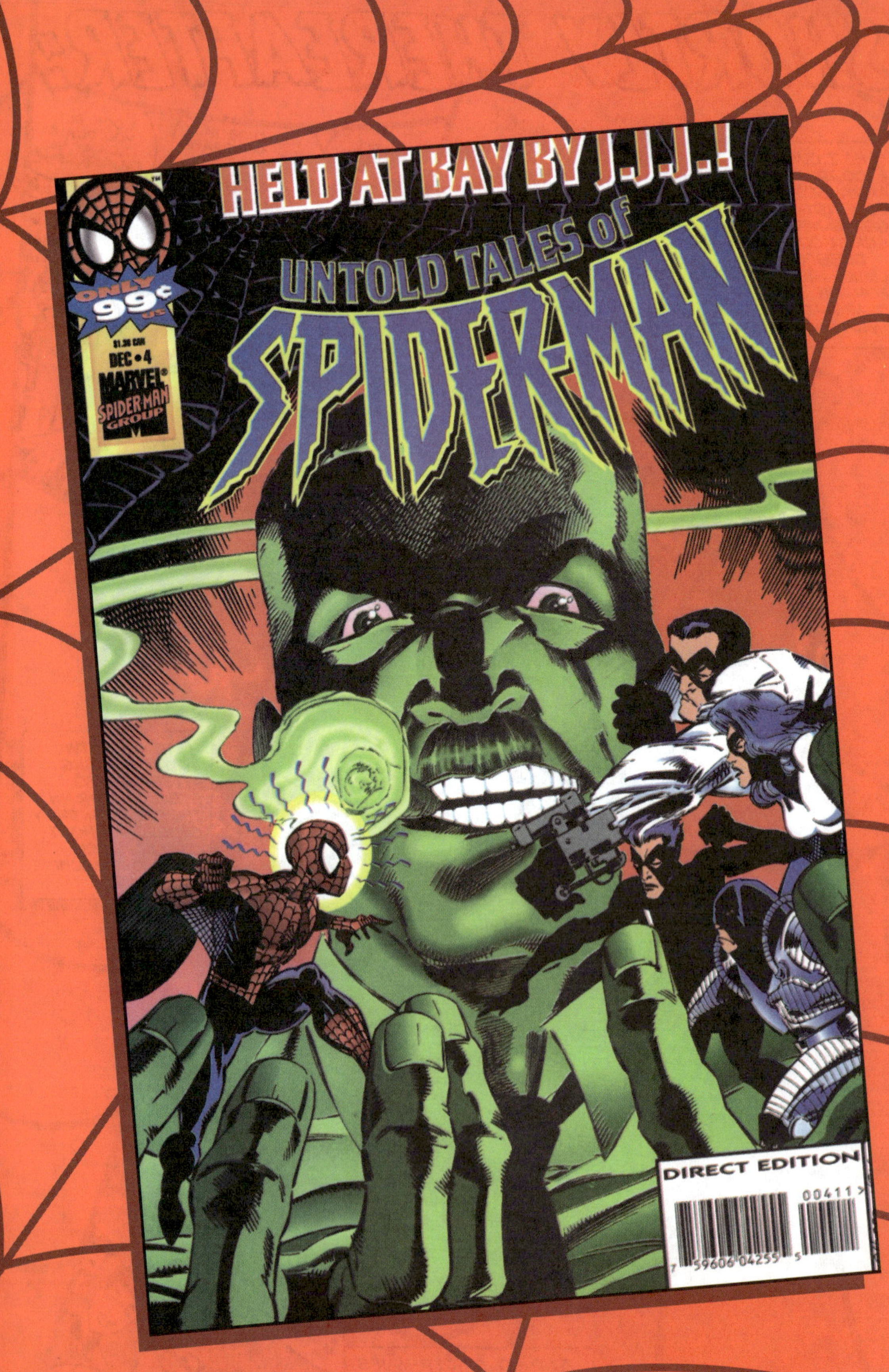
HELD AT BAY BY J.J.J.!
UNTOLD TALES OF
SPIDER-MAN
ONLY 99¢ US
$1.35 CAN
DEC • 4
MARVEL
SPIDER-MAN GROUP
DIRECT EDITION

Bitten by a radioactive spider, high school student **Peter Parker** gained the spider's powers, and soon became the costumed crimefighter the entire world would one day come to know as **Spider-Man!** In the early days of his career, when his amazing powers were still new to him, the teenaged Spider-Man struggled to learn about himself and his abilities, while trying to lead a **normal life!** It would **not** be easy...

STAN LEE PRESENTS... UNTOLD TALES OF SPIDER-MAN!

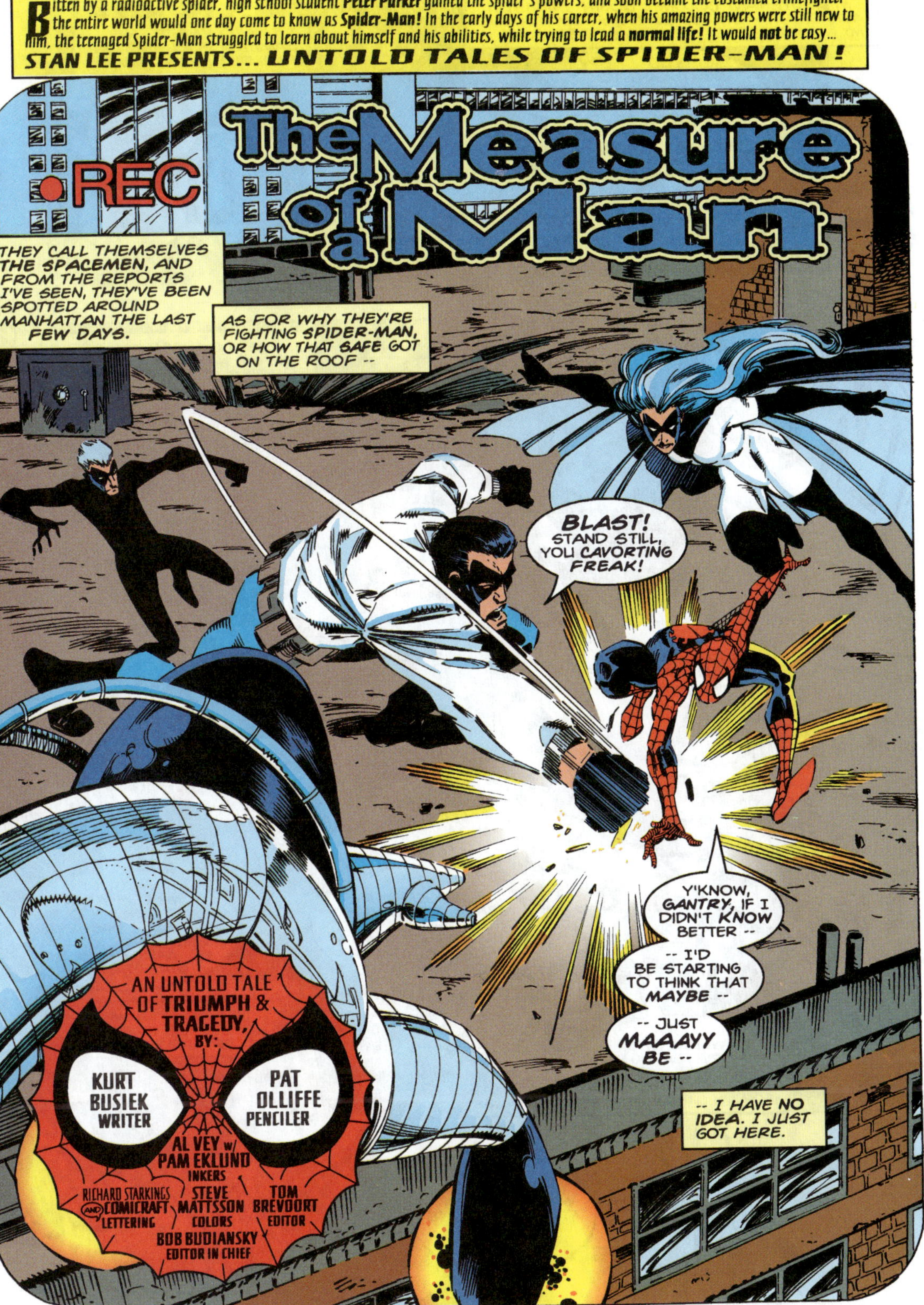

I'M LIEUTENANT COLONEL JOHN JAMESON, ASTRONAUT -- ON ASSIGNMENT FROM N.A.S.A. MY MAIN INTEREST HERE IS SPIDER-MAN.
YOU MIGHT WANT TO RADIO THE POLICE, CANYON -- THOUGH I DOUBT THEY'LL BE ABLE TO MAKE IT HERE BEFORE THIS IS OVER.
I TRY TO KEEEP THE CAMERA FOCUSED ON HIM, BUT IT'S NOT EASY.
CHECK. YOU STILL TAPING, SIR?
I'M STILL TAPING.
WRAK
-- YOU DON'T LIKE ME!
IT'S BREATHTAKING TO WATCH HIM, THOUGH.
Oh, WELL DONE, GANTRY! LEADING WITH YOUR CHIN LIKE THAT SET HIM UP PERFECTLY FOR MY LASER-BLASTS!
THERE'S DANGER ALL AROUND, BUT HE NEVER FREEZES UP, NEVER STOPS MOVING --
ONLY ONE PROBLEM, SATELLITE! IT'S KINDA HARD TO HIT A GUY --
-- WHO'S GOT A SPIDER-SENSE THAT LETS HIM KNOW WHERE YOUR BLASTS ARE AIMED PRACTICALLY BEFORE YOU DO!
Ah, BUT WHAT IF YOUR SPIDER-SENSE IS OVER-LOADED -- PRESENTED WITH DANGER FROM SO MANY DIFFRENT DIRECTIONS --
-- LIKE HE'S PLAYING HOPSCOTCH IN A MINEFIELD --
KRAM
-- THAT YOU CAN'T TELL WHERE THE NEXT ATTACK'S COMING FROM? WHAT DO YOU DO THEN?!
UHH!

WELL, ORBIT, MOSTLY I GET MY KEISTER HANDED TO ME, BUT I'M WORKING ON IT --!
YOU FORGOT ABOUT ME, SPIDER-MAN!
MY ENTIRE BODY'S AIRLESS, LIFELESS SPACE, AS YOU'RE ABOUT TO FIND OUT -- FROM THE INSIDE!
DO IT, VACUUM! THIS ROOF'S TOO GRIMY FOR HIM TO STICK TO FOR LONG!
Aw, CRIPES -- WHAT NOW?!
Huh --?
I'VE GOT A BETTER IDEA, GANTRY! YOU LIKE THE CONCEPT SO MUCH --
AND HE THINKS LIKE LIGHTNING -- EVEN IN THE MIDST OF CHAOS --
THWIPP
-- TAKING A DEADLY DANGER AND TURNING IT TO HIS ADVANTAGE!
SHUT IT DOWN, VACUUM! SHUT IT DOWN!
YOU GO!
I'M TRYING! BUT IT'S NOT EASY --
-- WHEN YOU'RE HALFWAY IN --!
ENOUGH!
SATELLITE! THE ROOF!
TRULY AMAZING.

THAT'S WHAT I LIKE ABOUT YOU, FEAR-LESS LEADER! WHEN THINGS AREN'T GOING YOUR WAY --
-- YOU GET CHILDISHLY DESTRUCTIVE!
Oh, NO! HIS LASERS --
CHOOM CHOOM CHOOM
KRSHMM
-- HE'S BRINGING THE WHOLE THING DOWN!
VERRY PERCEPTIVE, WEB-HEAD!
THEY ALL DISAPPEAR IN THE DUST AND RUBBLE, BUT I CAN'T BELIEVE SPIDER-MAN'S DEAD.
AND SURE ENOUGH, WHEN THE AIR CLEARS --
MANAGED TO DUCK UNDER A SUPPORT BEAM -- MISSED THE WORST OF IT!
BUT WOULDN'T YOU KNOW IT -- NO SIGN OF THE SPACE-MEN!
THE SAFE IS LATER FOUND WITH THE HINGES POPPED AND THE CASH MISSING -- BUT THERE'S NO WAY TO TELL WHO DID IT.
THE SMART MONEY WOULD BE ON SPIDER-MAN --

-- BUT THE SMART MONEY'S BEEN WRONG BEFORE.
SHOULD WE FOLLOW? HE MIGHT SWITCH BACK TO HIS NORMAL IDENTITY --
THAT'S NOT WHAT WE'RE HERE FOR, CANYON.
LET THE MAN KEEP HIS SECRETS.

THE NEXT MORNING, I CHECK IN WITH MY FATHER AND TELL HIM THE NEWS. HIS REACTION, REGRETFULLY, IS PREDICTABLE...
DAILY BUGLE
THIS IS BETRAYAL, JOHN! PURE, UNVARNISHED BETRAYAL!
I'VE JUST PRINTED A FRONT-PAGE STORY ACCUSING THAT WEB-HEADED WEASEL OF ROBBERY --
-- AND YOU TELL ME THAT N.A.S.A.'S CONSIDERING HIM AS A POTENTIAL ASTRONAUT?!
I TOLD YOU A WEEK AGO, DAD -- HIS REFLEXES, STRENGTH AND AGILITY MAKE HIM AN IDEAL CANDIDATE, AND WE'RE CONSIDERING HIM SERIOUSLY.
HE COULD CARRY OUT AN ASTRONAUT'S DUTIES BETTER THAN ANY NORMAL HUMAN COULD.
MY FATHER'S HATRED FOR SPIDER-MAN SEEMED TO START WHEN SPIDER-MAN GOT MORE PRESS THAN I DID, JUST BEFORE MY FIRST SPACEFLIGHT --

BAH! I WAS SURE YOU'D COME TO YOUR SENSES! HE'S A CRIMINAL!
THERE'S NO HARD EVIDENCE OF THAT!
I PROVED IT IN THE BUGLE A DOZEN TIMES OVER!
WITH ALL DUE RESPECT, SIR, EDITORIALS DON'T CONSTITUTE PROOF OF --
YOU'RE MAKING ME A LAUGHINGSTOCK, JOHN!
DAD, N.A.S.A. CAN'T JUST TAKE YOUR WORD FOR --
-- AND DEEPENED WHEN THE FLIGHT WENT AWRY -- AND SPIDER-MAN SAVED MY LIFE.

STILL, I'D HAVE THOUGHT IT WOULD HAVE FADED BY NOW, OR I'D NEVER HAVE SUGGESTED SPIDER-MAN TO N.A.S.A...
DON'T YOU HAVE ANY FAMILY PRIDE, SON? YOU'RE A JAMESON --
-- THE GLORY BELONGS TO YOU, NOT THAT MASKED MENACE!
IT'S NOT A QUESTION OF GLORY, DAD. THE JOB SHOULD GO TO WHOEVER'S BEST SUITED FOR IT.
RIGHT NOW, ALL I'M DOING IS OBSERVING SPIDER-MAN -- SO WE CAN DECIDE WHETHER TO APPROACH HIM. BUT PHYSICAL ABILITIES ASIDE --
-- SPIDER-MAN'S DEMONSTRATED CONSIDERABLE COURAGE -- CAPTURING DANGEROUS CRIMINALS -- RISKING HIS LIFE FOR OTHERS --
-:HARRUMPH!:- SO YOU KNOW ALL ABOUT HIM, DO YOU?
NO -- WE KNOW NOTHING ABOUT HIS BACKGROUND OR EDUCATION, OF COURSE. BUT I'VE BEEN GIVING IT A LOT OF THOUGHT --
-- TRYING TO IMAGINE WHAT SPIDER-MAN MUST BE LIKE UNDER THAT MASK. I'VE GOT TO FIGURE HE LIVES ALONE --
"-- HE'S TOO INDEPENDENT, TOO SELF-ASSURED TO DO OTHERWISE..."
PETER! YOU'RE NOT WEARING YOUR GLASSES!
THEY GOT BROKEN, AUNT MAY -- BUT IT'S OKAY. I DON'T NEED THEM ANY-MORE -- I CAN SEE JUST FINE!
NOW, PETER -- YOUR EYESIGHT IS NOTHING TO TRIFLE WITH. YOU DON'T WANT TO RISK PERMANENT DAMAGE BY --
I'VE GOT TO GET TO SCHOOL, AUNT MAY! CAN WE TALK ABOUT THIS WHEN I GET HOME?

BUT HE'S SUCH AN OUTGOING, GENIAL PERSON, JOKING ALL THE TIME --
-- HE MUST HAVE A LOT OF FRIENDS...
HEY, PETE! HOW'S IT GOIN', PAL? YOU WANT A RIDE TO SCHOOL?
Huh?
WELL, Uh, Gee -- SURE, FLASH! THANKS FOR AS --
THEN TAKE A BUS!!
VROOM
WHAT -- ? WHY, THAT ROTTEN, NO-GOOD -- !!

THAT WAS KINDA MEAN, FLASH--
AW, SO WHAT? SINCE WHEN DO YOU CARE ABOUT "PUNY" PARKER, TINY?
I'LL SHOW THAT MICROCEPHALIC MORON! HE DOESN'T KNOW WHO HE'S MESSING WITH!
A BALL OF WEBBING IN HIS TAILPIPE'LL TAKE THE WIND OUT OF HIS SAILS--!

AND ABOVE ALL, HE'S KNOWN AS AN ATHLETE.
I THINK ABOUT THE THINGS HE CAN DO-- THOSE AMAZING FEATS OF STRENGTH AND AGILITY --
-- AND I'VE GOT TO CONCLUDE THAT WHILE HE MAY BE ABLE TO KEEP HIS IDENTITY A SECRET...

"...THERE'S NO WAY HE COULD KEEP THOSE ABILITIES COMPLETELY TO HIMSELF --"
AW, WHO AM I KIDDING? AS SATISFYING AS IT WOULD BE TO TWIST FLASH THOMPSON'S TAIL --
-- I CAN'T RISK IT! AUNT MAY'S SO FRAGILE THESE DAYS --
-- IF ANYONE EVER EXPOSED MY IDENTITY AS SPIDER-MAN, THE SHOCK OF IT MIGHT KILL HER! I'VE GOT TO STAY MEEK, UNASSUMING PETER PARKER --
-- NO MATTER HOW HARD IT GETS.

-Hmph- SOUNDS LIKE YOU'VE WORKED UP QUITE THE PSYCHOLOGICAL PROFILE, SON! BUT I BET MY PRESSES SPIDER-MAN'S NOTHING LIKE --
MR. JAMESON! FREDERICK FOSWELL JUST CALLED FROM CITY HALL!
IT'S THE SPACEMEN --

" -- THEY'RE HOLDING A PRESS CONFERENCE!"
GREETINGS, GENTLEMEN AND LADIES OF THE PRESS!
WE'VE BEEN IN YOUR FAIR CITY LONG ENOUGH SO THAT WE REALLY SHOULD HAVE MADE A MORE FORMAL INTRODUCTION BEFORE NOW!
WE'RE THE SPACEMEN, AND AND WE'RE HERE TO ANSWER ANY QUESTIONS YOU MIGHT HAVE ABOUT US!
YOU SEE, JOHN? THIS IS WHAT IT'S ALL ABOUT --
-- HONESTY, INTEGRITY!
I'M STILL SKEPTICAL -- BUT THEN, I'M ONLY HERE AS AN OBSERVER --
-- SO I CONTINUE TO OBSERVE --
WE MUST REMAIN MASKED, FOR SECURITY REASONS, BUT WE CAN TELL YOU THIS MUCH ABOUT WHO WE ARE --
-- WE WERE PART OF A SECRET GOVERNMENT TASK FORCE --
"--THAT LAUNCHED A VERY SPECIAL SATELLITE INTO ORBIT AROUND EARTH!
" AN INDUCTION SATELLITE --
"--THAT ABSORBED MASSIVE QUANTITIES OF RADIATION FROM THE COSMIC RAY BELT -- AND TRANSMITTED IT DOWN TO EARTH --
"-- WHERE WE SUBJECTED OURSELVES TO THE DANGEROUS RADIATION, JUST AS THE WORLD-FAMOUS FANTASTIC FOUR DID --
"--ALLOWING IT TO CHANGE US -- TO IMBUE US WITH SUPER-POWERS --
"-- IN ORDER TO BE OF BETTER SERVICE TO OUR GREAT NATION!"

LADIES AND GENTLEMEN, WE ARE NOT VIGILANTES --
-- WE'RE HERE TO DO WHAT OUR GOVERNMENT AND CITIZENRY WANT OF US --
-- STARTING WITH OUR FIRST MISSION, WHICH SOME OF YOU HAVE ALREADY SEEN US WORKING ON --
-- THE APPREHENSION OF THE NOTORIOUS SPIDER-MAN!
NOW THIS IS WHAT SUPER HEROES SHOULD BE!
I'M NOT SO SURE, DAD -- I DON'T KNOW OF ANY GOVERNMENT AGENCY THESE GUYS ARE CONNECTED TO --
CLAP CLA-CLAPCLAP
-- AND YOU'D FIGURE N.A.S.A. WOULD KNOW OF ANY SATELLITE LAUNCH --!
PFAH! THEY SAID IT WAS A SECRET, DIDN'T THEY?
I'LL TELL YOU WHAT'S GOING TO HAPPEN -- THE BUGLE'S GOING TO GET BEHIND THE SPACEMEN! WE'LL MAKE SPIDER-MAN LOOK SO BAD --
-- N.A.S.A WOULDN'T HIRE HIM TO BE SO MUCH AS A JANITOR! AND YOU'LL REMAIN AMERICA'S TOP ASTRONAUT!
DAD -- I WISH YOU WOULDN'T --
TRUST YOUR OLD MAN, SON! I'LL WATCH OUT FOR YOUR BEST INTERESTS --
"-- EVEN IF YOU WON'T."
-- A HEARTY CHEER FOR DOING WHAT NEEDS TO BE DONE -- RIDDING THE CITY OF CRAVEN OPPORTUNISTS WHO TAKE THE LAW INTO THEIR OWN HANDS --
DAILY BUGLE
BUGLE PUBLISHER HAILS SPACEMEN
-- SOME COOKIES, PETER! A GROWING BOY NEEDS TO TAKE A BREAK EVERY NOW AND --
PETER! YOU LOOK SO TENSE! DO YOU FEEL WELL -- ?
IT'S OKAY, AUNT MAY. IT'S JUST A... SUDDEN HEADACHE --
-- AND YOU KNOW WHO I'M TALKING ABOUT --

SURE ENOUGH, IN THE DAYS THAT FOLLOW, SPIDER-MAN AND THE SPACEMEN CLASH SEVERAL MORE TIMES --
YOU WON'T GET AWAY WITH THIS SPIDER-MAN!
"GET AWAY WITH"? OF ALL THE COCKAMAMIE --
OOFF!
DAILY BUGLE
NEW YORK'S FINEST DAILY NEWSPAPER
SPACEMEN INTERRUPT BANK ROBBERY
SPIDER-MAN FLEES SCENE, ALONG WITH $30,000 CASH
-- AND THE BUGLE WEIGHS IN ENERGETICALLY ON THE SPACEMEN'S SIDE.
STILL --
WAKK
DAILY BUGLE
NEW YORK'S FINEST DAILY NEWSPAPER
SPACEMEN SPIDER-MAN EXCHANGE BLOWS ON WALL STREET
$250,000 IN NEGOTIABLE SECURITIES MISSING
-- IT'S CLEAR THAT SOMEONE'S USING THE BATTLES TO MASK A SERIES OF ROBBERIES. WITNESSES GIVE CONFUSED, CONTRADICTORY ACCOUNTS --
-- BUT I HAVE TO WONDER --
KLOW
DAILY BUGLE
NEW YORK'S FINEST DAILY NEWSPAPER
SPIDER-MAN SHOWS TRUE COLORS AT GALLERY OPENING
$50,000 IN CHARITY RECEIPTS STOLEN
-- ARE THE SPACEMEN RUNNING A SCAM --
THWIP
DON'T MOVE A MUSCLE, SPIDER-MAN -- WE'RE TAKING YOU IN!
Oh, I'M SURE YOU'D LIKE THAT, GANTRY --
-- OR EXPOSING ONE? COULD SPIDER-MAN'S PREVIOUS HEROICS HAVE JUST BEEN A COVER -- A FLASHY DISTRACTION FROM HIS TRUE ACTIVITIES -- ?

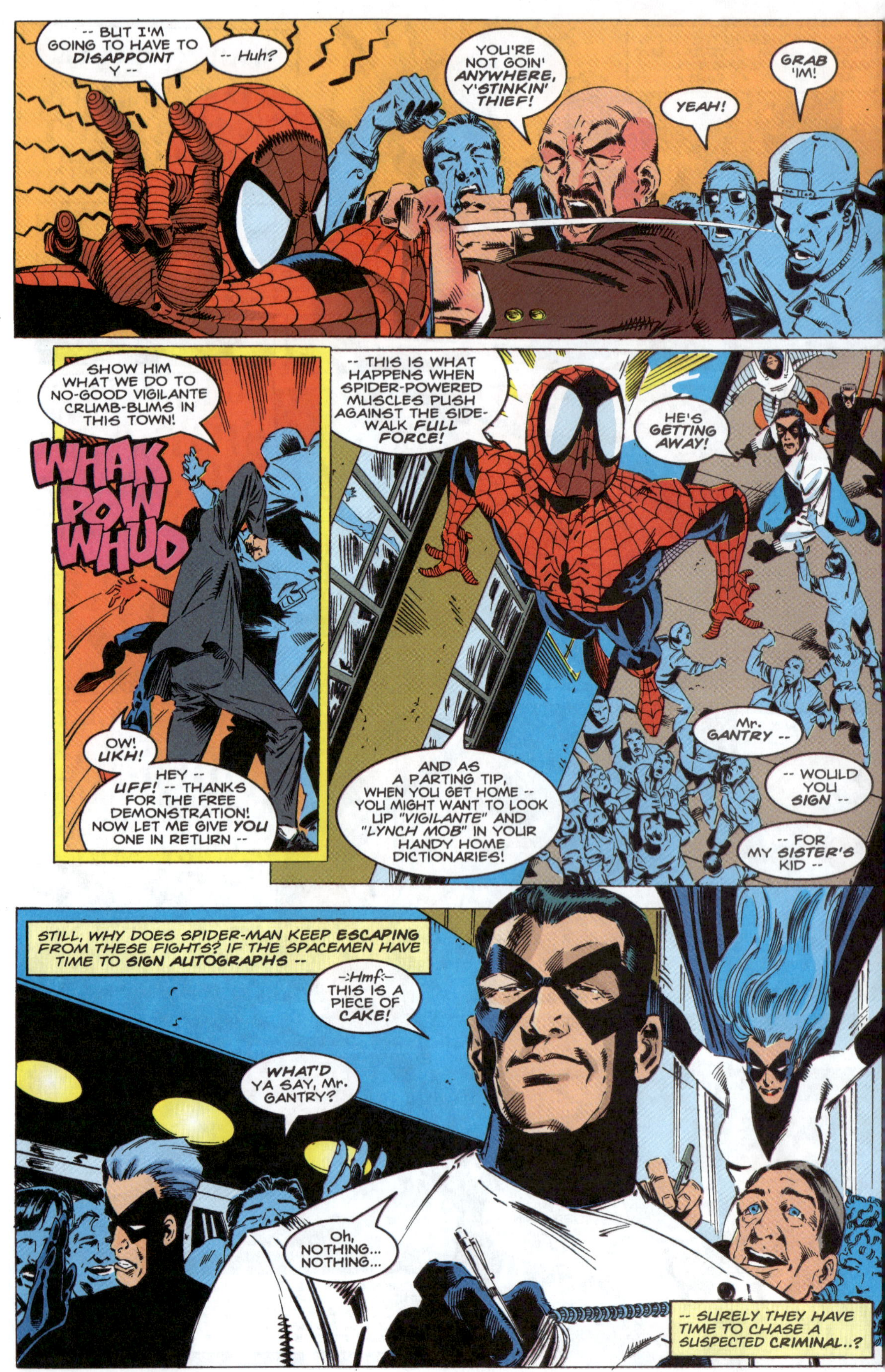
-- BUT I'M GOING TO HAVE TO DISAPPOINT Y --
-- Huh?
YOU'RE NOT GOIN' ANYWHERE, Y'STINKIN' THIEF!
YEAH!
GRAB 'IM!
SHOW HIM WHAT WE DO TO NO-GOOD VIGILANTE CRUMB-BUMS IN THIS TOWN!
WHAK POW WHUD
OW! UKH!
HEY -- UFF! -- THANKS FOR THE FREE DEMONSTRATION! NOW LET ME GIVE YOU ONE IN RETURN --
-- THIS IS WHAT HAPPENS WHEN SPIDER-POWERED MUSCLES PUSH AGAINST THE SIDE-WALK FULL FORCE!
HE'S GETTING AWAY!
AND AS A PARTING TIP, WHEN YOU GET HOME -- YOU MIGHT WANT TO LOOK UP "VIGILANTE" AND "LYNCH MOB" IN YOUR HANDY HOME DICTIONARIES!
Mr. GANTRY --
-- WOULD YOU SIGN --
-- FOR MY SISTER'S KID --
STILL, WHY DOES SPIDER-MAN KEEP ESCAPING FROM THESE FIGHTS? IF THE SPACEMEN HAVE TIME TO SIGN AUTOGRAPHS --
-Hmf- THIS IS A PIECE OF CAKE!
WHAT'D YA SAY, Mr. GANTRY?
Oh, NOTHING... NOTHING...
-- SURELY THEY HAVE TIME TO CHASE A SUSPECTED CRIMINAL..?

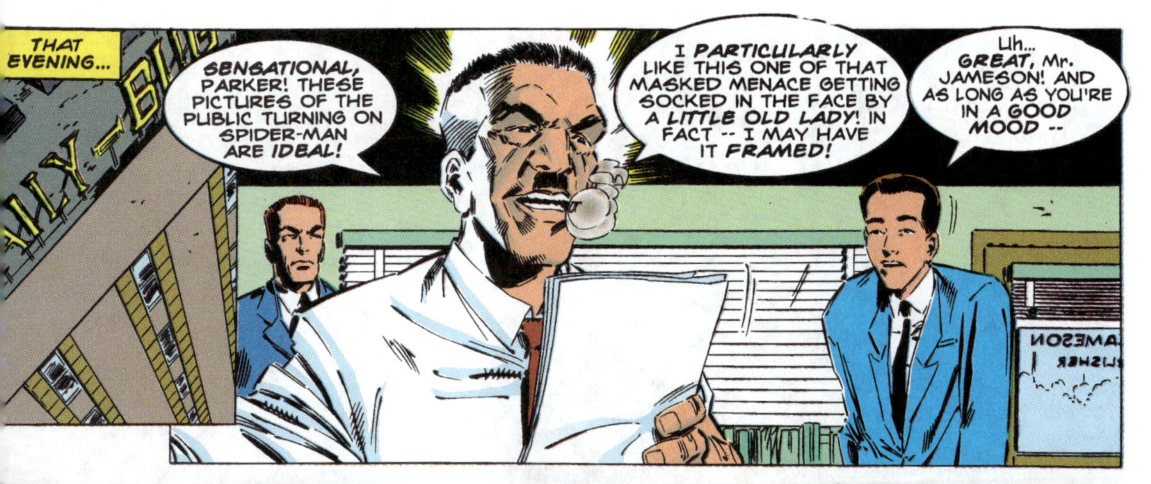
THAT EVENING...
SENSATIONAL, PARKER! THESE PICTURES OF THE PUBLIC TURNING ON SPIDER-MAN ARE IDEAL!
I PARTICULARLY LIKE THIS ONE OF THAT MASKED MENACE GETTING SOCKED IN THE FACE BY A LITTLE OLD LADY! IN FACT -- I MAY HAVE IT FRAMED!
Uh... GREAT, Mr. JAMESON! AND AS LONG AS YOU'RE IN A GOOD MOOD --

-- I'VE BEEN MEANING TO ASK IF BETTY BRANT COULD HAVE THE EVENING OFF THIS FRIDAY. SHE AND I HAVE BEEN PLANNING TO --
DON'T SAY ANOTHER WORD, MY BOY! I KNOW WHAT YOUNG LOVE'S LIKE!
Er... YOU DO?
I'M FEELING SO GOOD, I'LL NOT ONLY GIVE MISS BRANT THE NIGHT OFF, BUT I'LL GET YOU INTO THE EVENT OF THE SEASON --
-- MY LATEST ANTI-SPIDER-MAN LECTURE!
BRING YOUR CAMERA -- YOU CAN TAKE PICTURES FOR OUR COVERAGE OF THE EVENT, AND I'LL DEDUCT THE PRICE OF THE TICKETS FROM YOUR CHECK!

IT'S FUNNY -- PARKER HASN'T TURNED UP ON ANY WITNESS LISTS, BUT HE'S TAKEN PICTURES OF ALL THESE BATTLES. HE'S A PRETTY RESOURCEFUL KID.
NOW DON'T BOTHER TO THANK ME -- JUST GIVE YOUR GIRL THE HAPPY NEWS.
YOU'RE ALL HEART, Mr. JAMESON...
PERHAPS I SHOULD TALK TO HIM -- SEE IF HE KNOWS ANYTHING ABOUT SPIDER-MAN THAT WOULD BE HELPFUL...
YOU LOOK VERY HANDSOME WITHOUT YOUR GLASSES, PETER!
THANKS, BETTY -- BUT YOU MIGHT CHANGE YOUR MIND WHEN YOU HEAR WHERE WE'RE GOING FRIDAY NIGHT --!

SO, JOHN -- GIVEN UP THIS FOOLISH SPIDER-MAN THING YET?
DAD, I'M UNDER ORDERS -- TO OBSERVE AND MAKE A RECOMMENDATION--
HAH! WELL, WAIT'LL YOU SEE WHAT'S NEXT, SON --

"-- WAIT'LL YOU SEE WHAT'S NEXT!"
A TICKER-TAPE PARADE FOR THE SPACEMEN -- RIGHT DOWN FIFTH AVENUE.
WELL, ONE THING I'VE GOT TO SAY FOR MY FATHER -- HE DOESN'T DO THINGS BY HALVES!
The SPACEMEN
HEY, GWEN -- YOU WANT TO GET A SODA AFTER?
SURE, HARRY!
I'M CONCERNED ABOUT ALL THIS ADULATION FOR THE SPACEMEN, JONAH. YOU'RE WHIPPING THE PUBLIC INTO A FRENZY --
--FOR THE SPACEMEN AND AGAINST SPIDER-MAN!
AND WHILE MY RESEARCH INTO SPIDER-MAN IS INCONCLUSIVE AS YET, IT DOESN'T CONFIRM THAT THERE'S BEEN ANY CRIMINAL ACTIVITY BY HIM --
RESEARCH, SCHMESEARCH, CAPTAIN STACY! THE PEOPLE LOVE THIS --
The SPACEMEN

-- AND I DON'T SEE YOUR PRECIOUS SPIDER-MAN SHOWING UP HERE TO OBJECT, DO YOU?
HE'S PROBABLY AT HOME, HIDING UNDER THE BED -- IF HE'S HUMAN ENOUGH TO EVEN SLEEP IN A BED, THAT IS!
THAT'S RIDICULOUS, DAD!
NOBODY COULD TAKE THE KIND OF SMEAR CAMPAIGN YOU'VE BEEN DISHING OUT! THE WAY YOU'VE TURNED THE CITY AGAINST SPIDER-MAN --
--HE'D HAVE TO BE THE KIND OF MAN WHO DOESN'T CARE AT ALL ABOUT PUBLIC OPINION TO SHOW UP HERE!
HE'D HAVE TO BE COMPLETELY FOCUSED ON DOING WHAT HE THINKS IS RIGHT --
Hmph! I DON'T SEE PARKER IN THE CROWD!
IF HE DOESN'T GET PICTURES OF THIS TRIUMPH, I'LL --
-- NO MATTER WHAT THE REPERC --
-- UH, DAD --?
IT -- IT CAN'T BE --!
NICE DAY FOR A PARADE, GUYS! CAN ANYONE JOIN IN --
-- OR IS THIS FOR CROOKS ONLY?!
SPIDER-MAN!

THAT DOES IT, YOU WALL-CRAWLING SCOUNDREL -- YOU'VE THUMBED YOUR NOSE AT THE LAW LONG ENOUGH! THIS TIME YOU'RE GOING TO J --
WHAK
UHH!
SKIP THE POSTURING, GANTRY!
YOU NEVER ONCE WONDERED HOW I KEPT FINDING YOU WHENEVER YOU'D PULL A ROBBERY, DID YOU?
YOU MEAN HOW WE FOUND YOU!
SURE, SURE!
I WORKED UP A DEVICE TO TAP INTO YOUR SCRAMBLED RADIO SIGNALS! SO NOT ONLY DO I KNOW YOU PLANNED TO USE THIS PARADE AS A GETAWAY --
I ALSO KNOW WHERE YOU STASHED THE MONEY!
WHAT?!
YOU CAN'T -- I MEAN --
-- THE PUBLIC WILL NEVER BELIEVE SUCH LIES!
SPACEMEN --
PLAN S!
YOU TELL 'IM, GANTRY!
CLOBBER THAT WEB-SLINGIN' BUM!
GIVE 'IM ONE FER ME!
PLAN S! THAT MEANS I'LL GET HIM!
NO, SATELLITE -- I'LL GET HIM!
AH-AH, KIDDIES -- YOU'RE FORGETTING ABOUT MY SPIDER-SENSE!
NEITHER OF YOU IS --

-- GETTING... ME...
AW, NUTS! YOU USED MY SPIDER-SENSE TO HERD ME -- RIGHT INTO VACUUM!
WE SURE DID! SWALLOW US UP, BIG V!
I'VE REALLY GOT TO STOP EXPLAINING HOW MY POWERS WORK TO THE BAD GUYS.
GOOD ADVICE, SPIDER-MAN -- NOW LET ME TELL YOU HOW MINE WORK!
I FLY BY CREATING AN ORBITAL RELATIONSHIP BETWEEN MYSELF AND ANY OBJECT I CHOOSE -- IN EFFECT, ORBITING LIKE A SPACE-CRAFT!
BUT I CAN USE MY POWER ON THINGS OTHER THAN MYSELF! LIKE YOU FOR INSTANCE -- I'VE JUST PUT YOU IN ORBIT --
" --AROUND SATELLITE."
FINDING IT HARD TO BREATHE, SPIDER-MAN? I'M NOT SURPRISED --
--CONSIDERING VACUUM'S GOT NO AIR INSIDE HIM!
VERY WELL DONE, ORBIT! NOW ALL WE'VE GOT TO DO IS WAIT FOR SPIDER-MAN TO SUFFOCATE -- AND THEN WE TURN HIS BODY OVER TO THE POLICE!
NO TRIAL -- NO TESTIMONY -- THE CASE IS CLOSED, THE MONEY NEVER TURNS UP --
-- AND NOBODY'LL EVER FIGURE IT OUT!

HEY!
DON'T START SPENDING THE MONEY YET, YOU TWO -- HE'S STILL FIGHTING!
HE'S SNAGGED ME WITH HIS WEB --
-- AND THAT MEANS EVERY TIME HE ORBITS AROUND ME, IT GETS SHORTER --
-- AND HE GOES FASTER!
DO SOMETHING, GUYS! IF HE GOES FAST ENOUGH --
-- HE'LL REACH ESCAPE VELOCITY!
UFF!
KRASH
Ahh! THAT'S MUSIC TO MY EARS! SOUND DOESN'T TRAVEL IN A VACUUM -- BUT IT SURE IS SWEET OUT HERE!
GANTRY! ORBIT! NO!
YOU HIT THE FLOAT --!
Huh?
LOOK!
THE PARADE FLOAT -- THE PAPIER-MACHE MOON MOUNTAIN --
IT WAS STUFFED WITH CASH --!
THEN -- THE SPACE-MEN --

VACUUM! LOOK ALIVE, YOU SKINNY GEEK! SUCK ALL THIS CASH IN BEFORE THE CROWD GETS IT!
WE DIDN'T GO TO THE TROUBLE OF STEALING IT SO THESE STUMBLEBUMS COULD HAVE IT!
Huh? YOU HEAR THAT?!
THEN -- THEY'RE THE CROOKS!
UH-oh!
IT WAS THEM ALL ALONG -- NOT SPIDER-MAN!
PERRY MASON COULDN'T HAVE DONE IT BETTER! AT LEAST -- NOT IN A SKIN-TIGHT COSTUME, HE COULDN'T!
THANKS FOR THE CONFESSION, SATELLITE!
KRAT
UHH!
WE KNOW YOUR BODY'S IMPERVIOUS TO BULLETS, VACUUM, BUT YOUR FACE LOOKS PRETTY NORMAL! TELL ME --
-- CAN YOU TAKE A BULLET TO THE HEAD?!
Uh --
AND ON THAT CHEERY NOTE, I BID YOU ALL A FOND ADIEU, WITH JUST ONE FINAL QUESTION FOR THE PEANUT GALLERY!
HEY, JONAH! HOW DOES IT FEEL TO BE WRONG -- AGAIN?!
IT TURNED OUT THE SPACEMEN HAD LIED ABOUT HOW THEY GOT THEIR POWERS --

-- BUT BY THE TIME ALL THE DIFFERENT FEDERAL SECURITY AGENCIES HAD DISAVOWED THEM, IT WAS ALL OVER.
DAD? I WANTED TO SEE YOU, BEFORE I HEAD BACK. I THOUGHT YOU'D LIKE TO KNOW --
-- N.A.S.A.'S SCRAPPING THE IDEA OF SPIDER-MAN AS AN ASTRONAUT.
THEY WERE ALL EX- SPACE-PROGRAM TRAINEES -- WASHOUTS WHO'D USED THEIR INSIDER KNOWLEDGE TO STEAL SOME METEOR SAMPLES I BROUGHT BACK FROM A SPACE MISSION.
WHEN THEY UNSEALED THE STERILE CONTAINERS, THE METEORS CRACKED, GIVING OFF AN ALIEN GAS THAT GAVE THEM THEIR POWERS.
DESPITE HIS ABILITIES, PART OF ANY SPACE MISSION IS THE DATA WE GET ON HOW SPACE TRAVEL AFFECTS HUMANS --
-- AND NONE OF THE DATA WE'D GET ON SPIDER-MAN WOULD BE APPLICABLE TO ANYONE ELSE.
HE'S JUST TOO FAR OUTSIDE THE NORM.
THEY COULD HAVE BEEN THE HEROES THEY PRETENDED TO BE -- USED THEIR ABILITIES TO SERVE THEIR COUNTRY, AS THEY ONCE WANTED TO.
HE CAN'T BE A HERO... HE CAN'T BE THAT NOBLE...
DAD? DAD?
I'M GOING NOW, DAD...
IF HE'S A HERO, THEN WHAT DOES THAT MAKE ME...
...CIVIC LEADER... UPSTANDING CITIZEN... HAH...
NO... HE MUST BE A CRIMINAL... HE MUST HAVE AN ULTERIOR MOTIVE...
INSTEAD THEY LET THEMSELVES BE DRIVEN BY ANGER AND JEALOUSY, UNTIL IT WAS TOO LATE.
J. JONAH JAMESON PUBLISHER
THEY COULD HAVE BEEN HEROES...

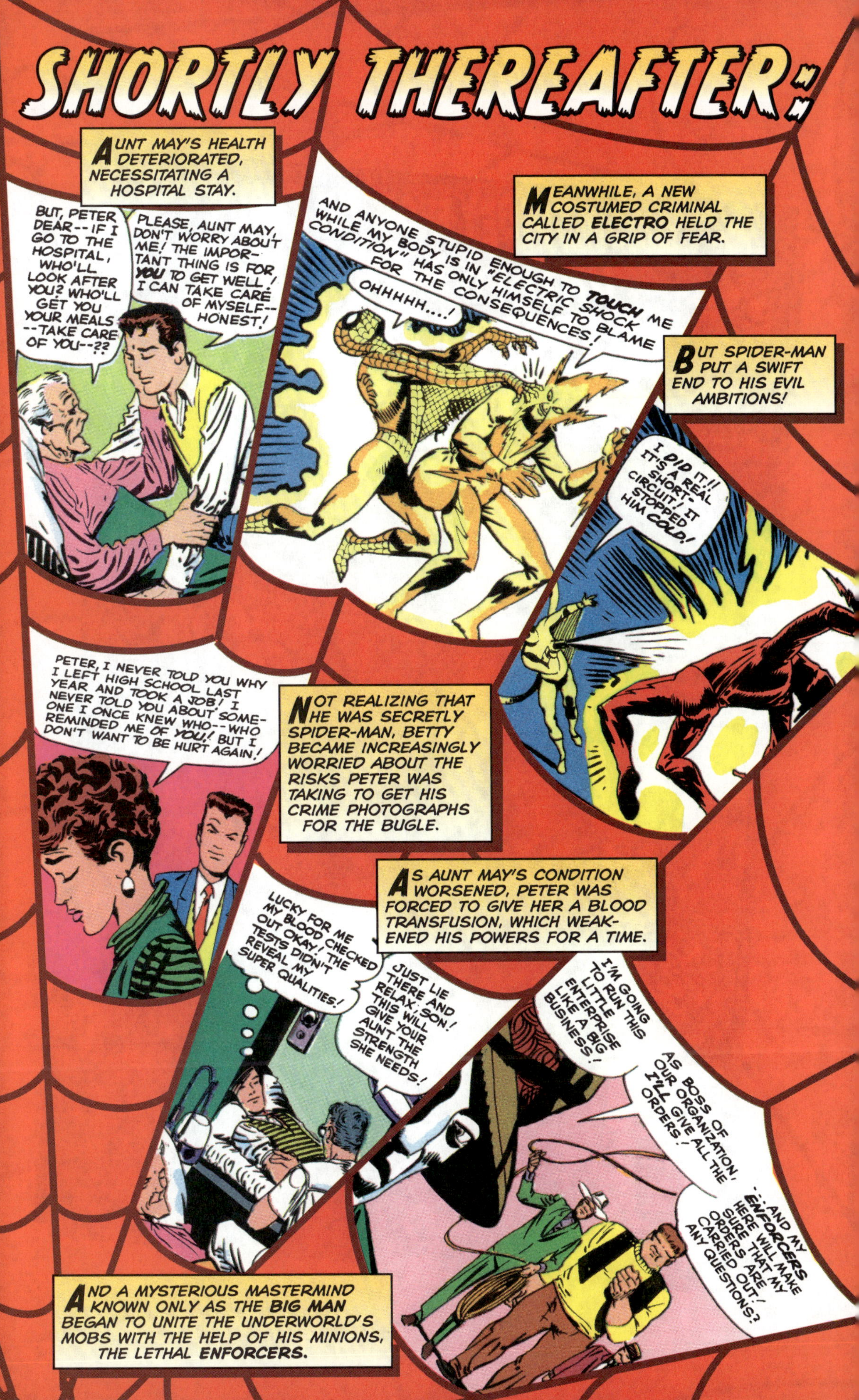
SHORTLY THEREAFTER:
AUNT MAY'S HEALTH DETERIORATED, NECESSITATING A HOSPITAL STAY.
BUT, PETER DEAR-- IF I GO TO THE HOSPITAL, WHO'LL LOOK AFTER YOU? WHO'LL GET YOU YOUR MEALS --TAKE CARE OF YOU--??
PLEASE, AUNT MAY, DON'T WORRY ABOUT ME! THE IMPORTANT THING IS FOR YOU TO GET WELL! I CAN TAKE CARE OF MYSELF-- HONEST!
MEANWHILE, A NEW COSTUMED CRIMINAL CALLED ELECTRO HELD THE CITY IN A GRIP OF FEAR.
AND ANYONE STUPID ENOUGH TO TOUCH ME WHILE MY BODY IS IN "ELECTRIC SHOCK CONDITION" HAS ONLY HIMSELF TO BLAME FOR THE CONSEQUENCES!
OHHHHH...!
BUT SPIDER-MAN PUT A SWIFT END TO HIS EVIL AMBITIONS!
I DID IT!! IT'S A REAL SHORT-CIRCUIT! IT STOPPED HIM COLD!
PETER, I NEVER TOLD YOU WHY I LEFT HIGH SCHOOL LAST YEAR AND TOOK A JOB! I NEVER TOLD YOU ABOUT SOMEONE I ONCE KNEW WHO-- WHO REMINDED ME OF YOU! BUT I DON'T WANT TO BE HURT AGAIN!
NOT REALIZING THAT HE WAS SECRETLY SPIDER-MAN, BETTY BECAME INCREASINGLY WORRIED ABOUT THE RISKS PETER WAS TAKING TO GET HIS CRIME PHOTOGRAPHS FOR THE BUGLE.
AS AUNT MAY'S CONDITION WORSENED, PETER WAS FORCED TO GIVE HER A BLOOD TRANSFUSION, WHICH WEAKENED HIS POWERS FOR A TIME.
LUCKY FOR ME MY BLOOD CHECKED OUT OKAY! THE TESTS DIDN'T REVEAL MY SUPER QUALITIES!
JUST LIE THERE AND RELAX, SON! THIS WILL GIVE YOUR AUNT THE STRENGTH SHE NEEDS!
I'M GOING TO RUN THIS LITTLE ENTERPRISE LIKE A BIG BUSINESS!
AS BOSS OF OUR ORGANIZATION, I'LL GIVE ALL THE ORDERS!
...AND MY ENFORCERS HERE WILL MAKE SURE THAT MY ORDERS ARE CARRIED OUT! ANY QUESTIONS?
AND A MYSTERIOUS MASTERMIND KNOWN ONLY AS THE BIG MAN BEGAN TO UNITE THE UNDERWORLD'S MOBS WITH THE HELP OF HIS MINIONS, THE LETHAL ENFORCERS.

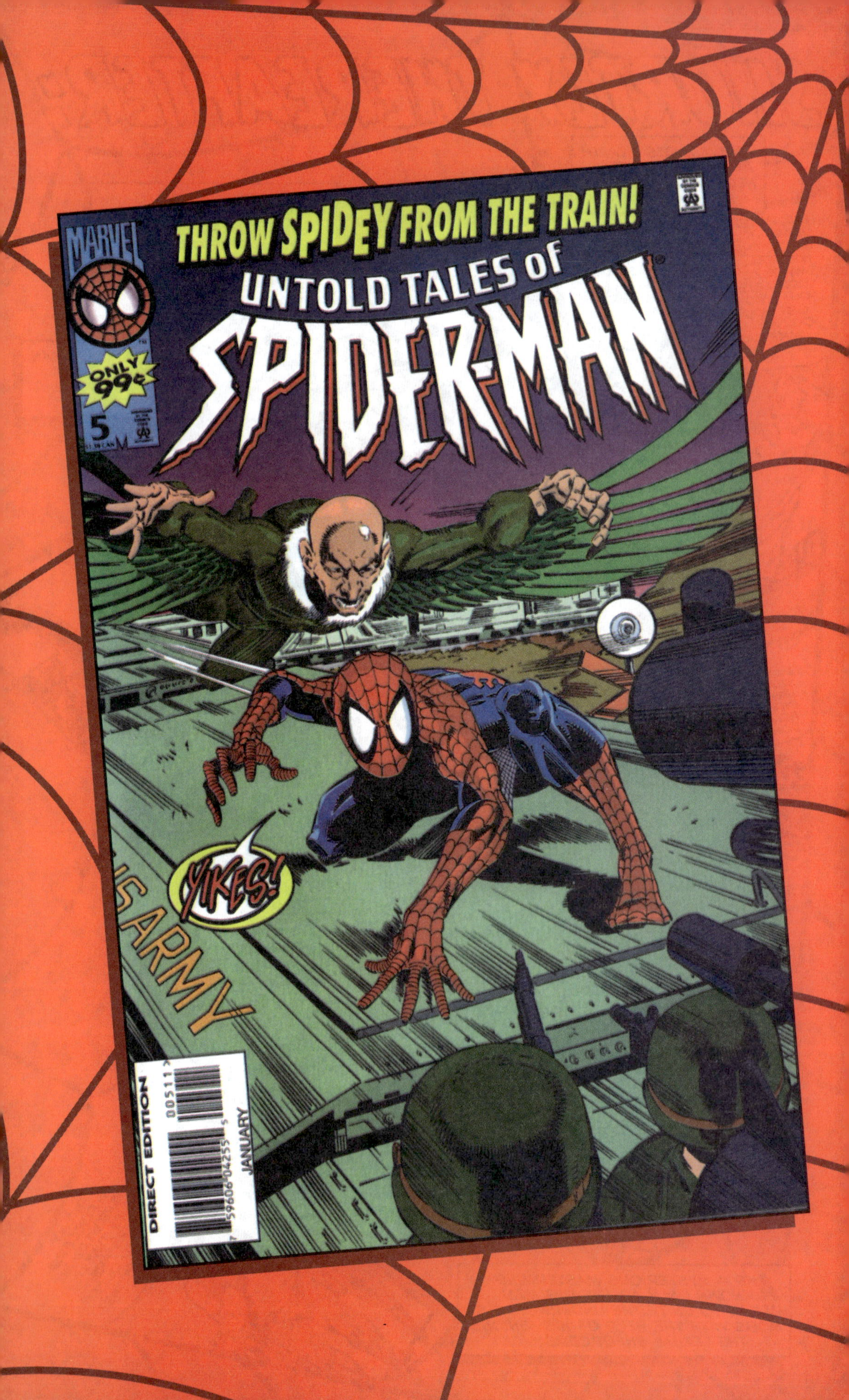
MARVEL
THROW SPIDEY FROM THE TRAIN!
UNTOLD TALES OF
SPIDER-MAN
ONLY 99¢
5
YIKES!
US ARMY
DIRECT EDITION
JANUARY

VULTURE ON THE WING!
HIGH-FLYING THRILLS, COURTESY OF:
KURT BUSIEK WRITER
PAT OLLIFFE PENCILER
AL MILGROM INKER
RICHARD STARKINGS AND COMICRAFT LETTERING
STEVE MATTSSON COLORS
TOM BREVOORT EDITOR
BOB BUDIANSKY EDITOR IN CHIEF
A TYPICAL EVENING IN MID-MANHATTAN...
YOU MAY HAVE DEFEATED ME BEFORE, SPIDER-MAN -- BUT NEVER AGAIN! INTERFERE WITH THE VULTURE'S PLANS --
-- AND YOU'LL DIE!
AW, VULTCH, VULTCH, VULTCH!
I COME ALL THIS WAY TO WELCOME YOU BACK TO THE CITY -- IN THE POURING RAIN NO LESS --
-- AND THIS IS THE RECEPTION I GET?!
AT LEAST, TYPICAL FOR THE AMAZING SPIDER-MAN!

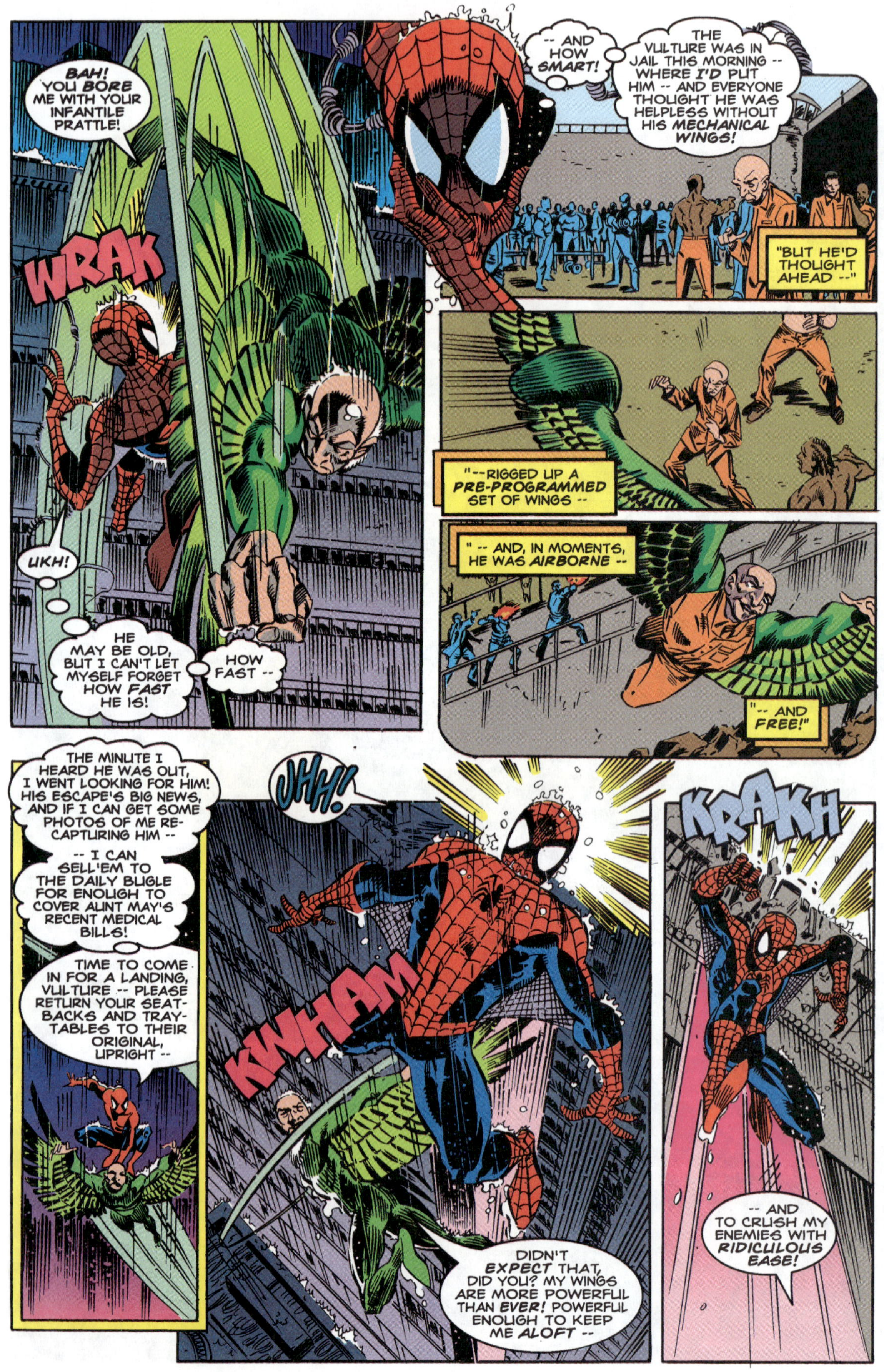
BAH! YOU BORE ME WITH YOUR INFANTILE PRATTLE!
WRAK
-- AND HOW SMART!
THE VULTURE WAS IN JAIL THIS MORNING -- WHERE I'D PUT HIM -- AND EVERYONE THOUGHT HE WAS HELPLESS WITHOUT HIS MECHANICAL WINGS!
"BUT HE'D THOUGHT AHEAD --"
"--RIGGED UP A PRE-PROGRAMMED SET OF WINGS --
" -- AND, IN MOMENTS, HE WAS AIRBORNE --
"-- AND FREE!"
UKH!
HE MAY BE OLD, BUT I CAN'T LET MYSELF FORGET HOW FAST HE IS!
HOW FAST --
THE MINUTE I HEARD HE WAS OUT, I WENT LOOKING FOR HIM! HIS ESCAPE'S BIG NEWS, AND IF I CAN GET SOME PHOTOS OF ME RE-CAPTURING HIM --
-- I CAN SELL'EM TO THE DAILY BUGLE FOR ENOUGH TO COVER AUNT MAY'S RECENT MEDICAL BILLS!
TIME TO COME IN FOR A LANDING, VULTURE -- PLEASE RETURN YOUR SEAT-BACKS AND TRAY-TABLES TO THEIR ORIGINAL, UPRIGHT --
UHH!
KWHAM
DIDN'T EXPECT THAT, DID YOU? MY WINGS ARE MORE POWERFUL THAN EVER! POWERFUL ENOUGH TO KEEP ME ALOFT --
KRAKH
-- AND TO CRUSH MY ENEMIES WITH RIDICULOUS EASE!

THAT **DOES** IT! I'VE DANCED AROUND WITH HIM -- KEPT HIM IN RANGE OF MY **AUTOMATIC CAMERA** LONG ENOUGH TO GET **PLENTY** OF GOOD SHOTS --

-- BUT ENOUGH'S **ENOUGH!**

THWIP

WHAT -- ?!

Oh, DON'T ACT SO **SURPRISED,** VULTURE -- THIS IS HOW I **ALWAYS** BEAT YOU! I GET CLOSE ENOUGH TO YOU TO PUT THE **KIBOSH** ON YOUR WINGS --

-- AND THAT'S **ALL SHE WROTE!**

NEVER!

LOOK!

HIS WINGS -- LOOK AT HOW **GRACEFULLY** HE SOARS!

Aw, C'MON, LADY -- HE'S A CROOK!

THEY **BOTH** ARE, IF YOU ASK ME! THE BUGLE SAYS --!

HERE WE GO AGAIN! I RISK MY LIFE MY LIFE TO CATCH A DANGEROUS CRIMINAL --

-- AND THANKS TO J. JONAH JAMESON'S EDITORIALS, THE PUBLIC'S AS SCARED OF ME AS THEY ARE OF THE BAD GUYS!

STILL, ONCE I CAPTURE HIM, MAYBE IT'LL CHANGE A FEW --

-- Oh, NO!

THAT ADVERTISING SIGN! IF I DON'T MOVE, AND PRONTO --

-- I'LL BE SLICED IN **HALF!**

The Best Blade in

HAH! AGE AND TREACHERY BEATS YOUTH AND ENTHUSIASM ANY DAY! YOU'RE SUCH A **FOOL,** SPIDER-MAN --

-- AND THAT'S WHY YOU MAY DELAY MY TRIUMPH, BUT STILL I PERSEVERE!
I'LL EVEN TELL YOU WHAT I'LL STEAL NEXT -- JUST TO PROVE TO YOU THAT THE KNOWLEDGE WILL DO YOU NO GOOD!
MY TARGET IS THE EXPERIMENTAL ATOMIC ACCELERATOR THE ARMY'S BRINGING THROUGH THE CITY BY TRAIN, TOMORROW NIGHT!
I EXPECT YOU TO CHALLENGE ME! I INVITE YOU TO!
BUT YOU'LL FAIL, SPIDER-MAN --
-- YOU'LL FAIL!
WE'LL SEE ABOUT THAT, VULTURE!
BLAST! HE SWOOPED UNDER MY WEB-LINE -- MISSED HIM!
AND HE'S TOO FAR AWAY FOR ANOTHER SHOT!
AND DOLLARS TO DONUTS HALF THE WITNESSES THINK I LET HIM GET AWAY -- THAT I'M IN CAHOOTS WITH HIM --
-- WHICH, I GUARANTEE, IS EXACTLY WHAT THEY'LL TELL THE REPORTERS AND THE POLICE WHEN THEY GET HERE!
Ah, WELL, NO SENSE BEATING MYSELF UP OVER IT! I'LL GET ANOTHER CRACK AT HIM --
-- AND IN THE MEAN-TIME, I'LL HAVE A CHECK FROM JOLLY JONAH TO KEEP ME WARM!
BUT...
Aw, NUTS! WHEN THE VULTURE SMASHED ME INTO THE WALL -- I MUST HAVE HIT THE CAMERA!
IT'S CRUSHED! USELESS!
NOW, I NOT ONLY WON'T GET THAT MONEY I NEED --
-- I'LL HAVE TO PAY TO GET MY CAMERA FIXED BEFORE I CAN EARN ANOTHER DIME! I'VE GOT TWO KINDS OF LUCK -- BAD AND WORSE!

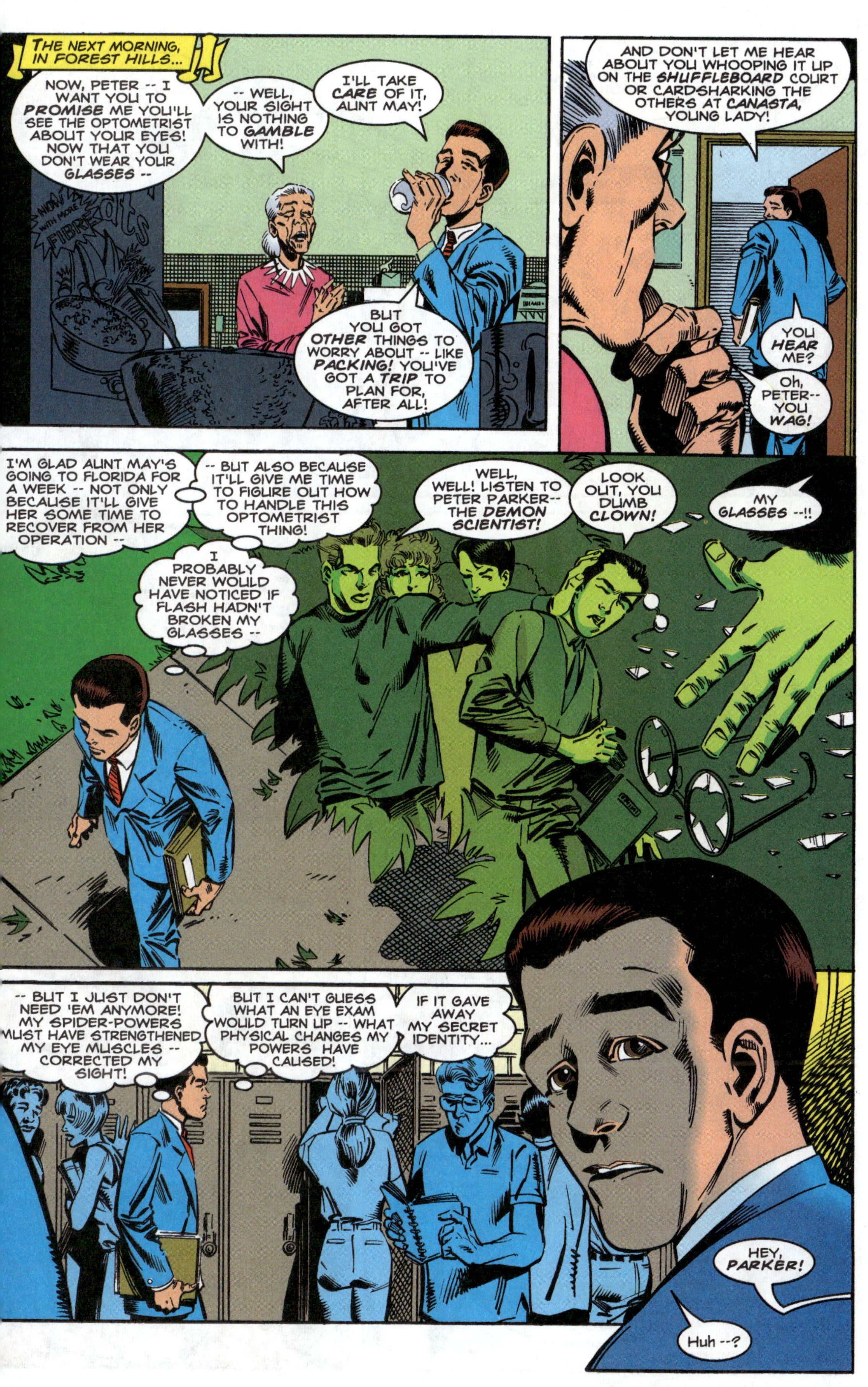
THE NEXT MORNING, IN FOREST HILLS...
NOW, PETER -- I WANT YOU TO PROMISE ME YOU'LL SEE THE OPTOMETRIST ABOUT YOUR EYES! NOW THAT YOU DON'T WEAR YOUR GLASSES --
-- WELL, YOUR SIGHT IS NOTHING TO GAMBLE WITH!
I'LL TAKE CARE OF IT, AUNT MAY!
BUT YOU GOT OTHER THINGS TO WORRY ABOUT -- LIKE PACKING! YOU'VE GOT A TRIP TO PLAN FOR, AFTER ALL!
AND DON'T LET ME HEAR ABOUT YOU WHOOPING IT UP ON THE SHUFFLEBOARD COURT OR CARDSHARKING THE OTHERS AT CANASTA, YOUNG LADY!
YOU HEAR ME?
Oh, PETER-- YOU WAG!
I'M GLAD AUNT MAY'S GOING TO FLORIDA FOR A WEEK -- NOT ONLY BECAUSE IT'LL GIVE HER SOME TIME TO RECOVER FROM HER OPERATION --
-- BUT ALSO BECAUSE IT'LL GIVE ME TIME TO FIGURE OUT HOW TO HANDLE THIS OPTOMETRIST THING!
I PROBABLY NEVER WOULD HAVE NOTICED IF FLASH HADN'T BROKEN MY GLASSES --
WELL, WELL! LISTEN TO PETER PARKER-- THE DEMON SCIENTIST!
LOOK OUT, YOU DUMB CLOWN!
MY GLASSES --!!
-- BUT I JUST DON'T NEED 'EM ANYMORE! MY SPIDER-POWERS MUST HAVE STRENGTHENED MY EYE MUSCLES -- CORRECTED MY SIGHT!
BUT I CAN'T GUESS WHAT AN EYE EXAM WOULD TURN UP -- WHAT PHYSICAL CHANGES MY POWERS HAVE CAUSED!
IF IT GAVE AWAY MY SECRET IDENTITY...
HEY, PARKER!
Huh --?

JUST THE MAN I WANTED TO SEE!
AND HOW ARE YOU ENJOYING OUR FINE ALMA MATER TODAY, PARKER? PULSE QUICKENING IN ANTICIPATION OF THAT CHEM QUIZ IN FOURTH PERIOD?
WHAT DO YOU WANT, FLASH?
WELL, I'LL TELL YOU. I'VE BEEN THINKING LONG AND HARD, TRYING TO FIGURE OUT HOW TO MAKE IT UP TO YOU FOR BREAKING YOUR GLASSES.
AND IT TOOK ME A WHILE, BUT I THINK I MANAGED TO FIX THEM.
YOU DIDN'T NEED TO DO THAT, FLASH --
OH, BUT I DID. NOW THE ONLY PROBLEM IS --
-- NOW THAT YOU'VE GOT THE BOTTOMS, WHAT DO I DO WITH THE REST OF THE COKE BOTTLES?!
OH, HA HA. VERY FUNNY, FLASH.
YOU KNOW, PARKER'S A PRETTY GOOD SPORT, PUTTIN' UP WITH ALL THE RIBBING HE GETS AROUND HERE!
HE MAY BE A BRAIN, BUT HE'S OKAY!
RM 202
AND YOU KNOW -- I NEVER NOTICED IT BEFORE, BUT HE'S NOT ALL THAT BAD-LOOKING WITHOUT THOSE GLASSES...
WHA-A-AT?! YOU CAN'T BE SERIOUS, LIZ!
WHADDYA MEAN HE'S NOT BAD-LOOKING? HE'S PARKER, FOR CRIPES' SAKE! HE'S SO --
-- SO PARKER!

A FEW
OURS
ATER...
GOOD THING I MANAGED TO HITCH A RIDE ON THAT TRAFFIC COPTER!
OTHERWISE 'D NEVER HAVE ADE IT ALL THE WAY UP TO THE RONX AND BACK URING LUNCH PERIOD!
D STATES
RMORY
BUT THIS IS WHERE THE SECURITY PREPARATIONS ARE BEING MADE FOR THE ATOMIC ACCELERATOR--
-- AND THERE'S THE MAN I'VE COME TO TALK TO --
--GENERAL THADDEUS "THUNDERBOLT" ROSS!
Eh?!
WHAT'S THE MEANING OF THIS INTRUSION?! IF YOU THINK YOU CAN INTIMIDATE ME --
FROM WHAT I'VE READ ABOUT YOU, SIR -- IT TAKES A LOT MORE THAN ME TO INTIMIDATE YOU! NO, I'M HERE TO WARN YOU --
-- THAT THE VULTURE INTENDS TO HIJACK YOUR ATOMIC ACCELERATOR -- AND HE PLANS TO STRIKE TONIGHT!
BAH! AS IF IT WEREN'T ENOUGH DEALING WITH UNPROFESSIONAL CIVILIAN SCIENTISTS, FOREIGN SPIES AND THE LIKE --
-- NOW I'VE GOT TO CONTEND WITH --
WAIT A MINUTE THERE, SON. WHAT MADE YOU COME ALL THE WAY UP HERE TO TELL ME ABOUT THIS?
WHAT'S IN IT FOR YOU?

I'M JUST DOING MY DUTY, SIR! I'M AWARE OF A THREAT TO YOUR CARGO, SO IT'S MY RESPONSIBILITY TO --
HMPH! I DON'T BELIEVE IT!
THE YOUNGER GENERATION DOESN'T KNOW THE MEANING OF THE WORD "RESPONSIBILITY," SON! NOBODY DOES ANY-THING FOR FREE ANYMORE!
YOU MUST BE HERE TO GET SOMETHING FROM ME, SO LET'S HAVE IT! SPEAK UP -- I'M A BUSY MAN!
WELL, ah, AS LONG AS YOU MENTION IT -- I COULD USE SOME WORK!
IF YOU NEED SOME, um, EXTRA PROTECTION FOR THE ACCELERATOR, I'M AVAILABLE -- AT, ah, REASONABLE RATES?
I KNEW IT! OF ALL THE UNMITIGATED GALL -- TRYING TO SHAKE DOWN THE U.S. ARMY BY MANUFACTURING BOGUS THREATS TO GET US TO HIRE YOU!
WELL, IT WON'T WORK, YOU HEAR ME?! THE CITY OF NEW YORK MAY TOLERATE YOUR EFFRONTERY -- BUT I DON'T!
M.P.'S -- ARREST THIS MAN!
OOPS, LOOK AT THE TIME!
GOTTA GO, GENERAL -- BUT IT'S BEEN GREAT TALKING TO YOU!
BLAM
HE'S MAKING A RUN FOR IT!
BLAM
BLAM
WE MUST GET TOGETHER FOR TEA AND COOKIES SOMETIME SOON!
DON'T LET HIM GET AWAY!
JERK! I HOPE THE ACCELERATOR DOES GET STOLEN -- IT'D SERVE THAT CLOSED-MINDED OLD BLOWHARD RIGHT!
AW, WHO AM I TRYING TO KID? I'LL STILL TRY TO STOP THE VULTURE -- NOT BECAUSE ROSS DESERVES IT, BUT BECAUSE THE VULTURE DOES!
BUT RIGHT NOW, I'VE GOT TO GET BACK TO SCHOOL --

" -- BEFORE I'M LATE FOR -- ->UGH<- -- GYM CLASS!"
MAN, I LOVE DODGE BALL! WHOMPIN' ON NERDS AND DWEEBS, AND DOING IT AS PART OF SCHOOL --
-- IS THIS A GREAT COUNTRY OR WHAT?
PARKER -- COULD YOU STAY FOR A FEW MINUTES WHILE THE OTHERS ARE SHOWERING AND CHANGING, TO HELP ME CLEAN UP?
BWAMP
OW!
SURE, Mr. MURCH -- ANYTHING TO GET ME OUT OF FLASH'S FIRING RANGE!
BUT AS PETER STRAIGHTENS UP THE GYMNASIUM...
NOT SO BAD-LOOKING, Huh? WELL, PARKER -- YOU'RE ABOUT TO LEARN THAT FLASH ISN'T THE ONLY ONE WHO CAN MAKE YOU LOOK LIKE A DOPE!
AND SOON...
"YOU'RE GONNA LOVE THIS, GUYS!
"WHILE PARKER WAS SHOWERING --
Huh?
-- I SWIPED HIS STREET-CLOTHES, HIS GYM UNIFORM --
-- HIS WHOLE DARNED GYM BAG!
P. Parker
HE HASN'T GOT A STITCH TO WEAR -- ISN'T IT GREAT?!

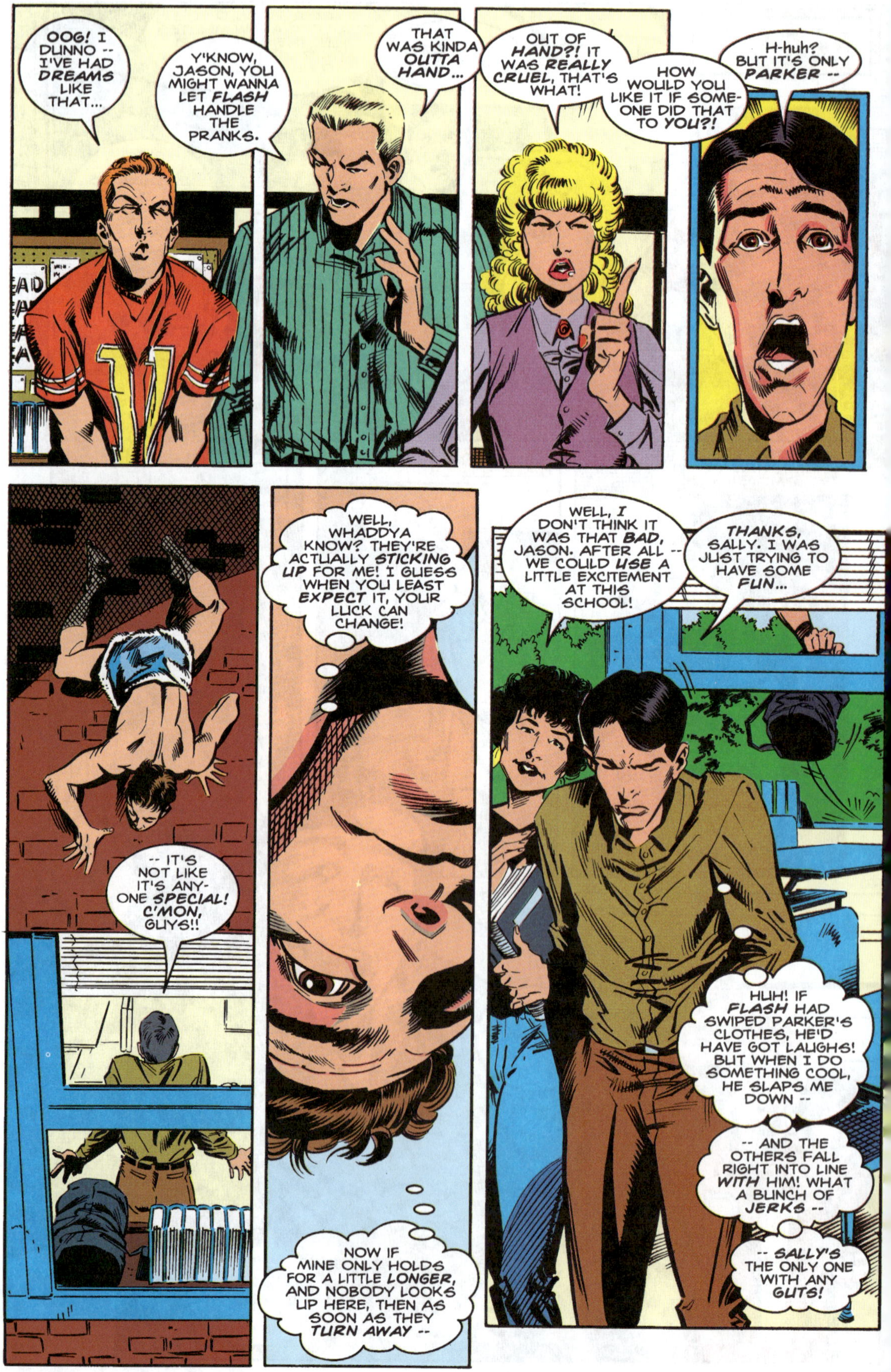

OOG! I DUNNO -- I'VE HAD **DREAMS** LIKE THAT...

Y'KNOW, JASON, YOU MIGHT WANNA LET **FLASH** HANDLE THE PRANKS.

THAT WAS KINDA **OUTTA HAND**...

OUT OF **HAND?!** IT WAS **REALLY CRUEL**, THAT'S WHAT!

HOW WOULD YOU LIKE IT IF SOME-ONE DID THAT TO **YOU?!**

H-huh? BUT IT'S ONLY **PARKER** --

-- IT'S NOT LIKE IT'S ANY-ONE **SPECIAL! C'MON,** GUYS!!

WELL, WHADDYA KNOW? THEY'RE ACTUALLY **STICKING UP** FOR ME! I GUESS WHEN YOU LEAST **EXPECT** IT, YOUR LUCK CAN CHANGE!

NOW IF MINE ONLY HOLDS FOR A LITTLE **LONGER**, AND NOBODY LOOKS UP HERE, THEN AS SOON AS THEY **TURN AWAY** --

WELL, **I** DON'T THINK IT WAS THAT **BAD**, JASON. AFTER ALL -- WE COULD **USE** A LITTLE EXCITEMENT AT THIS SCHOOL!

THANKS, SALLY. I WAS JUST TRYING TO HAVE SOME **FUN**...

HUH! IF **FLASH** HAD SWIPED PARKER'S CLOTHES, HE'D HAVE GOT LAUGHS! BUT WHEN I DO SOMETHING COOL, HE SLAPS ME DOWN --

-- AND THE OTHERS FALL RIGHT INTO LINE **WITH** HIM! WHAT A BUNCH OF **JERKS** --

-- **SALLY'S** THE ONLY ONE WITH ANY **GUTS!**

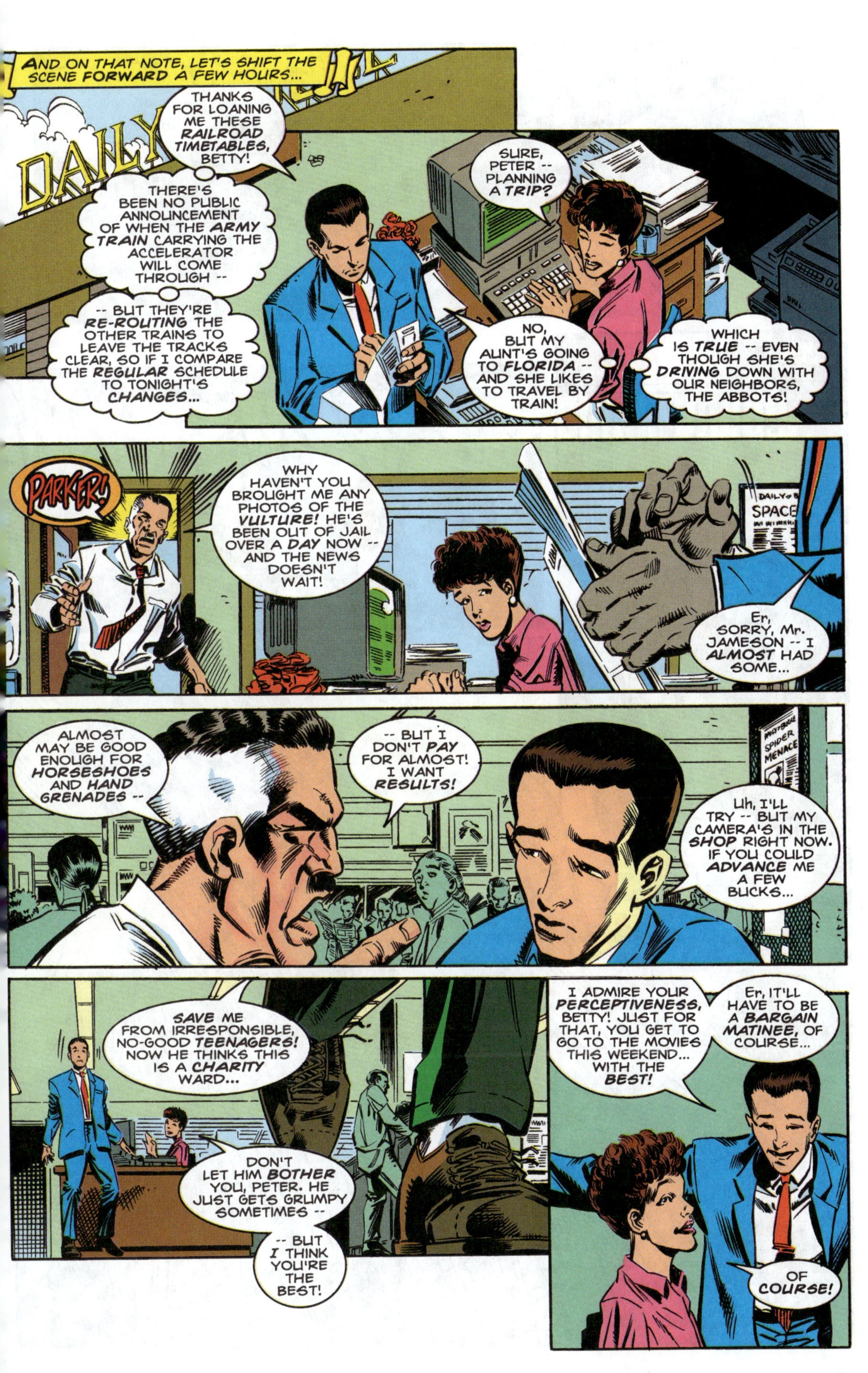
AND ON THAT NOTE, LET'S SHIFT THE SCENE FORWARD A FEW HOURS...
THANKS FOR LOANING ME THESE RAILROAD TIMETABLES, BETTY!
SURE, PETER -- PLANNING A TRIP?
THERE'S BEEN NO PUBLIC ANNOUNCEMENT OF WHEN THE ARMY TRAIN CARRYING THE ACCELERATOR WILL COME THROUGH --
-- BUT THEY'RE RE-ROUTING THE OTHER TRAINS TO LEAVE THE TRACKS CLEAR, SO IF I COMPARE THE REGULAR SCHEDULE TO TONIGHT'S CHANGES...
NO, BUT MY AUNT'S GOING TO FLORIDA -- AND SHE LIKES TO TRAVEL BY TRAIN!
WHICH IS TRUE -- EVEN THOUGH SHE'S DRIVING DOWN WITH OUR NEIGHBORS, THE ABBOTS!
PARKER!
WHY HAVEN'T YOU BROUGHT ME ANY PHOTOS OF THE VULTURE! HE'S BEEN OUT OF JAIL OVER A DAY NOW -- AND THE NEWS DOESN'T WAIT!
Er, SORRY, Mr. JAMESON -- I ALMOST HAD SOME...
ALMOST MAY BE GOOD ENOUGH FOR HORSESHOES AND HAND GRENADES --
-- BUT I DON'T PAY FOR ALMOST! I WANT RESULTS!
SPIDER MENACE
Uh, I'LL TRY -- BUT MY CAMERA'S IN THE SHOP RIGHT NOW. IF YOU COULD ADVANCE ME A FEW BUCKS...
SAVE ME FROM IRRESPONSIBLE, NO-GOOD TEENAGERS! NOW HE THINKS THIS IS A CHARITY WARD...
DON'T LET HIM BOTHER YOU, PETER. HE JUST GETS GRUMPY SOMETIMES --
-- BUT I THINK YOU'RE THE BEST!
I ADMIRE YOUR PERCEPTIVENESS, BETTY! JUST FOR THAT, YOU GET TO GO TO THE MOVIES THIS WEEKEND... WITH THE BEST!
Er, IT'LL HAVE TO BE A BARGAIN MATINEE, OF COURSE...
OF COURSE!

THAT NIGHT...
THAT'S GOTTA BE THE TRAIN -- THERE'S NOTHING SCHEDULED FOR THIS TRACK, EITHER PASSENGER OR FREIGHT! I'LL JUST HITCH A RIDE --
-- MAKE SURE IT DOESN'T HAVE ANY VULTURE TROUBLE, AT LEAST UNTIL IT LEAVES THE CITY!
BUT...
BRANG BRANG
ALARMS!
-- AS SOON AS I LANDED ON THE ROOF! THEY MUST HAVE INSTALLED PRESSURE SENSORS -- BEEN PREPARED FOR AN ATTACK --
INTRUDER! JUST AS WE WERE WARNED!
POOM
TAKE 'IM!
POOM
NO! WAIT!
BLAST! SOME SORT OF REINFORCED-ALLOY NET -- I CAN'T TEAR THROUGH IT!
I'M TRAPPED!

AND SOON, INSIDE THE SPEEDING TRAIN...
THIS IS EMBARRASSING -- NOW I NOW HOW CROOKS I CATCH FEEL!
IT WAS HIM, SIR -- AS YOU SUSPECTED IT WOULD BE!
WATCH HOW YOU WALK IN HERE, MAN! THE ACCELERATOR'S DELICATE -- JOSTLE IT TOO MUCH, AND IT COULD EXPLODE!
THAT'S WHY WE NEEDED THIS SPECIAL TRAIN TO TRANSPORT IT!
BUT AT LEAST WE DON'T HAVE TO WORRY ABOUT YOU -- Eh, Mr. RESPONSIBLE CITIZEN? THERE NEVER WAS ANY THREAT FROM THE VULTURE --
-- IT WAS JUST PETTY BLACKMAIL ON YOUR PART, AND WHEN WE DIDN'T FALL FOR IT --
GENERAL --
-- TURN AROUND.
Hm --?
GOOD EVENING, GENERAL ROSS!
WHILE YOUR MEN WERE SO ENTHUSIASTICALLY CAPTURING SPIDER-MAN, IT WAS CHILD'S PLAY TO GLIDE SILENTLY PAST THEM --
-- AND BOARD YOUR SO-WELL-PROTECTED TRAIN!
BUT I'M AFRAID I CAN'T STAY AND CHAT --
-- SO I'LL TAKE MY LEAVE OF YOU --
-- AND TAKE YOUR PRECIOUS ACCELERATOR AS A SOUVENIR!
THE ACCELERATOR! IT -- IT --
-- IF IT'S STRUCK AGAINST ANYTHING --!

DON'T WORRY, GENERAL -- I'LL GIVE YOUR TOY THE MOST GENTLE OF RIDES!
AFTER ALL, I WOULDN'T WANT ANYTHING TO HAPPEN TO IT --
--BEFORE I SELL IT TO THE HIGHEST BIDDER!
HE'S GONE!
BUT YOU -- I'LL SEE YOU ROT IN JAIL UNTIL YOU'VE GOT LONG GRAY WHISKERS! YOU MUST'VE BEEN IN ON IT WITH HIM -- DISTRACTING US WHILE HE --
SORRY TO DISAPPOINT YOU, GENERAL -- BUT NOW THAT I'VE GOT A DECENT GRIP ON THIS NET --
-- I'LL DECLINE YOUR KIND INVITATION, THANKS!
WHA--?
HE'S ESCAPING! GET HIM!
SURE, ROSS, SURE! THAT NET'LL TANGLE YOUR MEN UP -- SNARING THEM AS SURELY AS IT DID ME!
WHICH IS JUST AS WELL, SINCE I'M THE ONLY ONE ON THIS TRAIN EQUIPPED --

-- TO GO AFTER THE *VULTURE!*
I'M SORRY, SIR, BUT YOU'VE EXCEEDED YOUR *CARRY-ON* LIMIT --
Eh --?
-- MAY I *CHECK* THIS FOR YOU?!
SPIDER-MAN?!
DON'T *COMPOUND* YOUR FOOLISHNESS, BOY!
WRACK
I PLAYED YOU LIKE A VIOLIN -- TRICKED YOU INTO PROVIDING THE DIVERSION I NEEDED TO STEAL THE ACCELERATOR!
SO SLINK AWAY WITH YOUR *TAIL* BETWEEN YOUR LEGS -- BEFORE YOU EMBARRASS YOURSELF *FURTHER!*

YOU'VE CONVINCED ME, VULTURE! I'LL FALL TO MY DEATH IN SHAME --
-- BUT NOT BEFORE LUNCH! C'MON, I PACKED TWO PEANUT-BUTTER SANDWICHES AND A GARLIC PICKLE IN THERE --
-- NOT TO MENTION MY YOSEMITE SAM THERMOS!
PRATTLE ALL YOU WANT, IMBECILE --

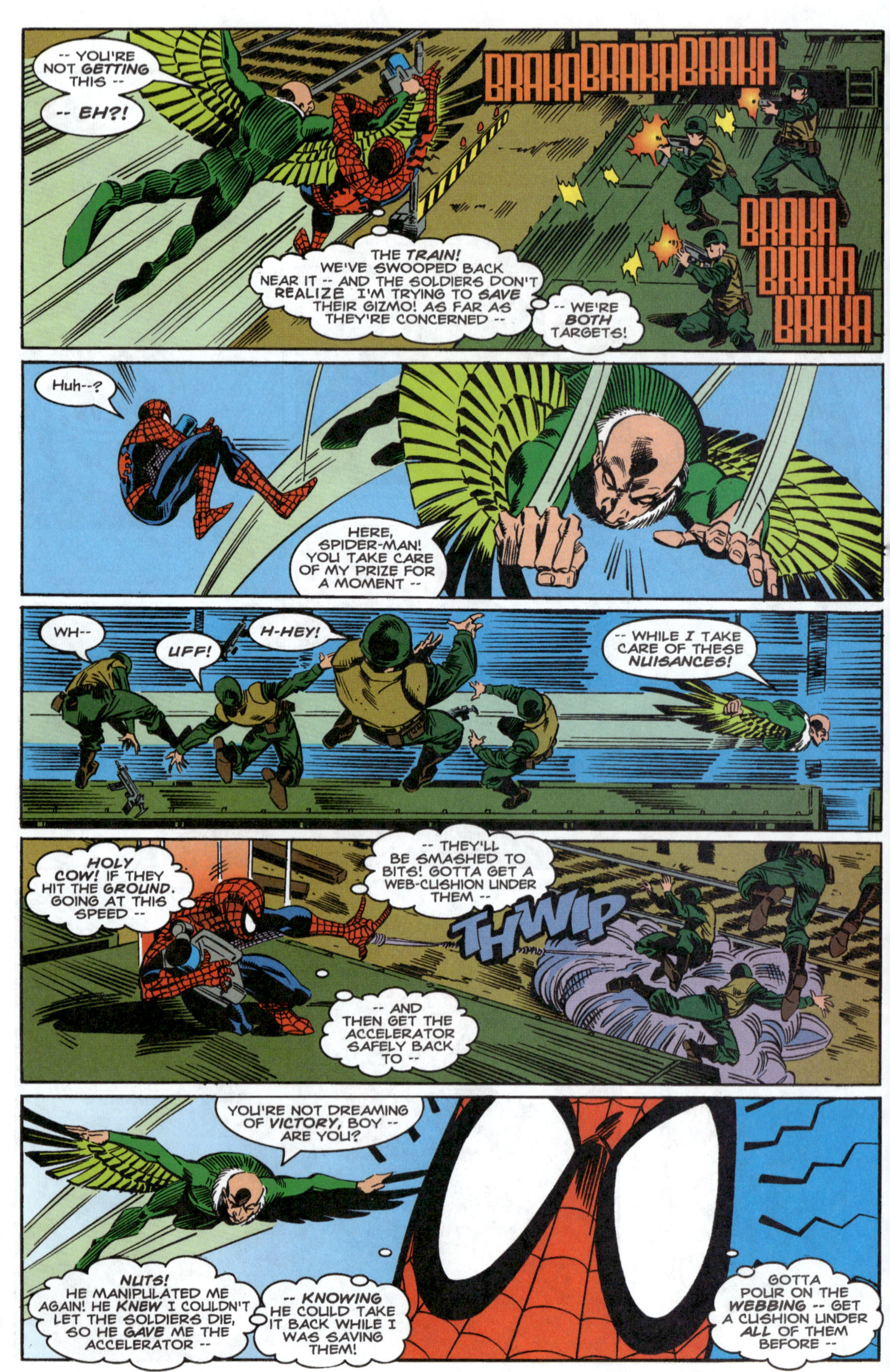
-- YOU'RE NOT GETTING THIS --
-- EH?!
BRAKA BRAKA BRAKA
BRAKA BRAKA BRAKA
THE TRAIN! WE'VE SWOOPED BACK NEAR IT -- AND THE SOLDIERS DON'T REALIZE I'M TRYING TO SAVE THEIR GIZMO! AS FAR AS THEY'RE CONCERNED --
-- WE'RE BOTH TARGETS!
Huh--?
HERE, SPIDER-MAN! YOU TAKE CARE OF MY PRIZE FOR A MOMENT --
WH--
UFF!
H-HEY!
-- WHILE I TAKE CARE OF THESE NUISANCES!
HOLY COW! IF THEY HIT THE GROUND. GOING AT THIS SPEED --
-- THEY'LL BE SMASHED TO BITS! GOTTA GET A WEB-CUSHION UNDER THEM --
THWIP
-- AND THEN GET THE ACCELERATOR SAFELY BACK TO --
YOU'RE NOT DREAMING OF VICTORY, BOY -- ARE YOU?
NUTS! HE MANIPULATED ME AGAIN! HE KNEW I COULDN'T LET THE SOLDIERS DIE, SO HE GAVE ME THE ACCELERATOR --
-- KNOWING HE COULD TAKE IT BACK WHILE I WAS SAVING THEM!
GOTTA POUR ON THE WEBBING -- GET A CUSHION UNDER ALL OF THEM BEFORE --

HAH! ONCE AGAIN, THE VULTURE IS TRIUMPHANT!
WHAKK
UHH!
YOU ARE... SERIOUSLY SOLD ON YOURSELF, VULTURE...
BUT OF COURSE! MY BATTLE-PLAN WAS EXCELLENT -- MY TACTICS EQUALLY SO! I'VE WIPED THE SLATE CLEAN OF MY PREVIOUS DEFEATS AT YOUR HANDS!
THINK ABOUT IT, SPIDER-MAN -- THERE IS NOTHING YOU CAN DO!
IF YOU FIRE YOUR INFERNAL WEBBING AT ME, I'LL HAUL YOU AWAY AND DASH YOUR BRAINS OUT ON THE ROCKS --
-- AND IF YOU STAY ON THE TRAIN, I SIMPLY FLY AWAY SCOT-FREE!
DON'T... BREAK AN ARM PATTING YOURSELF ON THE BACK, VULTURE...
...'CAUSE AS I LEARNED EARLIER TODAY...
THWIP

-- YOUR LUCK CAN CHANGE WHEN YOU LEAST EXPECT IT!
Eh? YOU'VE WEBBED THE ACCELERATOR?
NO MATTER -- YOU'RE TOO GROGGY TO PUT UP MUCH OF A FIGHT -- I'LL SIMPLY PULL YOU FROM THE TRAIN --
BETTER HOPE YOU CAN DO IT FAST, THEN --
-- OR HAVEN'T YOU LOOKED BEHIND YOU RECENTLY?
WHAT?!
A TUNNEL?!
"THAAAAT'S RIGHT! YOU KEEP HANGING ONTO THAT THING, AND IN SECONDS, YOU'RE GOING TO SMACK INTO SOLID ROCK!
"THE ACCELERATOR BLOWS UP --
"-- AND THERE ISN'T ENOUGH LEFT OF YOU TO STUFF A FEATHER PILLOW!

"SO, VULTURE --
"WHAT'S IT GONNA BE?"

SHORTLY...
BLAST HIS TREACHEROUS HIDE!
BUT SIR, HE DID SEEM TO BE FIGHTING AGAINST THE VULTURE --
A SHAM, SOLDIER! IT HAD TO BE! THEY WERE WORKING TOGETHER --
-- IT'S THE ONLY WAY THEY COULD HAVE --
NOK NOK
-- PULLED IT OFF --?
WELL, DON'T JUST STAND THERE, MAN --
-- OPEN IT!!
YESSIR!
AS THE HEAVY SLIDING DOOR OPENS, THERE'S AN INRUSH OF COLD AIR --
-- AND --
THE -- THE ACCELERATOR! IT'S SAFE!
BRING IT ON BOARD, SOLDIER!
BUT -- GENTLY --
-- GENTLY --

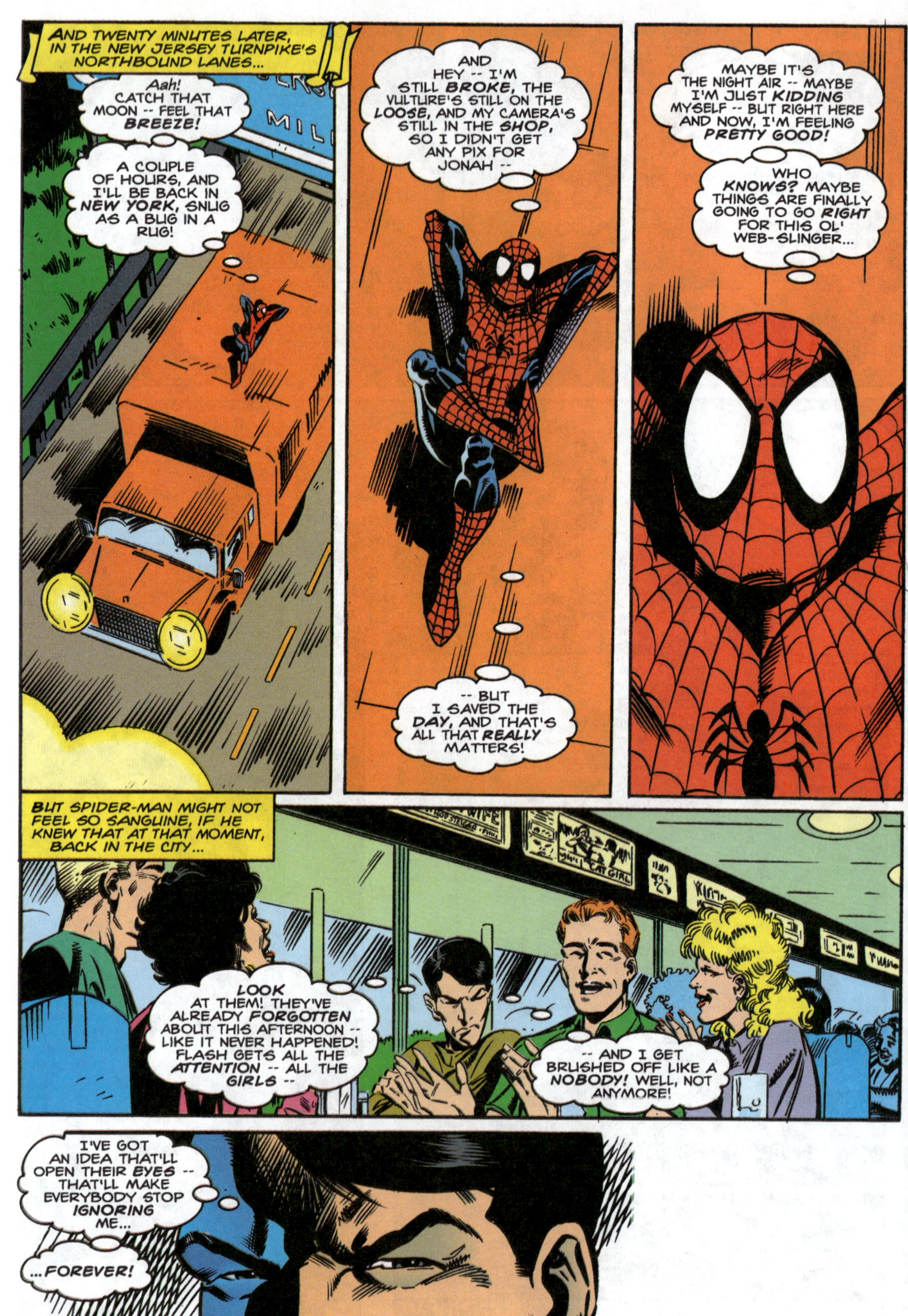

AND TWENTY MINUTES LATER, IN THE NEW JERSEY TURNPIKE'S NORTHBOUND LANES...
Aah! CATCH THAT MOON -- FEEL THAT BREEZE!
A COUPLE OF HOURS, AND I'LL BE BACK IN NEW YORK, SNUG AS A BUG IN A RUG!
AND HEY -- I'M STILL BROKE, THE VULTURE'S STILL ON THE LOOSE, AND MY CAMERA'S STILL IN THE SHOP, SO I DIDN'T GET ANY PIX FOR JONAH --
-- BUT I SAVED THE DAY, AND THAT'S ALL THAT REALLY MATTERS!
MAYBE IT'S THE NIGHT AIR -- MAYBE I'M JUST KIDDING MYSELF -- BUT RIGHT HERE AND NOW, I'M FEELING PRETTY GOOD!
WHO KNOWS? MAYBE THINGS ARE FINALLY GOING TO GO RIGHT FOR THIS OL' WEB-SLINGER...
BUT SPIDER-MAN MIGHT NOT FEEL SO SANGUINE, IF HE KNEW THAT AT THAT MOMENT, BACK IN THE CITY...
LOOK AT THEM! THEY'VE ALREADY FORGOTTEN ABOUT THIS AFTERNOON -- LIKE IT NEVER HAPPENED! FLASH GETS ALL THE ATTENTION -- ALL THE GIRLS --
-- AND I GET BRUSHED OFF LIKE A NOBODY! WELL, NOT ANYMORE!
I'VE GOT AN IDEA THAT'LL OPEN THEIR EYES -- THAT'LL MAKE EVERYBODY STOP IGNORING ME...
...FOREVER!

GUEST STARRING: THE HUMAN TORCH
FEB • 8
$1.95 US
$2.65 CAN
MARVEL
SPIDER-MAN GROUP
UNTOLD TALES OF
SPIDER-MAN
OLIFFE–VEY

IT'S SHAPING UP TO BE A DECENT MORNING -- I NAB A JEWEL THIEF BEFORE SCHOOL EVEN STARTS -- BUT THEN --
YOW!!
HEY, TORCH -- YOU NEARLY PLOWED RIGHT INTO ME, YOU KNOTHEAD! WHERE'S THE FIRE?
A TITANIC TEAM-UP, BROUGHT TO YOU BY:
KURT BUSIEK WRITER
PAT OLLIFFE PENCILER
AL VEY w/ PAM EKLUND INKERS
RICHARD STARKINGS AND COMICRAFT LETTERING
STEVE MATTSSON COLORS
TOM BREVOORT EDITOR
BOB BUDIANSKY EDITOR IN CHIEF
DOUBLE JEOPARDY
CAN'T TALK NOW, SPIDER-MAN!
GOTTA GET TO LaGUARDIA AIRPORT -- 'CAUSE IT WAS THE FIRST!

WHA-A-AT?! IS IT JUST ME, OR DID HE MAKE NO SENSE AT ALL?
MAYBE HIS BUDDIES IN THE FANTASTIC FOUR CAME TO THEIR SENSES AND KICKED HIM OUT...
YOU MEAN YOU AIN'T HEARD, SPIDEY? TH' TORCH IS MATCHIN' WITS WITH THAT WIZARD GUY AGAIN!
SORRY, PAL -- BUT WITH THE BIG MAN TAKING OVER ALL THE NEW YORK MOBS AND THE CRIME RATE GOING ASTRONOMICAL, I'VE BEEN A LITTLE TOO --
-- SAY, LOOKS LIKE YOU'RE RIGHT!
-- REPEATING THE TOP STORY OF THE HOUR --
-- THE MASTER CRIMINAL KNOWN AS THE WIZARD HAS BROKEN OUT OF JAIL, AND HIJACKED TELE-VISION BROADCASTS TO ISSUE A CHALLENGE.
HE'S THREATENED TO CAUSE DISASTERS THROUGHOUT THE CITY --
-- UNLESS THE HUMAN TORCH IS SMART ENOUGH TO FIGURE OUT HIS CLUES AND STOP THE DISASTERS BEFORE THEY HIT.
50% OFF
THE FIRST CLUE GIVEN WAS SIMPLY, "LaGUARDIA WAS THE FIRST." THE HUMAN TORCH, A MEMBER OF THE WORLD-FAMOUS FANTASTIC FOUR --
WAIT A MINUTE!
THERE ARE TWO ANSWERS TO THAT QUESTION! AND IF THE TORCH HAS BEEN FAKED OUT --
-- PEOPLE COULD DIE!
THE LOOT ON THAT CROOK'LL BE ENOUGH EVIDENCE FOR THE COPS TO BOOK HIM --
-- SO IT'S SAFE TO LEAVE HIM BEHIND --

-- WHILE I HIGH-TAIL IT TO **GRACIE MANSION**, WHERE SURE ENOUGH --

GAS!

RUN! RUN!

LaGUARDIA AIRPORT MAY HAVE BEEN THE FIRST MAJOR AIRPORT IN THE NEW YORK AREA --

-- BUT **FIORELLO LAGUARDIA**, WHOM THE AIRPORT'S NAMED AFTER, WAS THE FIRST IN A LONG LINE OF **MAYORS** WHO'VE LIVED HERE.

I WEB MYSELF A MAKESHIFT **GAS** MASK, AND --

Oh, YOO-HOO! LITTLE GAAAS BOMB! COME OUT, COME OUT, **WHERE-EVER** YOU ARE!

I FIND IT IN THE PUBLIC RELATIONS OFFICE.

EVEN THROUGH MY WEB-MASK, I CAN TELL IT'S HARMLESS -- MEANT TO FRIGHTEN PEOPLE MORE THAN **HURT** THEM --

THWIP

AS I HEAD FOR SCHOOL, I THINK IT OVER.
IT MAKES SENSE THAT THE WIZARD WOULD START OFF WITH SOMETHING HARMLESS, SINCE HE ISN'T DOING THIS FOR MONEY OR ANYTHING --
-- HE JUST WANTS TO MAKE THE TORCH LOOK BAD.
HE USED TO BE A CELEBRITY -- INVENTING FABULOUSLY EXPENSIVE LUXURIES LIKE HIS "AIR-CHAIR"--
-- SHOWING UP ON T.V., DOING THINGS LIKE PLAYING A COMPUTER AT CHESS AND WINNING --
IT'S AMAZING
-- OR PERFORMING FANTASTIC ESCAPES!
BUT AFTER SUPER HEROES LIKE THE F.F. BURST ON THE SCENE, SOMEHOW HE DIDN'T SEEM SO SPECIAL ANYMORE -- AND HIS BOOKINGS DECLINED.
HE DECIDED TO PROVE THAT HIS BRAINS WERE MORE IMPORTANT THAN SUPER-POWERS BY HUMILIATING THE TORCH --BUT EVERY TIME THEY'VE CLASHED, OL' MATCH-HEAD HAS FOUND A WAY TO DEFEAT HIM.
STILL, HE'S SMART AND TRICKY --

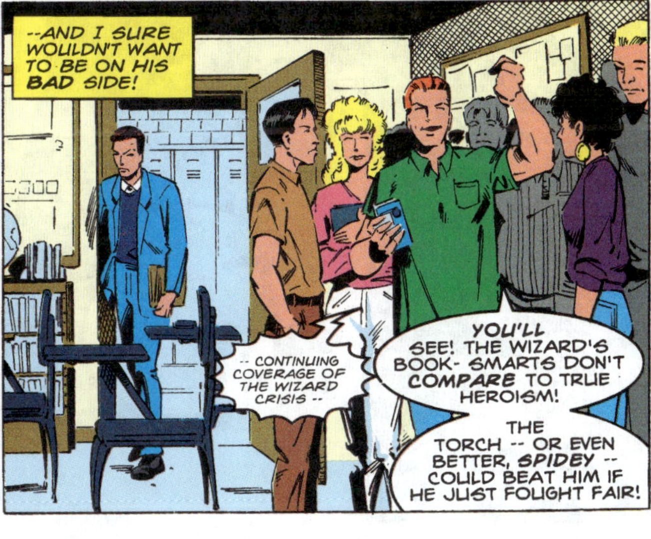

--AND I SURE WOULDN'T WANT TO BE ON HIS BAD SIDE!
-- CONTINUING COVERAGE OF THE WIZARD CRISIS --
YOU'LL SEE! THE WIZARD'S BOOK- SMARTS DON'T COMPARE TO TRUE HEROISM!
THE TORCH -- OR EVEN BETTER, SPIDEY -- COULD BEAT HIM IF HE JUST FOUGHT FAIR!

BRAINS COUNT FOR SOMETHING, FLASH --
-- OR THE WIZARD WOULDN'T HAVE PLANNED THIS FOR A DAY MISTER FANTASTIC AND GIANT-MAN ARE OUT OF THE CITY...
I DON'T CARE! IT'S ALL JUST SO EXCITING -- NO MATTER WHY IT'S HAPPENING!

Oh, SURE, LIZ! SO HOW 'BOUT PARKER HERE? THINK HE COULD BEAT THE WIZARD?
HE'S SO SMART HE DOESN'T DO ANYTHING BUT THINK!
IF ONLY YOU KNEW, FLASH --!
HEY, WHAT'S THIS --?
IN MY MATH BOOK -- A NOTE FROM AUNT MAY. SHE MUST'VE WRITTEN THIS BEFORE SHE WENT TO FLORIDA FOR A WEEK.
Peter -- I made an appointment for you with the optometrist -- for thursday at 4 p.m. Don't miss it -- you've got to take care of your eyes! Love, Aunt May
EVER SINCE MY GLASSES GOT BROKEN, SHE'S BEEN WANTING ME TO SEE A DOCTOR. I DON'T NEED 'EM ANY MORE, THANKS TO MY SPIDER-POWERS...
-- BUT IF AN EXAM SHOULD TURN UP SOMETHING, IT MIGHT JEOPARDIZE MY SECRET IDENTITY. I'VE GOT TO FIGURE OUT HOW TO --
-- Huh? ON FLASH'S RADIO -- THE WIZARD'S NEXT CLUE!
WHAT'S HE SAYING --?
Shh! Shh! I WANT TO HEAR THIS!
TURN IT UP A LITTLE!
-- WIZARD BROKE INTO TELE-VISION BROADCASTS A FEW MINUTES AGO --
-- TO TELL THE TORCH THAT HE'LL STRIKE NEXT AT "THE ONLY BUILDING IN MANHATTAN THAT ISN'T WRONG!"
THE TORCH MIGHT NOT UNDERSTAND THAT CLUE -- BUT I DO! I'VE GOT TO GET OUT THERE AND DEAL WITH IT!
Mrs. DOUGHTY?
ALL OF A SUDDEN I DON'T FEEL WELL -- MAY I BE EXCUSED TO GO TO THE NURSE'S OFFICE?

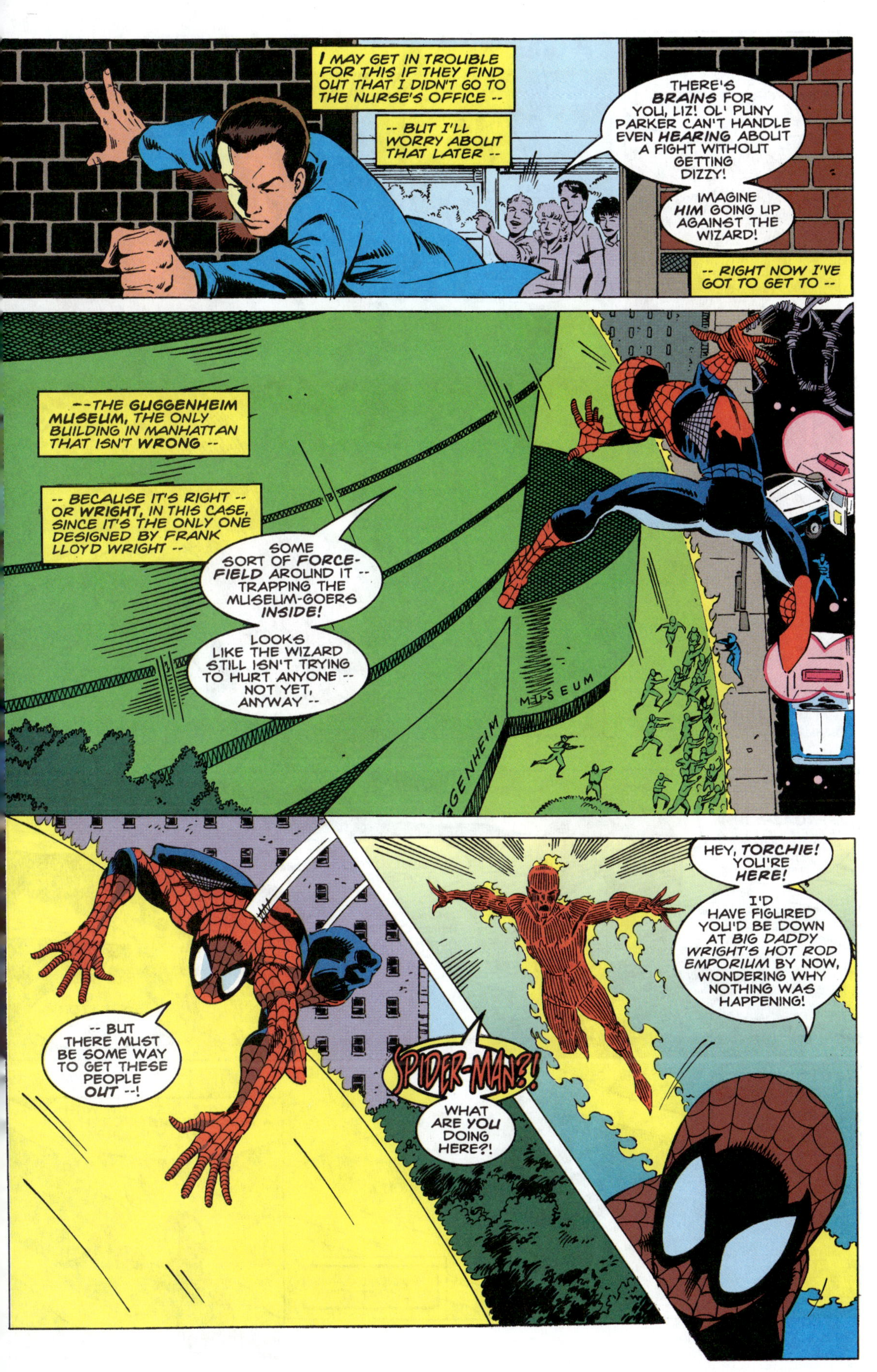
I MAY GET IN TROUBLE FOR THIS IF THEY FIND OUT THAT I DIDN'T GO TO THE NURSE'S OFFICE --
-- BUT I'LL WORRY ABOUT THAT LATER --
THERE'S BRAINS FOR YOU, LIZ! OL' PUNY PARKER CAN'T HANDLE EVEN HEARING ABOUT A FIGHT WITHOUT GETTING DIZZY!
IMAGINE HIM GOING UP AGAINST THE WIZARD!
-- RIGHT NOW I'VE GOT TO GET TO --
--THE GUGGENHEIM MUSEUM, THE ONLY BUILDING IN MANHATTAN THAT ISN'T WRONG --
-- BECAUSE IT'S RIGHT -- OR WRIGHT, IN THIS CASE, SINCE IT'S THE ONLY ONE DESIGNED BY FRANK LLOYD WRIGHT --
SOME SORT OF FORCE-FIELD AROUND IT -- TRAPPING THE MUSEUM-GOERS INSIDE!
LOOKS LIKE THE WIZARD STILL ISN'T TRYING TO HURT ANYONE -- NOT YET, ANYWAY --
GGENHEIM
MUSEUM
-- BUT THERE MUST BE SOME WAY TO GET THESE PEOPLE OUT --!
SPIDER-MAN?!
WHAT ARE YOU DOING HERE?!
HEY, TORCHIE! YOU'RE HERE!
I'D HAVE FIGURED YOU'D BE DOWN AT BIG DADDY WRIGHT'S HOT ROD EMPORIUM BY NOW, WONDERING WHY NOTHING WAS HAPPENING!

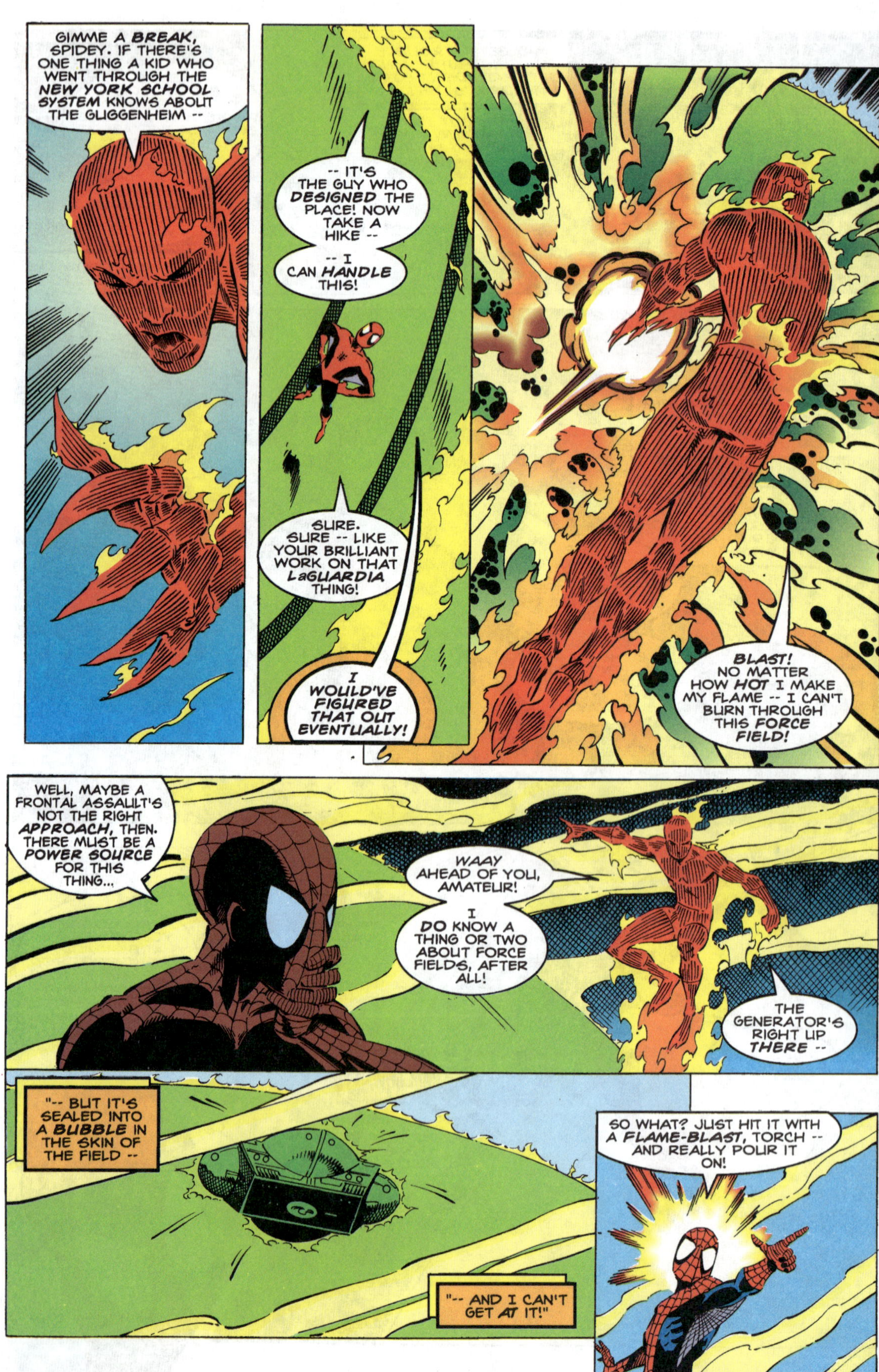
GIMME A BREAK, SPIDEY. IF THERE'S ONE THING A KID WHO WENT THROUGH THE NEW YORK SCHOOL SYSTEM KNOWS ABOUT THE GUGGENHEIM --
-- IT'S THE GUY WHO DESIGNED THE PLACE! NOW TAKE A HIKE --
-- I CAN HANDLE THIS!
SURE. SURE -- LIKE YOUR BRILLIANT WORK ON THAT LaGUARDIA THING!
I WOULD'VE FIGURED THAT OUT EVENTUALLY!
BLAST! NO MATTER HOW HOT I MAKE MY FLAME -- I CAN'T BURN THROUGH THIS FORCE FIELD!
WELL, MAYBE A FRONTAL ASSAULT'S NOT THE RIGHT APPROACH, THEN. THERE MUST BE A POWER SOURCE FOR THIS THING...
WAAY AHEAD OF YOU, AMATEUR!
I DO KNOW A THING OR TWO ABOUT FORCE FIELDS, AFTER ALL!
THE GENERATOR'S RIGHT UP THERE --
"-- BUT IT'S SEALED INTO A BUBBLE IN THE SKIN OF THE FIELD --
"-- AND I CAN'T GET AT IT!"
SO WHAT? JUST HIT IT WITH A FLAME-BLAST, TORCH -- AND REALLY POUR IT ON!

OKAY-- BUT I DON'T KNOW WHAT GOOD IT'LL DO! MY FLAME DOESN'T GET THROUGH AT ALL!
YEAH, BUT LOOK AT THE PEOPLE INSIDE!
THEY CAN SEE AND BREATHE OKAY -- AND THEY DON'T LOOK LIKE THEY'RE COLD!
SO THE FIELD LETS THROUGH LIGHT AND AIR-- AND APPARENTLY, HEAT!
I GET IT! MY FLAME MAY NOT GET THROUGH, BUT THE HEAT FROM IT DOES--
-- SO ALL I HAVE TO DO --
-- IS SUPERHEAT THE AIR AROUND THE GENERATOR --
-- UNTIL --
--PRESTO! NO MORE GENERATOR-- NO MORE FORCE FIELD!
NOT BAD -- BUT I CAN TAKE IT FROM HERE...
...SO AS SOON AS I LET YOU DOWN...
...FEEL FREE TO TAKE OFF!
TORCH! TORCH! Mr STORM!
Huh?
I'M FROM THE MAYOR'S OFFICE! WE'RE SETTING UP A BANK OF EXPERTS --
--OF RESEARCH LIBRARIANS AND HISTORY AND SCIENCE EXPERTS-- TO SOLVE THE CLUES FOR YOU!
WHAT?! YOU DON'T THINK I'M SMART ENOUGH TO BEAT THE WIZARD ON MY OWN?
WELL, YOU GO BACK TO THE MAYOR AND TELL HIM I'LL CALL IF I NEED YOUR GUYS--
--BUT SO FAR, THE WIZARD HASN'T COME UP WITH ANYTHING TOO TOUGH FOR SPIDEY AND ME TO HANDLE!
Huh? "SPIDEY AND ME"?
I THOUGHT I WAS BEING SENT TO THE SHOWERS--

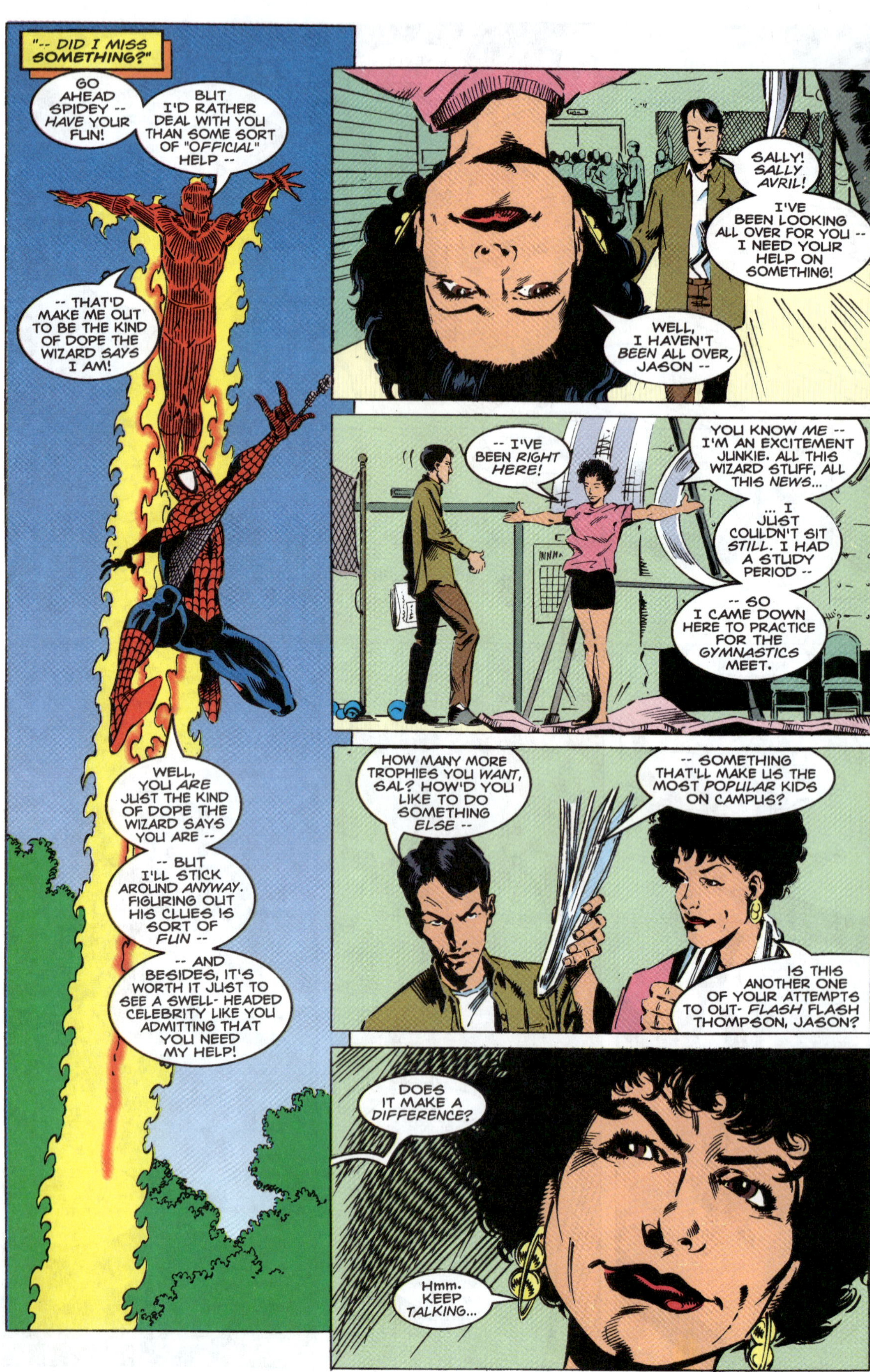
"-- DID I MISS SOMETHING?"
GO AHEAD SPIDEY -- HAVE YOUR FUN!
BUT I'D RATHER DEAL WITH YOU THAN SOME SORT OF "OFFICIAL" HELP --
-- THAT'D MAKE ME OUT TO BE THE KIND OF DOPE THE WIZARD SAYS I AM!
WELL, YOU ARE JUST THE KIND OF DOPE THE WIZARD SAYS YOU ARE --
-- BUT I'LL STICK AROUND ANYWAY. FIGURING OUT HIS CLUES IS SORT OF FUN --
-- AND BESIDES, IT'S WORTH IT JUST TO SEE A SWELL-HEADED CELEBRITY LIKE YOU ADMITTING THAT YOU NEED MY HELP!
SALLY! SALLY AVRIL!
I'VE BEEN LOOKING ALL OVER FOR YOU -- I NEED YOUR HELP ON SOMETHING!
WELL, I HAVEN'T BEEN ALL OVER, JASON --
-- I'VE BEEN RIGHT HERE!
YOU KNOW ME -- I'M AN EXCITEMENT JUNKIE. ALL THIS WIZARD STUFF, ALL THIS NEWS...
... I JUST COULDN'T SIT STILL. I HAD A STUDY PERIOD --
-- SO I CAME DOWN HERE TO PRACTICE FOR THE GYMNASTICS MEET.
HOW MANY MORE TROPHIES YOU WANT, SAL? HOW'D YOU LIKE TO DO SOMETHING ELSE --
-- SOMETHING THAT'LL MAKE US THE MOST POPULAR KIDS ON CAMPUS?
IS THIS ANOTHER ONE OF YOUR ATTEMPTS TO OUT-FLASH FLASH THOMPSON, JASON?
DOES IT MAKE A DIFFERENCE?
Hmm. KEEP TALKING...

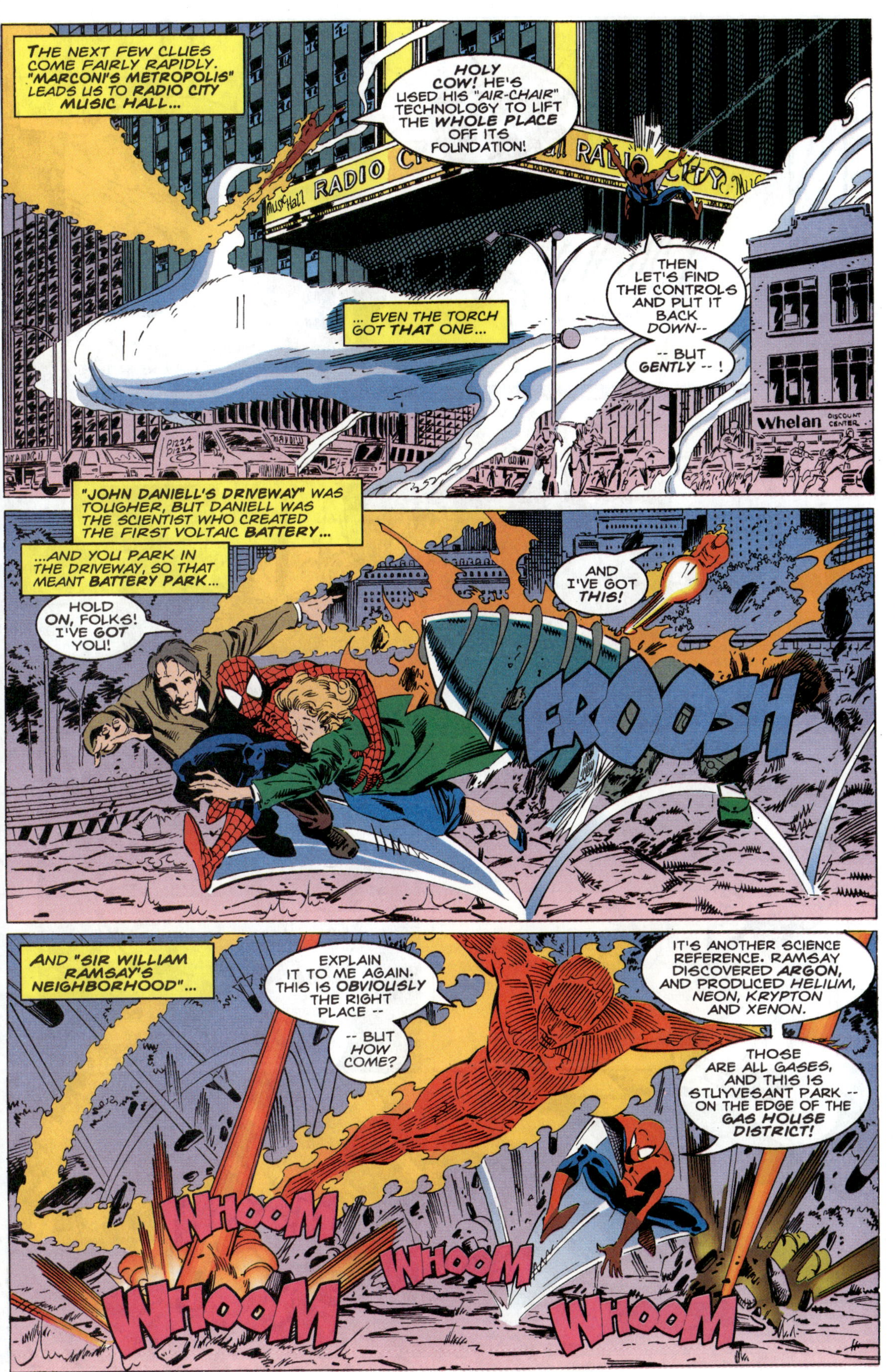
THE NEXT FEW CLUES COME FAIRLY RAPIDLY. "MARCONI'S METROPOLIS" LEADS US TO RADIO CITY MUSIC HALL...
HOLY COW! HE'S USED HIS "AIR-CHAIR" TECHNOLOGY TO LIFT THE WHOLE PLACE OFF ITS FOUNDATION!
RADIO CITY
...EVEN THE TORCH GOT THAT ONE...
THEN LET'S FIND THE CONTROLS AND PUT IT BACK DOWN--
-- BUT GENTLY -- !
Whelan DISCOUNT CENTER
"JOHN DANIELL'S DRIVEWAY" WAS TOUGHER, BUT DANIELL WAS THE SCIENTIST WHO CREATED THE FIRST VOLTAIC BATTERY...
...AND YOU PARK IN THE DRIVEWAY, SO THAT MEANT BATTERY PARK...
HOLD ON, FOLKS! I'VE GOT YOU!
AND I'VE GOT THIS!
FROOSH
AND "SIR WILLIAM RAMSAY'S NEIGHBORHOOD"...
EXPLAIN IT TO ME AGAIN. THIS IS OBVIOUSLY THE RIGHT PLACE --
-- BUT HOW COME?
IT'S ANOTHER SCIENCE REFERENCE. RAMSAY DISCOVERED ARGON, AND PRODUCED HELIUM, NEON, KRYPTON AND XENON.
THOSE ARE ALL GASES, AND THIS IS STUYVESANT PARK -- ON THE EDGE OF THE GAS HOUSE DISTRICT!
WHOOM
WHOOM
WHOOM
WHOOM

DAILY BUGLE
WHERE'S PARKER ?!
THE BIG MAN AND HIS ENFORCERS HAVE BEEN RUNNING NEW YORK RAGGED FOR DAYS --
-- AND NONE OF OUR PHOTOGRAPHERS HAVE MANAGED TO BRING IN A SINGLE PHOTO!
DAILY BUGLE
"BIG MAN" MOB LOOTS CITY
WIDESPREAD CRIME REPORTED
AND UNLIKE THE OTHER RAGS IN THIS TOWN --
-- THE DAILY BUGLE PROMISES PICTURE NEWS -- AND DELIVERS!
Eh? MISS BRANT?
I THOUGHT YOU'D LIKE TO KNOW, SIR -- SPIDER-MAN HAS BEEN SPOTTED HELPING THE HUMAN TORCH DEAL WITH THE THREAT OF WIZARD --
-- MAYBE PETER'S TRYING TO GET PHOTOS OF THAT!
Hm? WELL, THAT WOULDN'T BE SO BAD...
... ALL THOSE OTHER PAPERS CARRYING DRY HEADLINES, WHILE THE BUGLE HAS EXCLUSIVE EYEWITNESS COVERAGE --
--FRONT-PAGE PHOTOS, CLOSE-UP --
-- DIRECT FROM THE HEART OF THE DEADLIEST DANGER SPOTS IN THE CITY!
Er... YES... THE DEADLIEST DANGER SPOTS...
YOU ASK ME --
THE WIZARD'S REALLY REACHING WITH SOME OF THESE CLUES.
I MEAN -- ARGON?
YOU ASK ME --
CHOOM

-- HE'S GETTING MAD!
WHOOM
AND THE MADDER HE GETS, THE HARDER THE CLUES GET -- AND THE MORE DANGEROUS HIS TRICKS GET!
EVENTUALLY, WE'RE GOING TO MISS ONE, AND PEOPLE ARE GOING TO GET HURT -- UNLESS WE TAKE THE OFFENSIVE!
WELL, I'M ALL FOR THAT! C'MON --
"-- LET'S GET OVER TO THE BAXTER BUILDING BEFORE THE NEXT CLUE COMES IN!"
WOW!
DOUBLE-WOW! TRIPLE-WOW, EVEN!
EVERY TIME I SEE YOUR HEADQUARTERS, IT JUST GETS COOLER! I COULD SPEND A MONTH HERE, JUST FIGURING OUT WHAT SOME OF THESE MACHINES DO!
OKAY, OKAY -- SO YOU'RE NOT JUST A WALKING SCIENCE ENCYCLOPEDIA -- YOU'RE A COMPLETE GEEK, TOO!
SO WHAT DO WE DO?
WELL, THE WIZARD MUST BE DOING HIS BROADCASTING FROM A MOBILE LOCATION, OR THE F.C.C WOULD BE ABLE TO NAIL HIM EASILY.
SO TO FIND HIM, WE NOT ONLY NEED TO BE ABLE TO INTERCEPT HIS SIGNAL -- BUT TO TRIANGULATE ON IT!
I CAN TRY TO BUILD A TRACKING DEVICE...
SURE, SURE --

"--USE WHATEVER YOU NEED."
THIS EQUIPMENT IS AMAZING! YOU COULD PRACTICALLY BUILD A SPACESHIP IN HERE, SINGLE-HANDED -- IN A TENTH OF THE TIME IT WOULD TAKE N.A.S.A!
TELL ME SOMETHING I DON'T KNOW -- LIKE WHETHER YOU'RE GOING TO BE FINISHED ANY TIME THIS CENTURY!
IF REED WAS HERE...
WELL, PARDON ME FOR NOT BEING MISTER FANTASTIC, THE MOST BRILLIANT MIND IN THE COUNTRY! BUT JUST GIVE ME A FEW MORE SECONDS --
TOO LATE!
THE WIZARD JUST SEIZED THE AIRWAVES AGAIN --
"THE NEXT CLUE IS COMING NOW!"
HERE'S ONE THAT'S BENEATH EVEN YOU, TORCH! EVERYTHING YOU NEED TO KNOW IS IN THE PHRASE --
-- "ALWAYS WALKING THE PLANK!"
FINE! WITH A REFERENCE TO PIRATES LIKE THAT "WALKING THE PLANK" JAZZ, IT MUST BE SOMEWHERE ON THE WATERFRONT! I'LL JUST --
HOLD IT!
THE CLUE'S NOT ABOUT THE WATERFRONT -- OR PIRATES!
I THINK I KNOW WHAT HE MEANS, BUT WE'LL HAVE TO SPLIT UP --
I'VE GOT HIS SIGNAL KEYED INTO THE TRACKERS --
-- BUT BEFORE WE CAN FOLLOW IT UP, WE'LL HAVE TO FIGURE OUT HIS LATEST STUNT -- AND PUT A STOP TO IT!

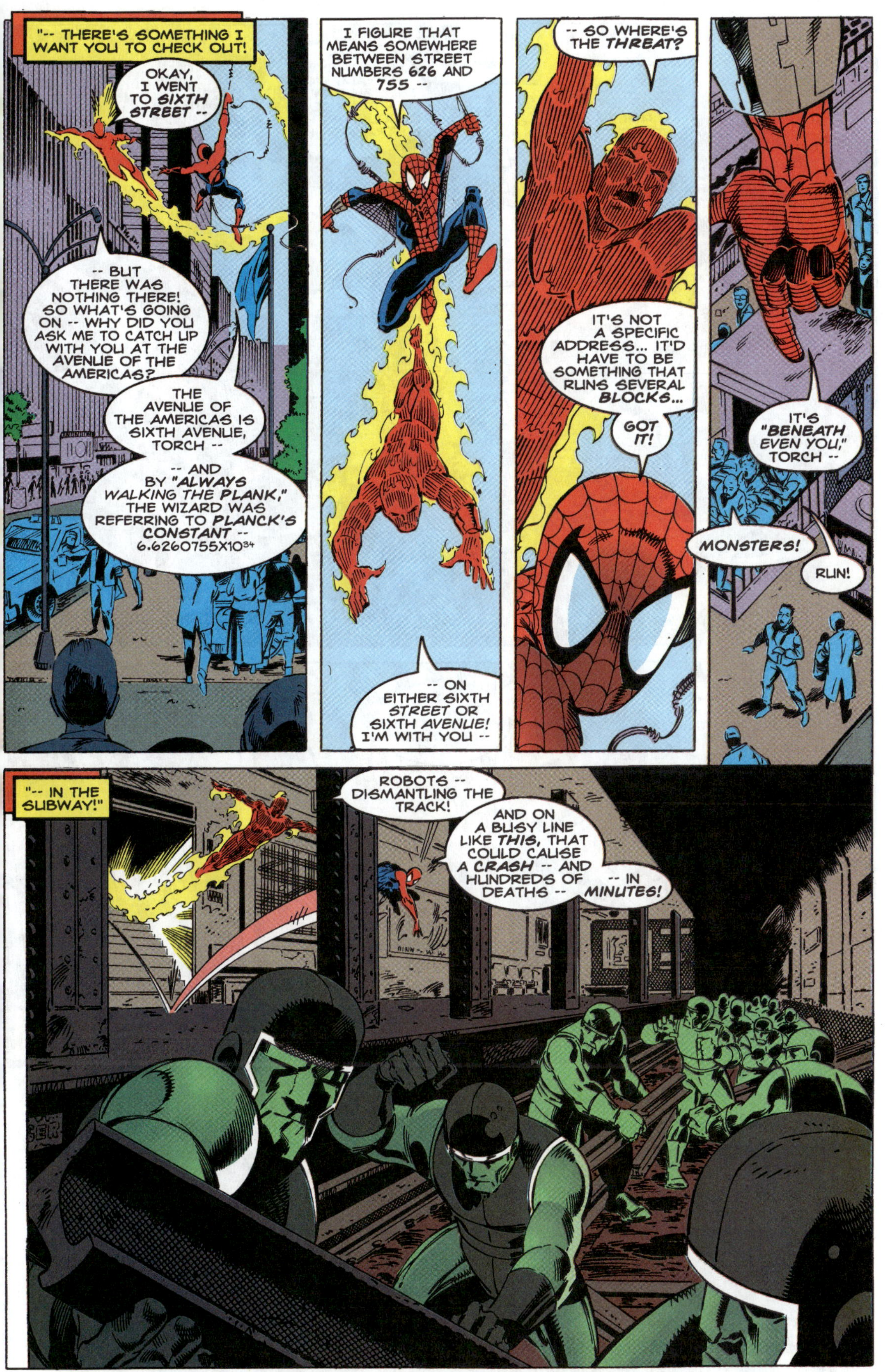
"-- THERE'S SOMETHING I WANT YOU TO CHECK OUT!
OKAY, I WENT TO SIXTH STREET --
-- BUT THERE WAS NOTHING THERE! SO WHAT'S GOING ON -- WHY DID YOU ASK ME TO CATCH UP WITH YOU AT THE AVENUE OF THE AMERICAS?
THE AVENUE OF THE AMERICAS IS SIXTH AVENUE, TORCH --
-- AND BY "ALWAYS WALKING THE PLANK," THE WIZARD WAS REFERRING TO PLANCK'S CONSTANT -- 6.6260755X10³⁴
I FIGURE THAT MEANS SOMEWHERE BETWEEN STREET NUMBERS 626 AND 755 --
-- ON EITHER SIXTH STREET OR SIXTH AVENUE! I'M WITH YOU --
-- SO WHERE'S THE THREAT?
IT'S NOT A SPECIFIC ADDRESS... IT'D HAVE TO BE SOMETHING THAT RUNS SEVERAL BLOCKS...
GOT IT!
IT'S "BENEATH EVEN YOU," TORCH --
MONSTERS!
RUN!
"-- IN THE SUBWAY!"
ROBOTS -- DISMANTLING THE TRACK!
AND ON A BUSY LINE LIKE THIS, THAT COULD CAUSE A CRASH -- AND HUNDREDS OF DEATHS --
-- IN MINUTES!

THE MOMENT WE ARRIVE, THE ROBOTS GIVE UP ON THEIR LITLE DEMOLITION JOB --
-- AND TURN THEIR ATTENTION TO US!
WELL, AT LEAST THEY'RE NOT RIPPING UP THE TRACKS ANY MORE!
YEAH, BUT THEY'VE ALREADY DONE ENOUGH DAMAGE! IF A TRAIN COMES THROUGH WITH THE TRACKS LIKE THIS --
FRASH
-- IT'LL BE A DISASTER!
THESE GUYS AREN'T ALL THAT STURDY, THOUGH! THINK YOU COULD HANDLE THEM ALONE --
-- WHILE I WORK ON THE TRACKS?
SURE, SURE!
WAK
YOU GO HAVE FUN, WHILE I DO ALL THE HEAVY WORK!
WHINE, WHINE, WHINE!
WHILE THE TORCH KEEPS THE ROBOTS' ATTENTION FIRMLY ON HIM --
-- I DO MY BEST TO GET THE TRACKS BACK IN PLACE.
BUT JUST AS I'M FINISHED --
OH, NO!
HERE COMES A TRAIN -- AND THE TRACKS AREN'T SPIKED IN YET!

TORCH!
I'LL WALTZ AROUND WITH THESE GUYS FOR A LITTLE BIT --
-- YOU GET THOSE TRACKS FASTENED DOWN -- NOW!

MAYBE YOU COULD CUT IT A LITTLE FINER NEXT TIME, SPIDEY?
THIS ISN'T EASY, YOU KNOW -- SPOT-WELDING THE TRACKS AND THEN DRAWING ENOUGH OF THE HEAT OUT OF THEM SO THE WELDS WILL HOLD --
-- ALL WITH A TRAIN RIGHT ON MY FLAMING BUTT!
HONK
HONK

WHOOM
KLAKT
KLAKT
KLAKT
WHEW! MADE IT!
KRAKT
AND THIS IS THE LAST OF THE LITTLE TIN TERRORS!

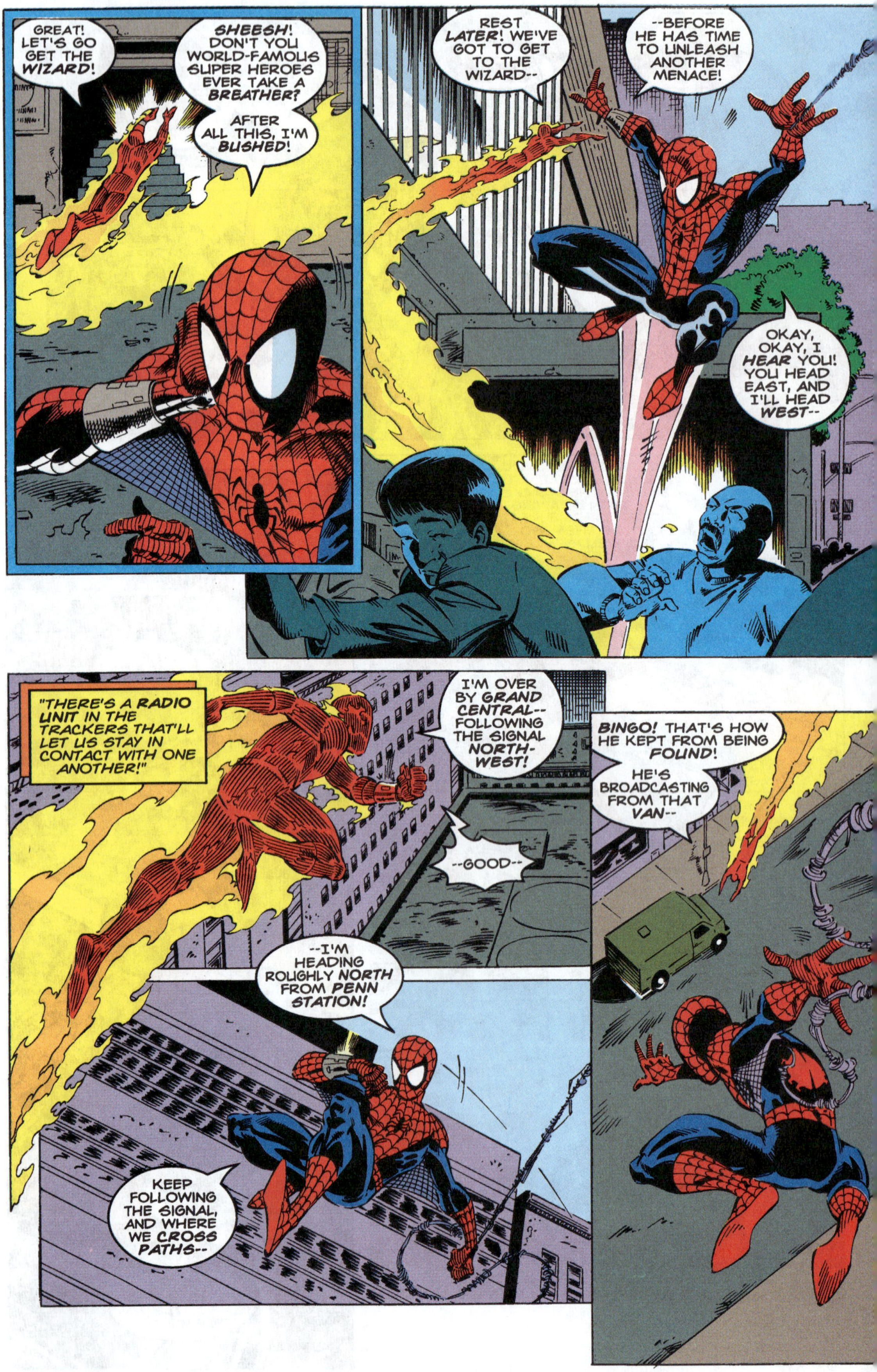

GREAT! LET'S GO GET THE *WIZARD*!

SHEESH! DON'T YOU WORLD-FAMOUS SUPER HEROES EVER TAKE A *BREATHER*?

AFTER ALL THIS, I'M *BUSHED*!

REST *LATER*! WE'VE GOT TO GET TO THE WIZARD--

--BEFORE HE HAS TIME TO UNLEASH ANOTHER MENACE!

OKAY, OKAY, I *HEAR* YOU! YOU HEAD EAST, AND I'LL HEAD *WEST*--

"THERE'S A RADIO UNIT IN THE TRACKERS THAT'LL LET US STAY IN CONTACT WITH ONE ANOTHER!"

I'M OVER BY *GRAND CENTRAL*-- FOLLOWING THE SIGNAL *NORTH-WEST*!

--GOOD--

--I'M HEADING ROUGHLY *NORTH* FROM *PENN STATION*!

KEEP FOLLOWING THE SIGNAL, AND WHERE WE *CROSS PATHS*--

BINGO! THAT'S HOW HE KEPT FROM BEING *FOUND*!

HE'S BROADCASTING FROM THAT *VAN*--

"-- AND AS LONG AS HE MOVES OFTEN ENOUGH, THE AUTHORITIES CAN'T GET A BEAD ON HIM!"
HAH!
THIS CLUE WILL TAKE HIM HOURS TO UNRAVEL -- IF HE EVEN RECOGNIZES THE EQUATION!
I'D GIVE ANYTHING TO SEE HIS FACE WHEN --

Eh--?!

HOW'S IT GOING, WIZ? HEARD ANY GOOD JOKES LATELY -- LIKE THE ONE ABOUT THE SUPER-GENIUS WHO GOT TROUNCED BY A COUPLE OF KIDS?
Ah-ah! HANDS AWAY FROM THE CONTROL PANELS!
BAH! THERE'S NO WAY AN EMPTY-HEADED YOUNGSTER LIKE YOU COULD HAVE FIGURED OUT MY CLUES!

SOME SCIENTIST -- SOMEONE WHO DEVOTES HIS TIME TO KNOWLEDGE, NOT MERELY BRAWLING -- MUST HAVE HELPED YOU!

HEY, HE DID SAY "A COUPLE OF KIDS!"
AND NOT ALL OF US MERE BRAWLERS ARE MUSCLE-BRAINED MORONS, YOU KNOW!
SPIDER-MAN!

IT'S NOT LONG BEFORE THE POLICE ARRIVE, AND...
"MUSCLE-BRAINED MORON," SPIDEY?
YEAH, WELL, YOU'RE THE ONE WHO WANTED TO LOOK FOR PIRATE SHIPS...
BAH! YOU BOTH GOT LUCKY! BOTH OF YOU!
SAY, WIZARD, AS LONG AS YOU'RE STILL HERE, I'M CURIOUS --
-- WHAT DID YOU HAVE PLANNED FOR THE CLOISTERS?
WHAT?!

YOU CAN'T HAVE SOLVED THAT EQUATION THAT FAST! YOU CAN'T! I'M SMARTER THAN YOU -- SMARTER THAN ANY COSTUMED CLOWN --
-- AND I'LL PROVE IT! YOU HEAR ME?!
I'LL PROVE IT!

SOUNDS LIKE YOU'VE MADE A NEW PAL, SPIDEY! AND, HEY, I GOTTA SAY-- I APPRECIATE THE HELP.

Ah, NOT REALLY, TORCH -- BUT IF I COULD GET ANOTHER PEEK AT REED RICHARDS'S LAB...

YOU WANNA COME TAKE A LOOK AT MY NEW CONVERTIBLE?

AW, FORGET IT! YOU'RE HOPELESS!

THAT'S WHAT I LIKE ABOUT YOU, TORCH -- YOU'RE SO GRACIOUS!

I DON'T TELL THE TORCH THE ONLY REASON I RECOGNIZED THAT LAST EQUATION WAS THAT I HAPPENED TO RUN ACROSS IT IN A PHYSICS TEXT RECENTLY --

-- WHY SPOIL THE ILLUSION?

THE WIZARD REALLY IS BRILLIANT, AND I SURE WOULDN'T LOOK FORWARD TO A REMATCH WITH HIM --

-- BUT FOR NOW, ALL'S WELL THAT ENDS WELL --

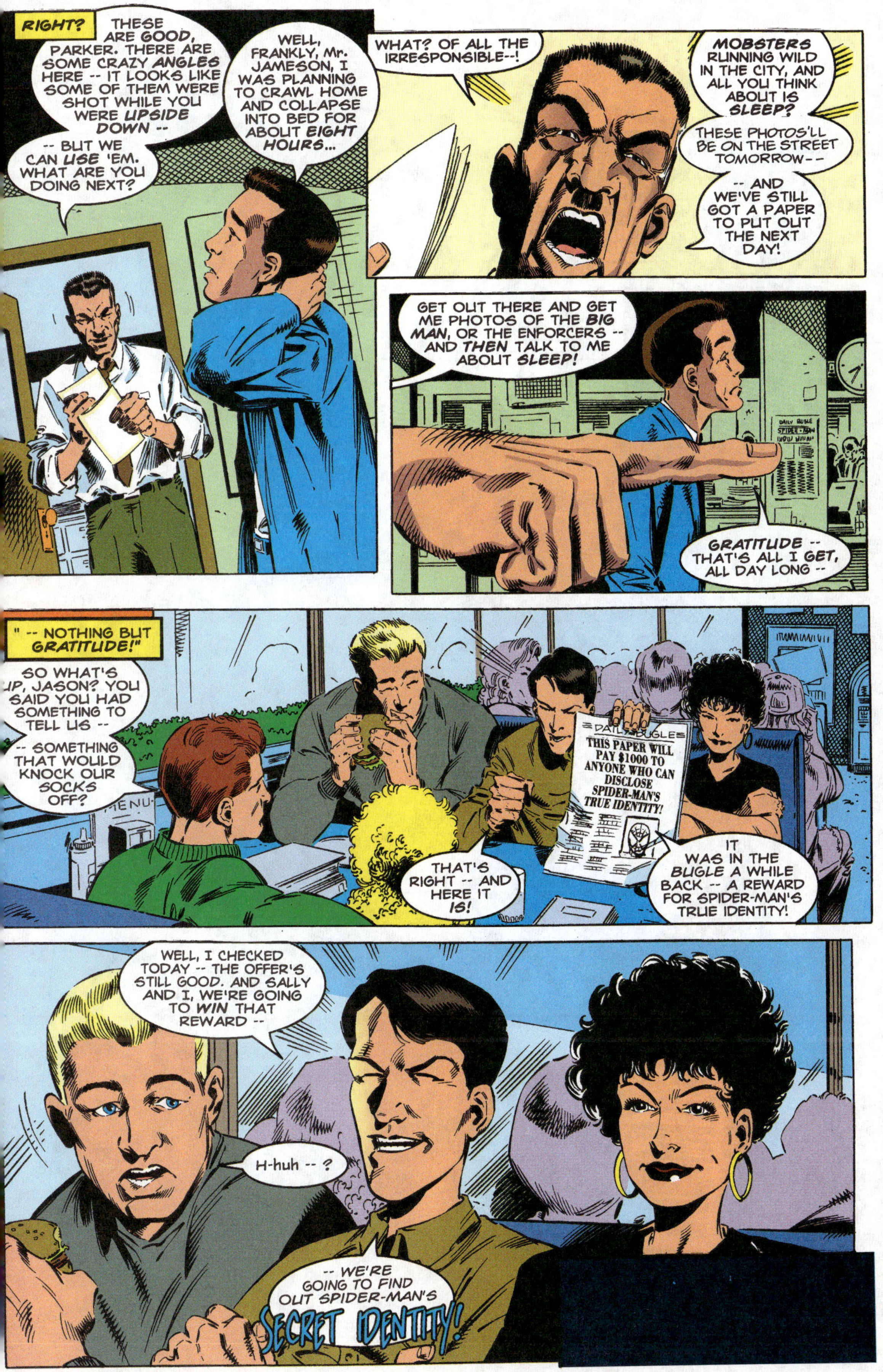

RIGHT?
THESE ARE *GOOD*, PARKER. THERE ARE SOME CRAZY *ANGLES* HERE -- IT LOOKS LIKE SOME OF THEM WERE SHOT WHILE YOU WERE *UPSIDE DOWN* --
-- BUT WE CAN *USE* 'EM. WHAT ARE YOU DOING NEXT?
WELL, FRANKLY, Mr. JAMESON, I WAS PLANNING TO CRAWL HOME AND COLLAPSE INTO BED FOR ABOUT *EIGHT HOURS*...

WHAT? OF ALL THE IRRESPONSIBLE--!
MOBSTERS RUNNING WILD IN THE CITY, AND ALL YOU THINK ABOUT IS *SLEEP?*
THESE PHOTOS'LL BE ON THE STREET TOMORROW--
-- AND WE'VE STILL GOT A PAPER TO PUT OUT THE NEXT DAY!

GET OUT THERE AND GET ME PHOTOS OF THE *BIG MAN*, OR THE ENFORCERS -- AND *THEN* TALK TO ME ABOUT *SLEEP!*
GRATITUDE -- THAT'S ALL I GET, ALL DAY LONG --

" -- NOTHING BUT *GRATITUDE!*"
SO WHAT'S UP, JASON? YOU SAID YOU HAD SOMETHING TO TELL US --
-- SOMETHING THAT WOULD KNOCK OUR SOCKS OFF?
DAILY BUGLE
THIS PAPER WILL PAY $1000 TO ANYONE WHO CAN DISCLOSE SPIDER-MAN'S TRUE IDENTITY!
THAT'S RIGHT -- AND HERE IT *IS!*
IT WAS IN THE *BUGLE* A WHILE BACK -- A REWARD FOR SPIDER-MAN'S TRUE IDENTITY!

WELL, I CHECKED TODAY -- THE OFFER'S STILL GOOD. AND SALLY AND I, WE'RE GOING TO *WIN* THAT REWARD --
H-huh -- ?
-- WE'RE GOING TO FIND OUT SPIDER-MAN'S
SECRET IDENTITY!

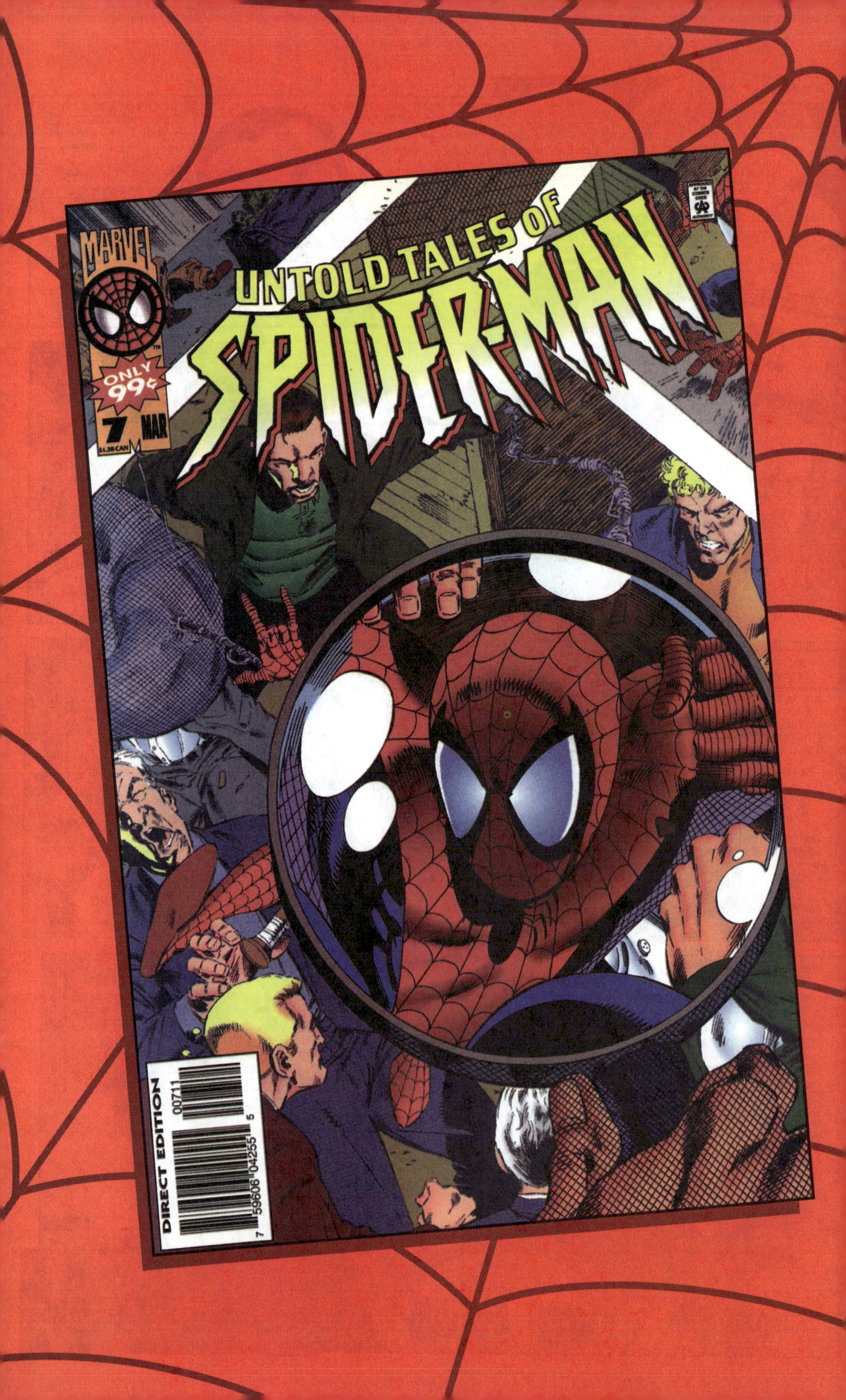
MARVEL
UNTOLD TALES OF
SPIDER-MAN
ONLY 99¢
7 MAR
$1.38 CAN
DIRECT EDITION

ON THE TRAIL OF THE AMAZING SPIDER-MAN!
MIDNIGHT --
-- on a night made for HORROR MOVIES!
It's MISTY and DARK and COLD, and the wind whispers around the rooftops of LOWER MANHATTAN --
-- and my SPIDER-SENSE is giving me this weird little prickly feeling on the back of my NECK --
A STIRRING TALE OF SUSPENSE & SECRETS, BY:
KURT BUSIEK WRITER
PAT OLLIFFE PENCILER
AL VEY w/ PAM EKLUND INKERS
RICHARD STARKINGS AND COMICRAFT LETTERING
STEVE MATTSSON COLORS
TOM BREVOORT EDITOR
BOB BUDIANSKY EXECUTIVE EDITOR
BOB HARRAS EDITOR IN CHIEF

-- so when I hear a SCRAPING noise behind me --
Huh?!

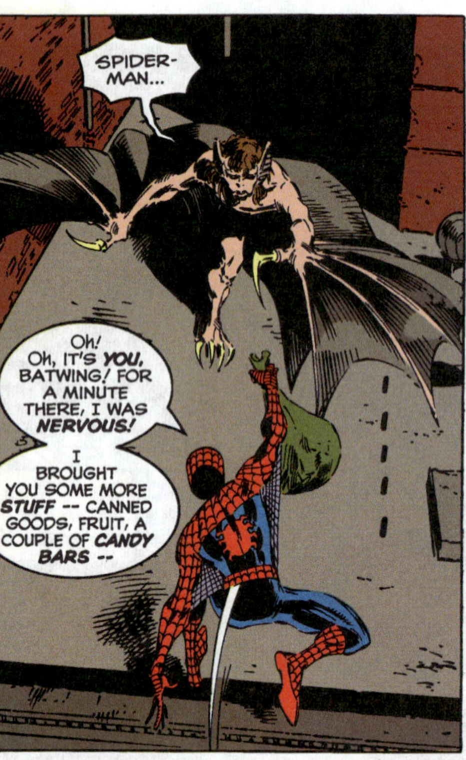
SPIDER-MAN...
Oh! Oh, IT'S YOU, BATWING! FOR A MINUTE THERE, I WAS NERVOUS!
I BROUGHT YOU SOME MORE STUFF -- CANNED GOODS, FRUIT, A COUPLE OF CANDY BARS --

AND THE PIECE DE RESISTANCE, THE CROWNING TOUCH -- THIS TIME I BROUGHT --
TA-DAAH!
-- A CAN OPENER!
THANK YOU. YOU... GOOD FRIEND...

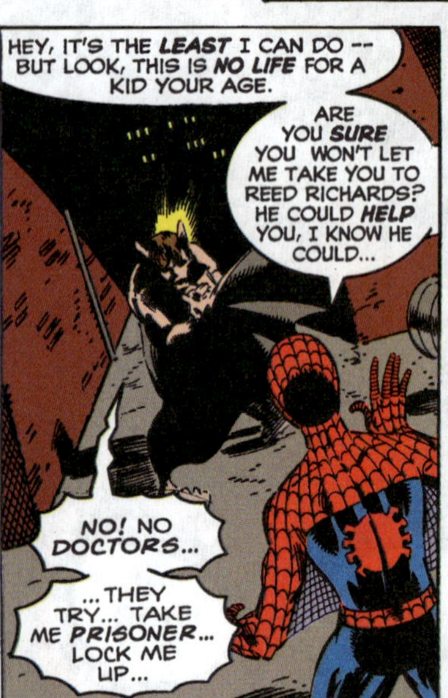
HEY, IT'S THE LEAST I CAN DO -- BUT LOOK, THIS IS NO LIFE FOR A KID YOUR AGE.
ARE YOU SURE YOU WON'T LET ME TAKE YOU TO REED RICHARDS? HE COULD HELP YOU, I KNOW HE COULD...
NO! NO DOCTORS...
...THEY TRY... TAKE ME PRISONER... LOCK ME UP...

HE'S NOT LIKE THAT, HONEST. AND HE MIGHT NOT EVEN NEED YOU --
-- JUST A BLOOD SAMPLE WOULD BE A START...
NEEDLES... DRUG ME... CATCH ME...

WELL, DANG!

The poor little GUY.
He's just a KID -- who got accidentally turned into this HALF-BAT CREATURE the same time he lost his father . It must be AWFUL --
-- and there's got to be a way I can HELP him. He's so scared...

"C'MON, C'MON, WHAT'S HE DOING?!"
"HE'S JUST STANDING THERE, WHILE THE BAT-GUY FLIES OFF!"
"IT LOOKS LIKE HE'S THINKING ABOUT SOMETHING --!"
WELL, MAYBE WE SHOULD DO SOME THINKING, TOO, SALLY. THIS ISN'T THE SAFEST PART OF TOWN, ESPECIALLY IN THE MIDDLE OF THE NIGHT...
Oh, WHERE IS YOUR SENSE OF ADVENTURE, JASON? THIS IS SO EXCITING! AND BESIDES --
-- YOU'RE THE ONE WHO WANTED TO BECOME A BIG WHEEL AT SCHOOL BY EXPOSING SPIDER-MAN'S SECRET I.D. AND COLLECTING THAT REWARD FOR IT!
Oh, NOW LOOK WHAT YOU'VE MADE ME DO! I LOST SIGHT OF HIM -- AND NOW HE'S GONE!
WHERE'D HE GO? WHERE'D HE GO?
Oh, I DON'T KNOW...
...YOU MIGHT TRY LOOKING BEHIND YOU.
NOW -- WHAT ARE YOU KIDS DOING HERE?
I knew my spider-sense was reacting to SOMETHING.
And it wasn't Batwing, because he's no THREAT to me. So it had to be something else. Something NEARBY...

I do my best to keep from LAUGHING as they explain themselves. They're so RESPECTFUL --
-- but so DETERMINED.
-- AND THE DAILY BUGLE'S OFFERED A $1000 REWARD FOR YOUR SECRET IDENTITY, SO WE FIGURED --
-- WHY NOT TAKE A CRACK AT IT?
AND HAVE YOU CONSIDERED WHAT MIGHT HAPPEN TO YOU IF I REALLY AM THE RUTHLESS CRIMINAL FINK THE BUGLE SAYS I AM?
Uh --
W-WELL --
WELL, THEN --
MY FEET!
THWIP
-- IT'S A GOOD THING FOR YOU I'M NOT, EH?
SO LONG!
HE'S GETTING AWAY!
SALLY! DON'T YOU DARE LEAVE ME STUCK HERE ALONE!
SALLY!

THE NEXT AFTERNOON...
MIDTOWN HIGH SCHOOL
-- AND THEN WE TURNED AROUND, AND THERE HE WAS, CROUCHED ABOVE US --
-- SIX FEET TALL IF HE'S AN INCH --
-- AND THOSE EYES -- I KNOW THAT RED PART'S A MASK, BUT I WOULDN'T BE AT ALL SURPRISED TO FIND OUT THAT THOSE EYES WERE REAL...
ANYWAY -- HE CREPT SLOWLY TOWARD US, AND WE WERE ROOTED TO THE SPOT, NOT SURE WHETHER HE WAS GONNA KILL US OR NOT!
YOU COULD TELL HE WANTED TO -- THAT IF WE'D SHOWN THE TINIEST BIT OF FEAR, JUST FOR A SPLIT SECOND...
...HE'D HAVE BEEN ON US, TEARING US FROM LIMB TO LIMB --
HOLD IT! SPIDEY'S NOT LIKE THAT, AND YOU KNOW IT! HE'S ONE OF THE GOOD GUYS -- HE WOULDN'T KILL ANYONE!
NOT JUST FOR FOLLOWIN' HIM AROUND, ANYWAY!
WERE YOU THERE, FLASH? DID YOU SEE IT?
I TELL YOU, HE'S A VICIOUS FIEND! HE'S IN LEAGUE WITH THAT BATWING MONSTER FOR SURE, AND --
NOW WAIT A SEC, JASON. I READ ABOUT BATWING IN THE PAPER, AND HE'S NO MONSTER. HE'S JUST A LITTLE KID, AND HE ISN'T OUT TO HURT ANYBODY.
THEY RAN EXCERPTS FROM HIS DIARY, AND IT WAS HEARTBREAKING..!
HMPH!

-- HE'S JUST **ANGRY** BECAUSE SPIDEY WEBBED HIS SHOES TO THE ROOF AND IT TOOK AN **HOUR** TO GET LOOSE. SPIDER-MAN WAS PERFECTLY NICE --

-- HE DIDN'T STRANGLE **ANY** BABY DUCKS OR EAT **ANYONE'S** BRAIN, NOT WHILE WE WERE THERE. ISN'T THAT **RIGHT,** JASON?

FINE, WHATEVER. ***I*** COULD TELL, EVEN IF YOU COULDN'T. HE'S A **MENACE,** AND HE BELONGS BEHIND **BARS** --

-- AND WE'LL **FIND OUT** WHO HE IS FOR **REAL** -- **WHEREVER** HE'S HIDING!

HAH! What I wouldn't give to see their FACES --

-- if they found out Spidey's right under their noses, as puny ol' Peter Parker, and they never KNEW it!

Still, this could be trouble, if they keep it up. I'll have to figure out something to do about it --

-- but not right now.

NEW **BUSINESS!** RIGHT IN THE **NEIGHBORHOOD** -- NO NEED TO MAKE LONG TRIPS OUT OF YOUR WAY ANYMORE.

A-1 EYE CLINIC

FLYER, MISTER?

UH, THANKS.

I've seen these all over the neighborhood -- tacked up to TELEPHONE POLES or in STORE WINDOWS.
It's funny --

-- ever since my GLASSES got broken, Aunt May's been bugging me to get an EYE TEST. I can see just fine --
-- but I've been worried that our USUAL eye doctor would notice something DIFFERENT about my eyes --

-- something that might expose me as SPIDER-MAN.
But if I go to this NEW guy, I can get a clean bill of health, and if there's anything strange -- well, he's never SEEN me before --

-- so where's the HARM? Heck, I don't even have to give him my REAL NAME!
-- YOU SEEING ME ON SUCH SHORT NOTICE, Dr. WINSLOW.
A PLEASURE, Mr. PALMER, A PLEASURE. WE'RE EAGER TO SERVE THE COMMUNITY!
A-1
CLINIC
NOW, IF YOU'LL JUST STEP THIS WAY?
WOW --
"-- THIS IS SOME SET-UP, DOC! IT LOOKS LIKE SOMETHING OUT OF A FRANKENSTEIN MOVIE!"
IT'S THE VERY LATEST EQUIPMENT, SIR. IT'S TOTALLY HARMLESS, I ASSURE YOU --
-- BUT ALLOWS US TO TEST YOUR VISION FASTER AND MORE ACCURATELY THAN EVER, AND BEST OF ALL, IT'S TOTALLY AUTOMATED.
THE PROCESS IS ENTIRELY MECHANICAL -- NO HUMAN JUDGMENT, AND THEREFORE NO RISK OF HUMAN ERROR.
SOUNDS GOOD TO ME, DOC -- FOR A COUPLE OF REASONS. SO WHAT DO I DO?
YOU JUST SIT THERE, Mr. PALMER --
-- AND LET THE MACHINE DO EVERYTHING!
SHHHK
All I see are weird, shifting colored BLOBS OF LIGHT --
-- and then, suddenly, my SPIDER-SENSE goes off --
-- and then --

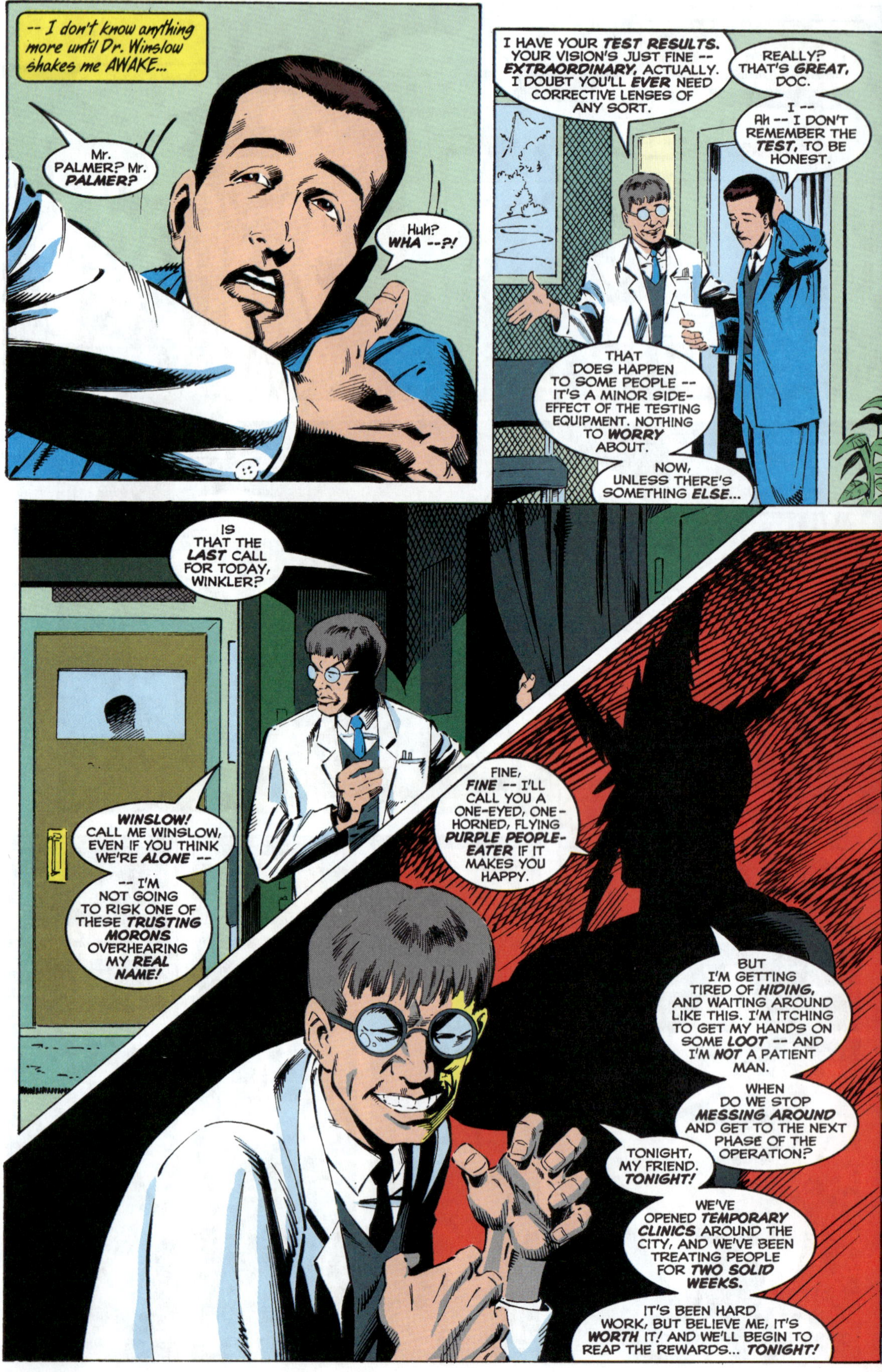
-- I don't know anything more until Dr. Winslow shakes me AWAKE...
Mr. PALMER? Mr. PALMER?
Huh? WHA --?!
I HAVE YOUR TEST RESULTS. YOUR VISION'S JUST FINE -- EXTRAORDINARY, ACTUALLY. I DOUBT YOU'LL EVER NEED CORRECTIVE LENSES OF ANY SORT.
REALLY? THAT'S GREAT, DOC.
I -- AH -- I DON'T REMEMBER THE TEST, TO BE HONEST.
THAT DOES HAPPEN TO SOME PEOPLE -- IT'S A MINOR SIDE-EFFECT OF THE TESTING EQUIPMENT. NOTHING TO WORRY ABOUT.
NOW, UNLESS THERE'S SOMETHING ELSE...
IS THAT THE LAST CALL FOR TODAY, WINKLER?
WINSLOW! CALL ME WINSLOW, EVEN IF YOU THINK WE'RE ALONE --
-- I'M NOT GOING TO RISK ONE OF THESE TRUSTING MORONS OVERHEARING MY REAL NAME!
FINE, FINE -- I'LL CALL YOU A ONE-EYED, ONE-HORNED, FLYING PURPLE PEOPLE-EATER IF IT MAKES YOU HAPPY.
BUT I'M GETTING TIRED OF HIDING, AND WAITING AROUND LIKE THIS. I'M ITCHING TO GET MY HANDS ON SOME LOOT -- AND I'M NOT A PATIENT MAN.
WHEN DO WE STOP MESSING AROUND AND GET TO THE NEXT PHASE OF THE OPERATION?
TONIGHT, MY FRIEND. TONIGHT!
WE'VE OPENED TEMPORARY CLINICS AROUND THE CITY, AND WE'VE BEEN TREATING PEOPLE FOR TWO SOLID WEEKS.
IT'S BEEN HARD WORK, BUT BELIEVE ME, IT'S WORTH IT! AND WE'LL BEGIN TO REAP THE REWARDS... TONIGHT!

I'm feeling pretty good -- I've got a piece of paper that'll make Aunt May stop worrying about my EYESIGHT --
-- and I've got a dinner date with the lovely and charming Betty Brant --
CRIME WAVE! READ ABOUT THE CRIME WAVE!
CAN ANYONE STOP THE BIG MAN AND HIS ENFORCERS?! CRIME WAVE!
DAILY BUGLE
CRIME WAVE
-- and all I've got to do is brave the DRAGON'S LAIR to rescue the fair princess --
PARKER!
TELL ME YOU'VE GOT SOME CRIME PHOTOS FOR ME!
Uh, SORRY, Mr. J. -- I'M DRY. I JUST STOPPED BY TO PICK UP BETTY.
OF ALL THE INCOMPETENT, IRRESPONSIBLE EXCUSES FOR A FREELANCER!
THE BIG MAN'S TAKEN OVER THE MOBS AND IS PULLING CRIMES LEFT AND RIGHT -- AND NOBODY'S SO MUCH AS SEEN HIM?
MAYBE THERE IS NO BIG MAN, JONAH. MAYBE HE WAS JUST MADE UP BY THE CROOKS SO THE COPS'D HAVE SOMEONE TO CHASE FOR AWHILE...
YOU KNOW, I WOULDN'T PUT IT PAST SPIDER-MAN TO PULL A TRICK LIKE THAT, FOSWELL --
-- TO DISTRACT US FROM HIS SHENANIGANS BY SENDING US ON A WILD GOOSE CHASE!
AND YOU, PARKER -- DON'T THINK YOU CAN MAKE A HABIT OF SUCH FLIMSY EXCUSES! GET ME PHOTOS OF SOMETHING NEWSWORTHY --
-- OR BY GODFREY, I'LL GET SOMEONE WHO CAN!
I'LL DO MY BEST, Mr. JAMESON...

"...I'LL DO MY **BEST**."

SORRY IT'S ONLY **FAST FOOD**, BETTY -- BUT UNTIL I SELL JONAH SOME MORE PHOTOS, THIS IS ALL I CAN **AFFORD**.

THIS IS **FINE**, PETER -- I DON'T WANT YOU TAKING ANY **UNNECESSARY RISKS** ON MY ACCOUNT.

WHEN I THINK ABOUT WHAT YOU MUST **GO THROUGH** TO GET SOME OF THESE PHOTOS...

AW, C'MON, BETTY! YOU CAN'T BE WORRIED ABOUT A **DYNAMIC HE-MAN PHOTOGRAPHER** LIKE **ME**! IF I EVER RAN INTO THE BIG MAN'S GANG --

BILLY BURGER

-- WHY, I'D JUST TAKE THEIR GUNS **AWAY** FROM THEM AND --

UUUHH...

PETER!

PETER, ARE YOU **ALL RIGHT?!**

I'M FINE... I'M **FINE**. THINGS JUST... WENT A LITTLE **GRAY** THERE, FOR A SECOND...

WE'D BETTER CALL IT A **NIGHT**, PETER. YOU'VE OBVIOUSLY BEEN WORKING TOO HARD -- YOU NEED TO GET SOME **SLEEP** BEFORE YOU MAKE YOURSELF **ILL!**

IF YOU **SAY** SO, BETTY...

-- BUT ARE YOU **SURE** THAT WITH MY AUNT MAY IN FLORIDA FOR A WHILE, YOU'RE NOT JUST TAKING OVER HER JOB OF **FUSSING** OVER ME..?
OH, PETER...
...IT'S JUST... YOU TAKE SO MANY **RISKS**, AND YOU SEEM TO **ENJOY** IT, AND...

...AND I DON'T WANT TO **LOSE** YOU... NOT **YOU**, TOO!
And she walks off before I can ask her what she MEANS by that.
BETTY?
GET SOME **SLEEP**, PETER...
...FOR ME, IF NOT FOR YOURSELF...

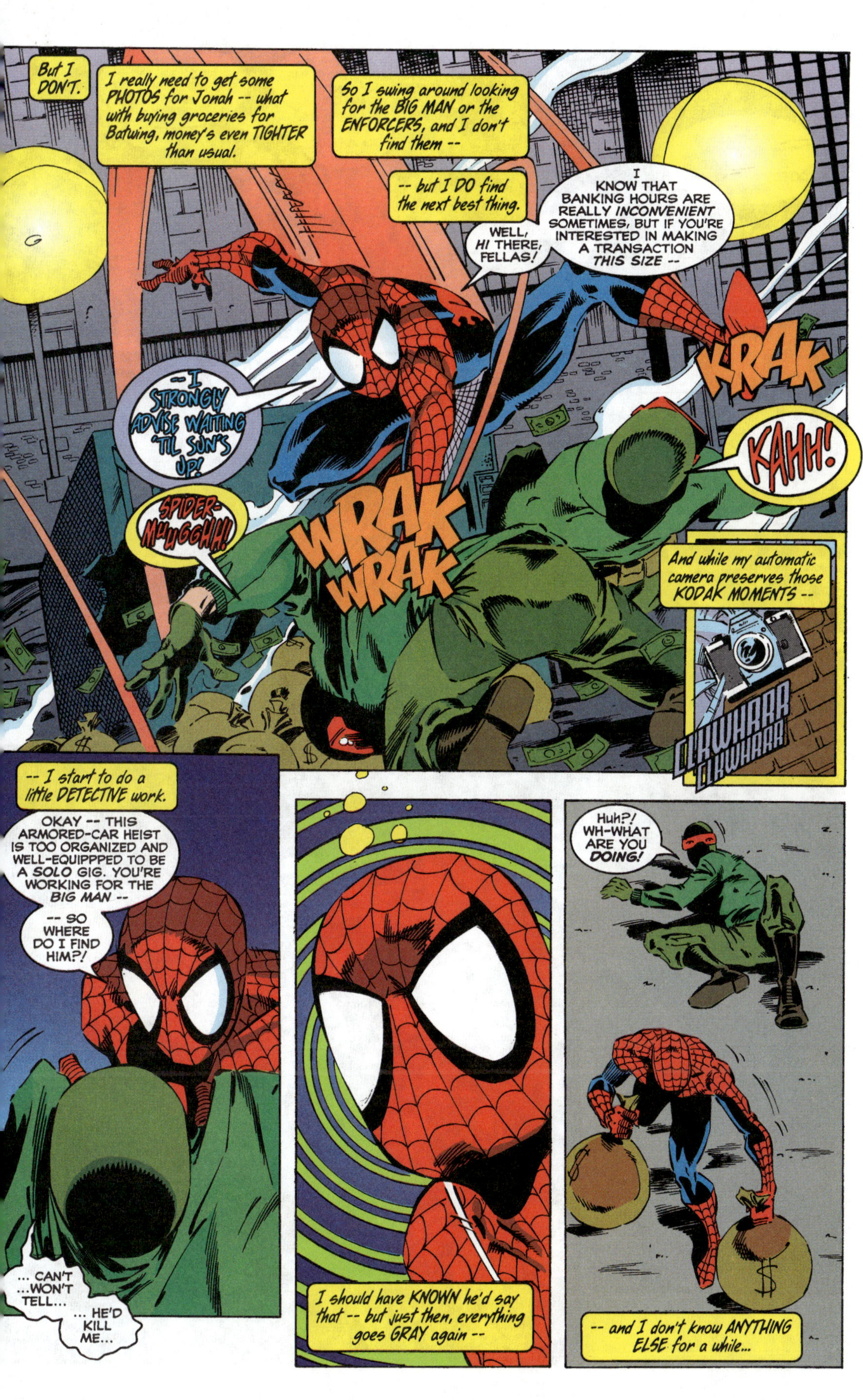

But I DON'T.
I really need to get some PHOTOS for Jonah -- what with buying groceries for Batwing, money's even TIGHTER than usual.
So I swing around looking for the BIG MAN or the ENFORCERS, and I don't find them --
-- but I DO find the next best thing.
WELL, HI THERE, FELLAS!
I KNOW THAT BANKING HOURS ARE REALLY INCONVENIENT SOMETIMES, BUT IF YOU'RE INTERESTED IN MAKING A TRANSACTION THIS SIZE --
KRAK
-- I STRONGLY ADVISE WAITING 'TIL SUN'S UP!
KAHH!
SPIDER-MUUGGHH!
WRAK WRAK
And while my automatic camera preserves those KODAK MOMENTS --
CLKWHRRR CLKWHRRR
-- I start to do a little DETECTIVE work.
OKAY -- THIS ARMORED-CAR HEIST IS TOO ORGANIZED AND WELL-EQUIPPPED TO BE A SOLO GIG. YOU'RE WORKING FOR THE BIG MAN --
-- SO WHERE DO I FIND HIM?!
... CAN'T ...WON'T TELL... ... HE'D KILL ME...
I should have KNOWN he'd say that -- but just then, everything goes GRAY again --
Huh?! WH-WHAT ARE YOU DOING!
-- and I don't know ANYTHING ELSE for a while...

HE -- HE'S STEALING THE MONEY?! BUT -- THAT DOESN'T MAKE ANY SENSE!
I KNEW IT! HE IS A CROOK -- JUST LIKE THE BUGLE SAYS!
I DON'T BELIEVE IT! THERE MUST BE SOME OTHER EXPLANATION! NOW COME ON --
-- WE'VE GOT TO GO AFTER HIM!
GIVE ME A SEC, SALLY -- I'M NOT USED TO DRIVING MY DAD'S JEEP!
HECK, I SHOULDN'T EVEN BE DRIVING IT -- I ONLY HAVE MY LEARNER'S PERMIT AFTER ALL!
JUST SHUT UP AND DRIVE, JASON --
" -- WE CAN'T LOSE SPIDEY!"
JASON, LOOK!
IT'S NOT JUST SPIDER-MAN -- THERE ARE PEOPLE COMING FROM ALL DIRECTIONS, CONVERGING ON THAT DERELICT THEATER!
AND IT LOOKS LIKE THEY'RE ALL CARRYING MONEY -- OR JEWELRY -- OR SOMETHING!
COME ON --

"-- LET'S FIND A WAY IN!"
IT'S POETRY, ELECTRO -- SHEER POETRY!
A SIMPLE SET OF MENTAL COMMANDS, IMPLANTED DURING AN "EYE EXAM" -- AND THESE PEOPLE BECOME OUR WILLING PUPPETS!
AS LONG AS MY MACHINE BROADCASTS ITS SIGNAL, THEY'LL DO ANYTHING WE ASK -- EVEN ROB THEIR OWN HOMES!
YEAH, I'VE GOT TO ADMIT --
-- WHEN YOU FIRST ASKED ME TO THROW IN WITH YOU ON THIS, IN CASE YOU NEEDED A LITTLE SECURITY, I THOUGHT YOU WERE CRACKERS.
NOW I'M SURE OF IT -- BUT I CAN'T ARGUE WITH THE RESULTS! THIS IS ONE SWEET --
-- DISASTER!
WHAT? WHAT IS IT?
LOOK! IN THE BACK -- JUST COMING IN --!
SPIDER-MAN?! BUT WHY -- HOW COULD HE HAVE KNOWN --
WAAIIIT A MINUTE! HE'S NOT HERE TO BUST US --
-- HE'S AS ZONKED OUT AS ALL THE OTHERS!
THEN -- ONE OF THE PATIENTS WE "TESTED" OVER THE LAST COUPLE OF WEEKS MUST HAVE BEEN HIM, IN HIS TRUE IDENTITY!
AND NOW HE'S OURS -- AS SURELY AS ANY OF THESE OTHER SHEEP!

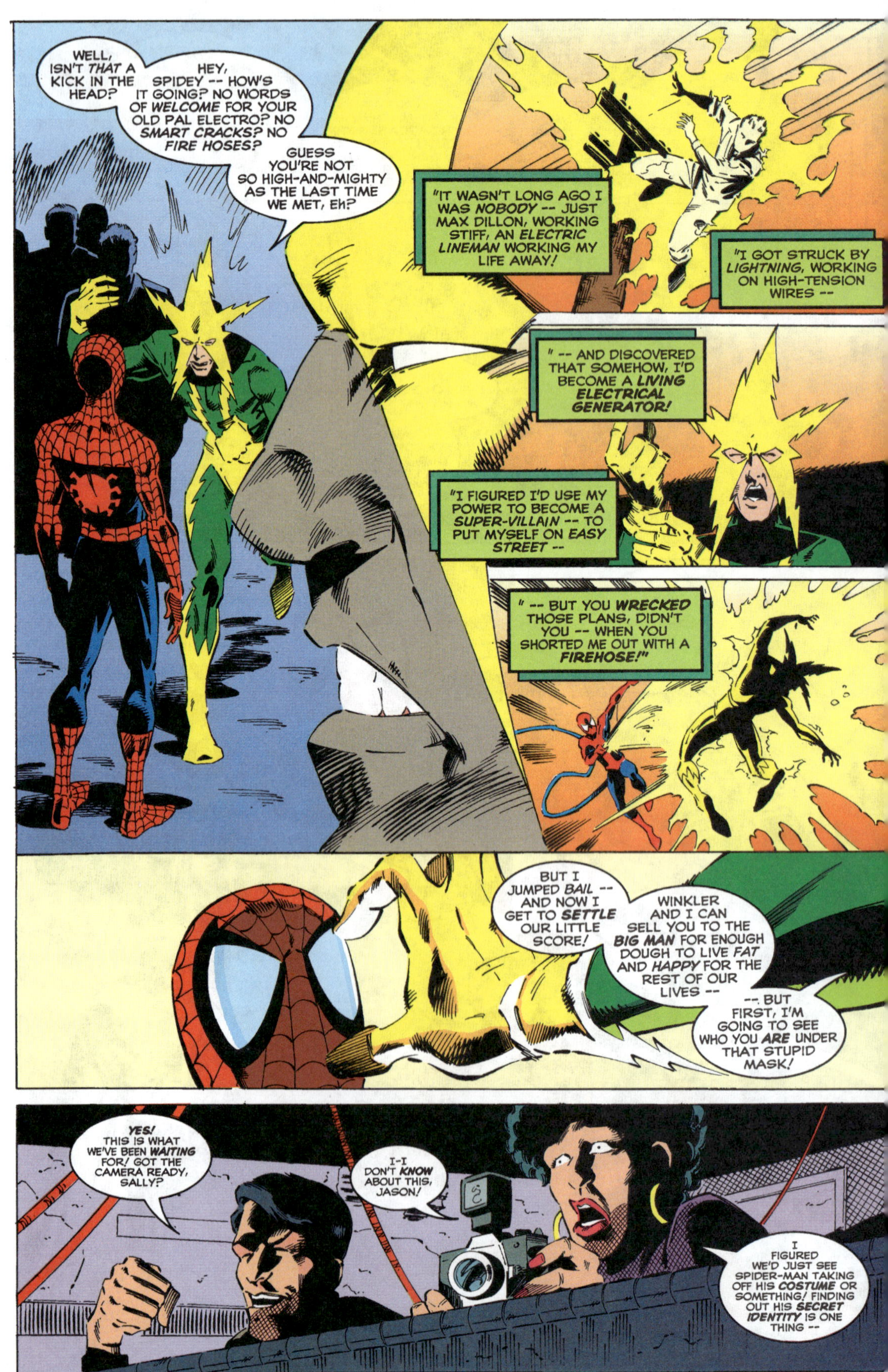
WELL, ISN'T THAT A KICK IN THE HEAD?
HEY, SPIDEY -- HOW'S IT GOING? NO WORDS OF WELCOME FOR YOUR OLD PAL ELECTRO? NO SMART CRACKS? NO FIRE HOSES?
GUESS YOU'RE NOT SO HIGH-AND-MIGHTY AS THE LAST TIME WE MET, EH?
"IT WASN'T LONG AGO I WAS NOBODY -- JUST MAX DILLON, WORKING STIFF, AN ELECTRIC LINEMAN WORKING MY LIFE AWAY!
"I GOT STRUCK BY LIGHTNING, WORKING ON HIGH-TENSION WIRES --
" -- AND DISCOVERED THAT SOMEHOW, I'D BECOME A LIVING ELECTRICAL GENERATOR!
"I FIGURED I'D USE MY POWER TO BECOME A SUPER-VILLAIN -- TO PUT MYSELF ON EASY STREET --
" -- BUT YOU WRECKED THOSE PLANS, DIDN'T YOU -- WHEN YOU SHORTED ME OUT WITH A FIREHOSE!"
BUT I JUMPED BAIL -- AND NOW I GET TO SETTLE OUR LITTLE SCORE!
WINKLER AND I CAN SELL YOU TO THE BIG MAN FOR ENOUGH DOUGH TO LIVE FAT AND HAPPY FOR THE REST OF OUR LIVES --
-- BUT FIRST, I'M GOING TO SEE WHO YOU ARE UNDER THAT STUPID MASK!
YES! THIS IS WHAT WE'VE BEEN WAITING FOR! GOT THE CAMERA READY, SALLY?
I-I DON'T KNOW ABOUT THIS, JASON!
I FIGURED WE'D JUST SEE SPIDER-MAN TAKING OFF HIS COSTUME OR SOMETHING! FINDING OUT HIS SECRET IDENTITY IS ONE THING --

-- BUT LETTING CRIMINALS KNOW IT --
-- I JUST DON'T KNOW!
FPASHH
H-Huh --?!
WHAT? THAT SUDDEN LIGHT -- ?
The world starts coming back into FOCUS, and the first thing I see --
WHOA! ELECTRO!
WHAT ARE YOU DOING HERE?!
AND COME TO THINK OF IT -- WHERE IS HERE, ANYWAY?
BLAST IT, WINKLER -- YOU SAID THAT MACHINE OF YOURS WOULD KEEP ITS VICTIMS UNDER CONTROL!
IT DOES! IT DID! BUT IT'S OPTICALLY ACTIVATED -- SO THAT FLASH OF LIGHT MUST HAVE SNAPPED HIM OUT OF IT!
GET HIM, PEOPLE -- ATTACK, ATTACK!
HE CAN'T BE ALLOWED TO ESCAPE -- NOT WITH WHAT HE'S SEEN!
ATTACK...
ATTACK...

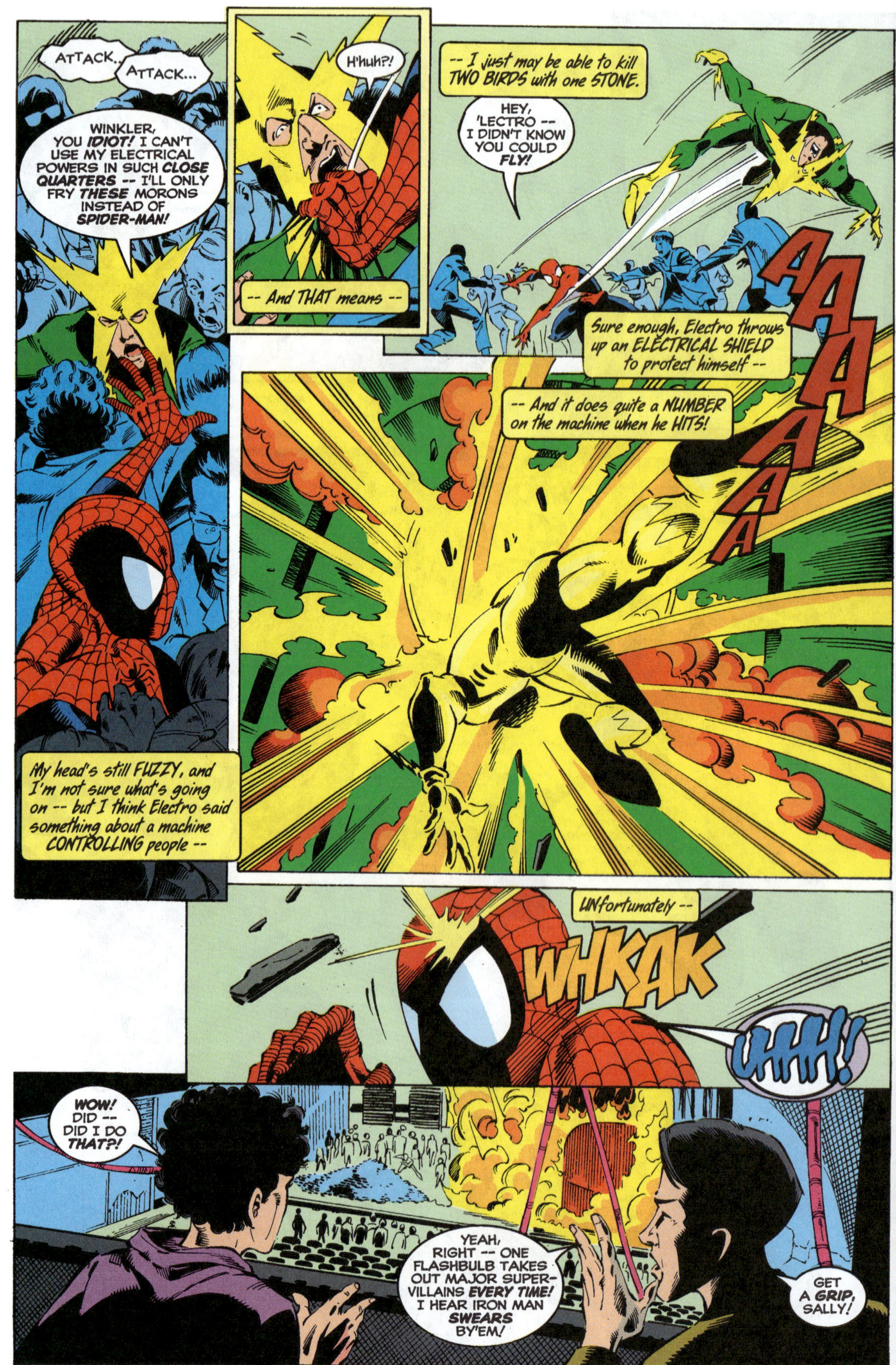
ATTACK..
ATTACK...
WINKLER, YOU IDIOT! I CAN'T USE MY ELECTRICAL POWERS IN SUCH CLOSE QUARTERS -- I'LL ONLY FRY THESE MORONS INSTEAD OF SPIDER-MAN!
H'huh?!
-- And THAT means --
-- I just may be able to kill TWO BIRDS with one STONE.
HEY, 'LECTRO -- I DIDN'T KNOW YOU COULD FLY!
AAAAAAAA
Sure enough, Electro throws up an ELECTRICAL SHIELD to protect himself --
-- And it does quite a NUMBER on the machine when he HITS!
My head's still FUZZY, and I'm not sure what's going on -- but I think Electro said something about a machine CONTROLLING people --
UNfortunately --
WHKAK
UHH!
WOW! DID -- DID I DO THAT?!
YEAH, RIGHT -- ONE FLASHBULB TAKES OUT MAJOR SUPER-VILLAINS EVERY TIME! I HEAR IRON MAN SWEARS BY'EM!
GET A GRIP, SALLY!

THEY'RE COMING TO THEIR SENSES! I'D BETTER GET OUT OF HERE --
-- BEFORE ANYONE RECOGNIZES ME!
WH -- WH --
WHERE -- HOW -- ?
I never do see that "WINKLER" guy that Electro was shouting about, but I've got enough to deal with --
-- Namely, the downside of throwing an ELECTRICALLY POWERED bad guy into a BIG ELECTRIC DOOHICKEY!
THAT'S IT, SPIDER-MAN! THAT'S ENOUGH!
I CAN FEED OFF THE MAIN POWER CABLE TO THIS THING -- SOAK UP ENOUGH JUICE TO BLAST YOU OUT OF MANHATTAN AND ALL THE WAY TO JERSEY!
YOU'VE GOT NOTHING TO HIDE BEHIND -- NOWHERE TO DODGE --
-- AND THERE IS JUST NO WAY YOU CAN OUTRUN LIGHTNING! MAKE NO MISTAKE, SPIDER-MAN --
-- YOU'RE ABOUT TO DIE!
I'm still woozy from whatever MIND-CONTROL I was under -- still reeling from getting conked on the SKULL in the explosion --
-- forget dodging, I can barely STAND --

-- but --
KRAKK
UKH!
HE'S ALL YOURS, SPIDEY! TAKE HIM!
I --
-- WHO --
I take a DEEP BREATH while Electro stumbles -- plant my FEET -- and --
KPOW
Oh, NICE MOVE, SALLY!
YOU COULD'VE GOTTEN YOURSELF KILLED -- OR DID IT SLIP YOUR MIND THAT YOU'RE NOT A SUPER HERO?
GIMME A BREAK, IONELLO! I'M ON THE SCHOOL GYMNASTICS TEAM -- I KNOW HOW TO SWING ON A ROPE!
THAT'S NOT WHAT I MEANT!
HOLD UP A MINUTE, KIDS -- I'VE GOT AN IDEA!
LET ME SEE THAT CAMERA FOR A SEC --

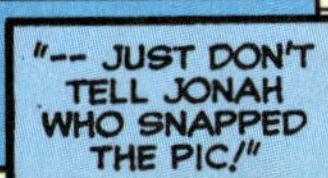

"-- JUST DON'T TELL JONAH WHO SNAPPED THE PIC!"

DAILY BUGLE

NEW YORK'S FINEST DAILY NEWSPAPER

SCHOOL KIDS FOIL SUPER-VILLAIN

Jason Ionello

Sally Avril

Midtown High students Jason Ionello and Sally Avril stand over the unconscious body of the super-villain known as Electro. More than a million dollars in cash and valuables was recovered by the pair.

Two Queens Teenagers Pull the Plug on Electro

It all worked out just FINE. Jonah got a story -- the money got recovered --
C'MON, JASE -- TELL IT AGAIN!
THERE WE WERE, ME AND SALLY -- WATCHING FROM THE SHADOWS, AS ELECTRO PREPARED TO UNMASK SPIDER-MAN!
BUT COULD WE LET IT HAPPEN? NO!

-- and Jason and Sally got all the ATTENTION they'd been looking for, and THEN some!
HEY, FLASH -- YOU'RE NOT GOING TO STICK AROUND AND LISTEN?

Huh? NAH -- AFTER YOU'VE HEARD IT SEVENTEEN TIMES, IT KIND OF LOSES ITS APPEAL. OR AT LEAST IT DOES FOR ME.
I THOUGHT YOU MIGHT BE SORE, WHAT WITH SALLY AND JASON STEALING YOUR THUNDER. YOU'RE USUALLY THE BIG GUY AROUND HERE...
Aw, I DON'T MIND. THEY DID SOMETHING PRETTY COOL -- THEY DESERVE TO HAVE A FUSS MADE OVER THEM.
I DON'T SUPPOSE YOU'D EVER TAKE A CRACK AT EXPOSING SPIDER-MAN'S SECRET IDENTITY..?
ARE YOU KIDDING? NO WAY!
LISTEN, IF SPIDEY WANTS TO KEEP HIS IDENTITY A SECRET, I'M SURE HE HAS A GOOD REASON, AND THAT'S ALL I NEED TO KNOW!
I'D NEVER DO THAT TO SPIDEY -- NEVER!
YOU KNOW, FLASH, YOU MAY BE NOTHING BUT A BIG DUMB APE --
-- BUT SOMETIMES, YOU'RE DOWNRIGHT OKAY!
Huh? SOMEBODY WANT TO TELL ME WHAT THAT WAS ALL ABOUT?
Jonah even bought my ARMORED-CAR ROBBERY PHOTOS, for an inside page, so I can take Betty out to a REAL restaurant this Friday.
Like the bard said, all's well that ENDS well...
-- that is, if you can count on it ENDING...
SO THIS IS IT, RIGHT? NO MORE CHASING AROUND AFTER SPIDER-MAN ALL NIGHT, RIGHT?
HEY, IT WAS YOUR IDEA, JASON. IF YOU SAY WE'RE THROUGH, WE'RE THROUGH. BESIDES --
-- I'VE GOT A WHOLE NEW IDEA NOW...

SHORTLY THEREAFTER:
AFTER A RUN-IN WITH THE ENFORCERS, BETTY BRANT SWIFTLY LEFT TOWN.
I CAN'T LET HIM FALL INTO THE HANDS OF THE ENFORCERS BECAUSE OF ME!
THERE'S ONLY ONE THING TO DO... I'VE GOT TO LEAVE! NEVER SEE HIM AGAIN!
GOOD WORK, MONTANA! AND NOW, GET RID OF SPIDER-MAN ONCE AND FOR ALL! I CAN'T HAVE HIM TRYING TO INTERFERE WITH MY PLANS!
THE BIG MAN! AND THE ENFORCERS! I'VE GOT YOU ALL TOGETHER!
SPIDER-MAN FOUGHT A SERIES OF SKIRMISHES WITH THE ENFORCERS...
CORRECTION, MY FRIEND! IT IS WE WHO HAVE YOU! GET HIM, OX!
...EVENTUALLY DISMANTLING THEIR ORGANIZATION.
KEEP AFTER HIM! HE'S TIRING! HE'S ONLY HUMAN! YOU'RE WEARING HIM DOWN!
RELAX, BIG MAN-- THEY'RE DOIN' OKAY WITHOUT A CHEER-LEADER!
SORRY, SPIDER-MAN! I DON'T FIGHT BY YOUR RULES! I KNOW WHEN TO MAKE MY EXIT!
DESPITE THE WALL-CRAWLER'S BEST EFFORTS, THE BIG MAN HIMSELF ESCAPED...
...ONLY TO BE SUBSEQUENTLY UNMASKED BY THE POLICE AS BUGLE REPORTER FREDERICK FOSWELL.
DON'T TRY TO SNEAK OUT OF HERE, FOSWELL! WE HAVE THE PLACE SURROUNDED! YOU MIGHT AS WELL COME ALONG PEACEFULLY!
FREDERICK FOSWELL?! BUT I THOUGHT IT WAS JONAH?? HOW CAN LITTLE FOSWELL BE THE BIG MAN?
FOSWELL?
HERE'S A LETTER FROM AUNT MAY! SHE'S HAVING A FINE TIME IN FLORIDA!
BUT NOTHING FROM BETTY! NOT EVEN A CARD!
BUT EVEN WITH THE ENFORCERS BEHIND BARS, BETTY'S WHERE-ABOUTS REMAINED A MYSTERY TO THE CONFUSED AND CON-CERNED SPIDER-MAN.

...COMES the HEADSMAN!
MARVEL
UNTOLD TALES OF SPIDER-MAN
ONLY 99¢
8 APR
$1.38 CAN
DIRECT EDITION
59606 04255 5

THIS IS THE STORY OF A BOY -- A BOY WHO'LL BE VERY IMPORTANT TO THE AMAZING SPIDER-MAN, AS BOTH HIS BEST FRIEND AND HIS MOST FEARED ENEMY. BUT FOR NOW, IT'S JUST THE STORY OF A BOY...
HARRY'S STORY
...A BOY AND HIS FATHER...
FINAL
Daily Globe
BIG MAN UNMASKED
Spider-Man Helps Police Capture Notorious Enforcers; Crime Boss Revealed to be Daily Bugle Employee
HEY, DAD --
The Big Man, masked crimelord (artist's rendition)
#DS5368BW
Frederick Foswell, Bugle employee and the Big Man's true face
The Enforcers -- from left to right: Montana, the Ox, and Fancy Dan (artist's renditions)
A TALE OF FAMILY, FRIENDS & THE FUTURE, BY:
KURT BUSIEK WRITER
PAT OLLIFFE BREAKDOWNS
PAM EKLUND & AL MILGROM FINISHES
RICHARD STARKINGS AND COMICRAFT LETTERING
STEVE MATTSSON COLORS
TOM BREVOORT EDITOR
BOB HARRAS EDITOR IN CHIEF

I'M HARRY OSBORN -- THE SON OF NORMAN OSBORN, HEAD OF OSBORN INDUSTRIES.
THE KIDS AT SCHOOL THINK LIFE MUST BE PRETTY COOL, BEING THE SON OF A MILLIONAIRE WHO CAN BUY ANYTHING, OR GO ANYWHERE --
-- TAKE A LOOK AT THIS! SPIDER-MAN HELPED THE COPS CATCH THE ENFORCERS -- AND THE BIG MAN HAS BEEN CAPTURED, TOO!
ACTUALLY, IT'S MORE LIKE THE COPS HELPED SPIDER-MAN, SINCE --
HARRY!
HOW MANY TIMES HAVE I TOLD YOU NOT TO INTERRUPT ME WHEN I'M WORKING? I'M A BUSY MAN --
-- I JUST CAN'T CLOSE DOWN THE BUSINESS EVERY TIME YOU READ SOME STUPID THING IN THE NEWSPAPER!
4TH QUARTER PROJECTIONS
-- BUT, WELL --
BUT -- I KNEW YOU'D BEEN CLIPPING THE CRIME NEWS RECENTLY, SO I THOUGHT YOU'D WANT TO --
WELL, QUIT THINKING!
HONESTLY, I DON'T KNOW HOW YOU CAN BE SO STUPID --!
WHAT -- WHAT'S HAPPENED TO YOU, DAD --?
YOU'VE CHANGED -- YOU'RE SO ANGRY ALL THE TIME NOW --
-- SOMETIMES... SOMETIMES IT'S NOT SO GREAT.
I'M JUST SICK OF HAVING SUCH A WHINY, STUPID, USELESS SON! NOW GET OUT --
-- I'VE GOT WORK TO DO!
O-OKAY...

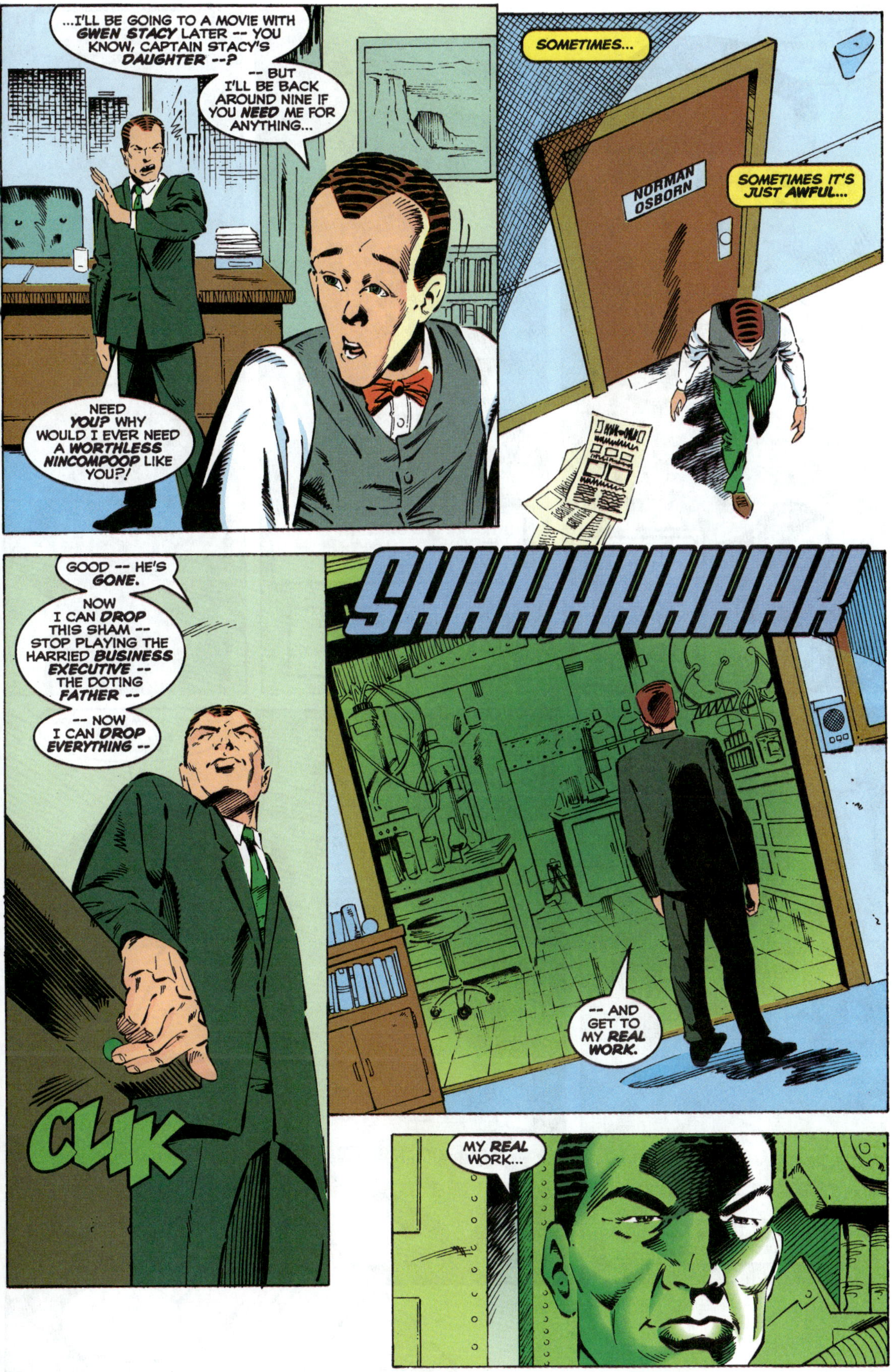

...I'LL BE GOING TO A MOVIE WITH GWEN STACY LATER -- YOU KNOW, CAPTAIN STACY'S DAUGHTER --?
-- BUT I'LL BE BACK AROUND NINE IF YOU NEED ME FOR ANYTHING...
NEED YOU? WHY WOULD I EVER NEED A WORTHLESS NINCOMPOOP LIKE YOU?!

SOMETIMES...
NORMAN OSBORN
SOMETIMES IT'S JUST AWFUL...

IT WASN'T SO LONG AGO OPPORTUNITY STRUCK, WAS IT?
THAT STROMM, MY IDIOT PARTNER, WAS FOOLISH ENOUGH TO EMBEZZLE MONEY FROM THE COMPANY --
"-- LEAVING ME FREE TO HAVE HIM JAILED, AND TAKE COMPLETE CONTROL OF THE FIRM... AND ALL OF STROMM'S NOTES!
"STROMM WAS BRILLIANT -- AND WHEN I TRIED TO ANALYZE HIS WORK, I CREATED A CHEMICAL EXPLOSION --
"-- AN EXPLOSION THAT LEFT ME SEETHING WITH POWER -- AND SEEING MORE CLEARLY THAN EVER BEFORE!
"THE WORLD BELONGS TO THE STRONG --
"-- SO I HIRED THE SCORCHER TO STEAL ME MORE SECRETS --
"-- PLANS FOR EXPERIMENTAL ELECTRONICS EQUIPMENT, COMPACT TURBINE ENGINES, EXPLOSIVES --
"-- PLANS I CAN MAKE FAR BETTER USE OF THAN THE FOOLS WHO CREATED THEM COULD EVER HOPE TO.
"I'VE WORKED LONG AND HARD FOR THIS MOMENT --"
VULTURE ATTACK
BUGLE
DAILY RECORD-LEDGER
WHO IS THE BIG MAN?
POST-BULLETIN
IS CRIME GOING "SUPER"?
"THUG" THATCHER INDICTED, STEEL MOB SMASHED
-- AND NOW I'M READY TO ACT, READY TO STRIKE!
ALL I NEED IS THE RIGHT MOMENT --

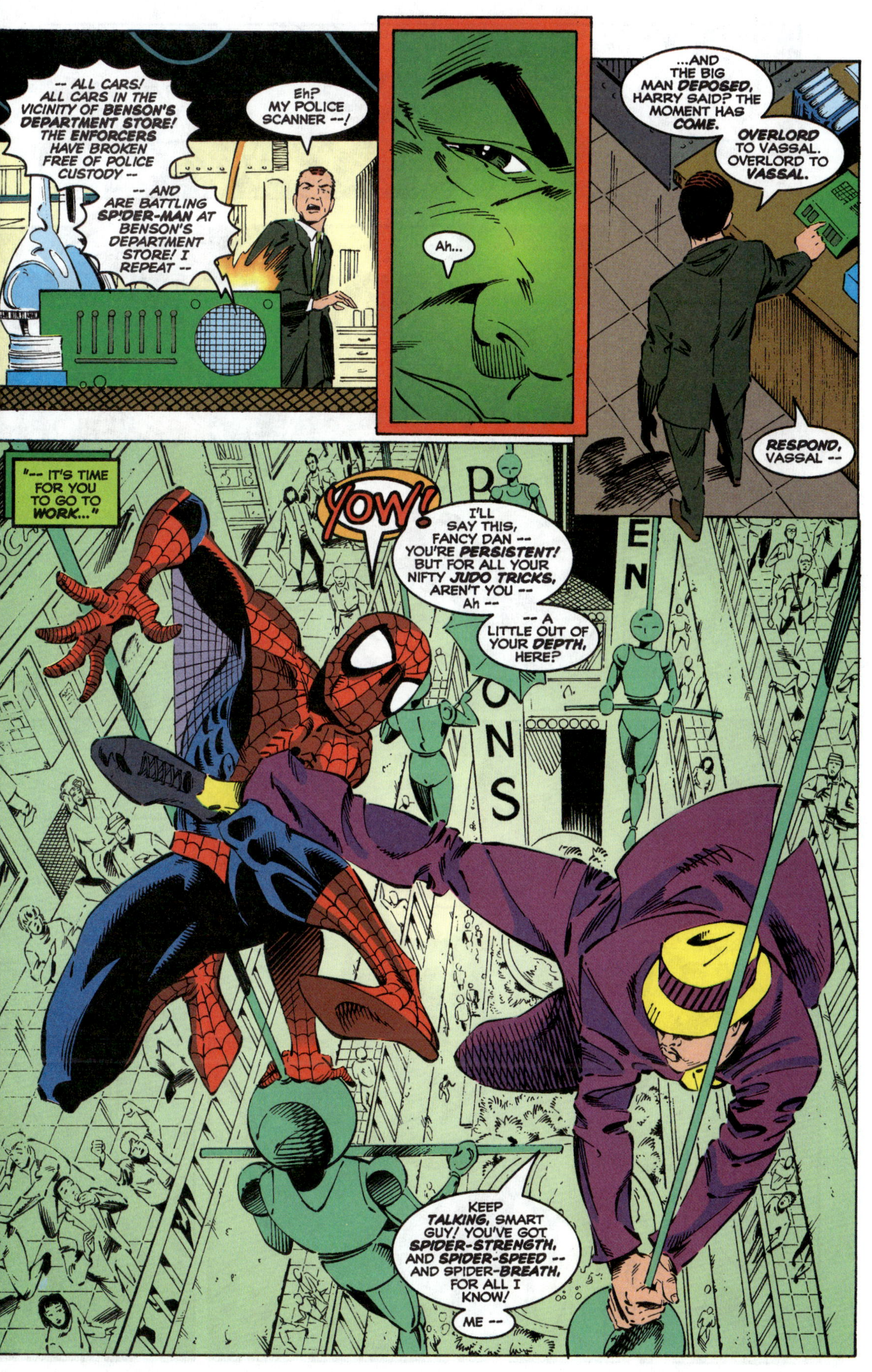
-- ALL CARS! ALL CARS IN THE VICINITY OF BENSON'S DEPARTMENT STORE! THE ENFORCERS HAVE BROKEN FREE OF POLICE CUSTODY --
-- AND ARE BATTLING SPIDER-MAN AT BENSON'S DEPARTMENT STORE! I REPEAT --
Eh? MY POLICE SCANNER --!
Ah...
...AND THE BIG MAN DEPOSED, HARRY SAID? THE MOMENT HAS COME.
OVERLORD TO VASSAL. OVERLORD TO VASSAL.
RESPOND, VASSAL --
"-- IT'S TIME FOR YOU TO GO TO WORK..."
YOW!
I'LL SAY THIS, FANCY DAN -- YOU'RE PERSISTENT! BUT FOR ALL YOUR NIFTY JUDO TRICKS, AREN'T YOU -- Ah --
-- A LITTLE OUT OF YOUR DEPTH, HERE?
KEEP TALKING, SMART GUY! YOU'VE GOT SPIDER-STRENGTH, AND SPIDER-SPEED -- AND SPIDER-BREATH, FOR ALL I KNOW!
ME --

SPIDER-MAN'S FIGHTING THEM! BUT -- ISN'T HE A CRIMINAL, TOO?!
NO -- THE DAILY GLOBE SAYS --
FORGET THE PAPERS -- THEY'RE IN ON IT, TOO! IT WAS A REPORTER BOSSING THOSE GUYS AROUND BEFORE --
-- WHY NOT SPIDER-MAN NOW?!
-- ALL I'VE GOT IS PARTNERS!
Uh-oh!
A LITTLE TIP FOR YOU, WISE GUY!
IT'S HARD TO DODGE WHEN YOU'RE ALREADY IN MID-AIR!
LEMME AT 'IM, MONTANA!
HOLD YER HORSES, OX! OL' MONTANA'S GOIN' T'SHOW THIS BOY A FEW THINGS ABOUT HOG-TYIN' -- WITH HIM AS THE HOG!
Oh, REALLY?
WELL, I'VE GOT A FEW THINGS TO TEACH YOU ABOUT WEB-SLINGING --
AAAH!
-- THE FIRST LESSON'S ABOUT WHEN TO LET GO! OOPS --
-- WELL, WE CAN TRY THAT AGAIN LATER!
MONTANA, YOU --
-OOF!
SLAM
HAPPY LANDINGS, GUYS! AND HEY, FOR THOSE OF YOU IN OUR STUDIO AUDIENCE HAVING TROUBLE KEEPING SCORE --
-- THOSE ARE THE BAD GUYS!
SPLOOSH

C'MERE, YOU!
JUST LEMME GET CLOSE ENOUGH -- AN' I'LL WIPE THAT SMILE OFF YER FACE!
BOY, OX --
-- YOU REALLY ARE AS DUMB AS YOU LOOK, AREN'T YOU?
Huh?
FIRST, I DON'T HAVE A SMILE ON MY FACE -- I DON'T EVEN HAVE A MOUTH!
SECOND --
-- KEEPING IN MIND THAT THERE'S NO ORNAMENTAL FOUNTAIN UNDER US, LIKE THERE WAS UNDER MONTANA AND FANCY DAN --
-- HERE I AM!
NOW WHAT WAS IT YOU WANTED TO GET CLOSE ENOUGH FOR?
Ah --
-- Ah --
SKZAKK
"SKZAKK?" WHO SAID "SKZ --
Uh-oh! THAT ELEVATOR --!
AAAAAAAA

SOMEONE'S CUT THE **CABLE** -- AND BUSTED THE **EMERGENCY BRAKES**, TO BOOT!

GOTTA MOVE **FAST**, BEFORE IT --

AAAH!

FEELS LIKE... I TORE MY **ARMS**... OUT OF THEIR **SOCKETS**...

BUT **STILL**...

THWIP

...WHO WANTS TO BET THAT TOMORROW'S BUGLE EXPLAINS HOW I ***"TERRORIZED AN ELEVATOR FULL OF INNOCENT SHOPPERS"***?!

NOW TO FIND OUT **WHO** CUT THE --

IT WAS **I**, SPIDER-MAN!

CALL ME... *the* **HEADSMAN!**

I'VE SAID IT **BEFORE** AND I'LL SAY IT **AGAIN** --

--*Uh-oh!*

SWATT

OH, MAN... HE'S FASTER THAN HE LOOKS...
HE'S DOWN! LET'S GET HIM!
HOLD, ENFORCERS!
AND WHOSE LITTLE BOY ARE YOU?
DOES IT MATTER? I SAVED YOU FROM CAPTURE, AND YOU OWE ME.
MEET ME AT THIS ADDRESS AT TEN O'CLOCK SHARP!
NOW GO --
-- I'LL TAKE CARE OF SPIDER-MAN!

SHUUKK
AAH!
M-MY FACE --!
YOU'RE GOOD, BOY! GOOD ENOUGH TO KEEP YOUR HEAD ON YOUR SHOULDERS --
-- BUT NOT SO GOOD AS TO ESCAPE DAMAGE ENTIRELY. Eh?
IF -- IF ANYONE SEES --!
HAHAHAHAHA
RUN, SPIDER-MAN! RUN LIKE THE SCARED RABBIT YOU ARE! AND KNOW THAT IF WE MEET AGAIN --
-- IT'LL GO FAR WORSE FOR YOU!
WHY IS HE RUNNING? ISN'T HE GOING TO PROTECT US?
SPIDER-MAN'S TURNED COWARD! OR MAYBE --
-- MAYBE HE DOES HAVE SOMETHING TO HIDE!
YEAH, YEAH, YEAH!
SOME DAYS --

"-- SOME DAYS YOU JUST CAN'T WIN FOR LOSING!"
I JUST WISH I COULD HELP HIM IN SOME WAY, YOU KNOW? I WISH I COULD DO SOMETHING FOR HIM --
-- SHOW HIM I'M NOT THE USELESS KID HE THINKS I AM!
I KNOW, HARRY. SOMETIMES, WHEN MY DAD'S WRAPPED UP IN ONE OF HIS POLICE CASES --
BENSON'S
-- WELL, IT'S ALL I CAN DO TO MAKE HIM REMEMBER TO EAT!
YOUR DAD. I USED TO THINK MY DAD WAS LIKE YOUR DAD, GWEN, BUT --
MAYBE IT'D BE BETTER IF YOU DON'T THINK ABOUT IT SO MUCH, HARRY. LET'S TALK ABOUT SOMETHING ELSE, LIKE WHAT MOVIE WE'RE GOING TO --
--SAAH!
H-huh--?!
Oh! SORRY, SORRY --
-- I WASN'T LOOKING WHERE I WAS --
--GUHH!
UFF!
KRAK
WHUMP

-- SO THERE I AM, GOING OUT FOR A LONG BOMB, WHEN --
-- HEY!
LOOK AT THAT, FLASH -- A ROLL OF FILM, OUT FOR AN AFTERNOON STROLL. NOT SOMETHING YOU SEE EVERY DAY...
TEK
TEK
TEK
HEY! I NEED THAT, JASON! THAT'S MINE!
Oh, AND THE FILM HAS A PET -- PETER PARKER, MIDTOWN HIGH'S FAVORITE TOTAL NONENTITY!
WHAT IS IT, PARKER -- YOUR AUNT SEND BACK VACATION SNAPS FROM FLORIDA AND YOU'RE DESPERATE TO SEE THE CANASTA LEAGUE IN ACTION?
NEVER MIND, JASON!
JUST GIVE IT BACK -- I DON'T HAVE TIME TO LISTEN TO YOU FLAPPING YOUR JAW!
NAB
WELL, HE WAS IN A MOOD, WASN'T HE--?
Aw, WHO CARES? LET'S GET INTO BENSON'S --
-- AND FIND OUT IF THERE'S ANYTHING LEFT TO SEE FROM THE SPIDEY FIGHT! MAYBE WE CAN GET A SOUVENIR OR SOMETHING!
YOU COMING, SALLY?
Hm? SURE, SURE -- RIGHT BEHIND YOU.
I THINK I RECOGNIZE THE BIG GUY -- HE'S QUARTERBACK FOR SOME HIGH SCHOOL IN QUEENS THAT TROUNCED STANDARD ALL LAST SEASON.
Oh WELL, IT'S NOT IMPORTANT. LET'S GET TO THAT MOVIE, SHALL WE?
SURE, HARRY. I JUST WONDER --

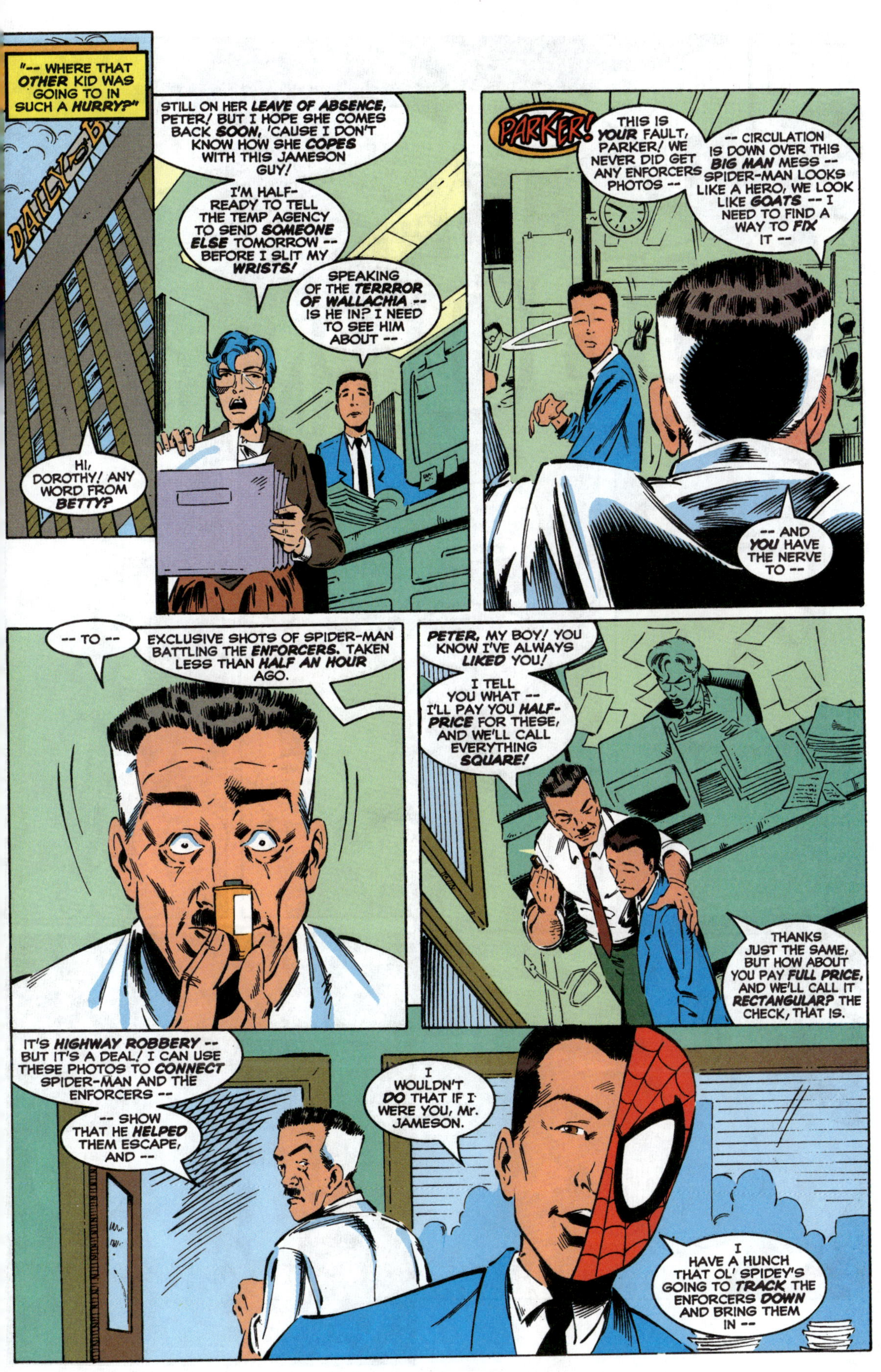
"-- WHERE THAT OTHER KID WAS GOING TO IN SUCH A HURRY?"
DAILY B
HI, DOROTHY! ANY WORD FROM BETTY?
STILL ON HER LEAVE OF ABSENCE, PETER! BUT I HOPE SHE COMES BACK SOON, 'CAUSE I DON'T KNOW HOW SHE COPES WITH THIS JAMESON GUY!
I'M HALF-READY TO TELL THE TEMP AGENCY TO SEND SOMEONE ELSE TOMORROW -- BEFORE I SLIT MY WRISTS!
SPEAKING OF THE TERRROR OF WALLACHIA -- IS HE IN? I NEED TO SEE HIM ABOUT --
PARKER!
THIS IS YOUR FAULT, PARKER! WE NEVER DID GET ANY ENFORCERS PHOTOS --
-- CIRCULATION IS DOWN OVER THIS BIG MAN MESS -- SPIDER-MAN LOOKS LIKE A HERO, WE LOOK LIKE GOATS -- I NEED TO FIND A WAY TO FIX IT --
-- AND YOU HAVE THE NERVE TO --
-- TO --
EXCLUSIVE SHOTS OF SPIDER-MAN BATTLING THE ENFORCERS. TAKEN LESS THAN HALF AN HOUR AGO.
PETER, MY BOY! YOU KNOW I'VE ALWAYS LIKED YOU!
I TELL YOU WHAT -- I'LL PAY YOU HALF-PRICE FOR THESE, AND WE'LL CALL EVERYTHING SQUARE!
THANKS JUST THE SAME, BUT HOW ABOUT YOU PAY FULL PRICE, AND WE'LL CALL IT RECTANGULAR? THE CHECK, THAT IS.
IT'S HIGHWAY ROBBERY -- BUT IT'S A DEAL! I CAN USE THESE PHOTOS TO CONNECT SPIDER-MAN AND THE ENFORCERS --
-- SHOW THAT HE HELPED THEM ESCAPE, AND --
I WOULDN'T DO THAT IF I WERE YOU, Mr. JAMESON.
I HAVE A HUNCH THAT OL' SPIDEY'S GOING TO TRACK THE ENFORCERS DOWN AND BRING THEM IN --

"-- AND SOON!"
IT'S NOT FAIR.
DAD'S LOCKED HIMSELF IN HIS LAB AGAIN, AND HE WON'T EVEN TALK TO ME.
I DON'T EVEN KNOW WHAT I DID WRONG. IF HE'D TELL ME, I'D FIX IT. WHAT-EVER IT IS.
IF HE'D JUST TELL ME...
OSBORN CH
CRNK
Huh? WHAT'S THAT?
THE LOADING DOCK'S CLOSED! THERE SHOULDN'T BE ANYB --
THIS IS TH'PLACE, Huh? DON'T LOOK LIKE MUCH.
IT'S NOT WHAT'S ON THE OUTSIDE THAT MATTERS, OX -- EXCEPT IN YOUR CASE.
COME ON -- LET'S GET INSIDE.
THAT -- THAT WAS THE ENFORCERS!
B-BUT --
-- WHAT ARE THEY DOING HERE?
THEY COULD HURT MY DAD --
WHAT DO I DO --?!
Huh?!
SPIDER-MAN! HE MUST BE LOOKING FOR THEM! WELL --
-- I'D BETTER MAKE SURE HE FINDS THEM, THEN!

PFOON
AN OSBORN #4 DISTRESS FLARE!
PART OF THE OSBORN CATALOG FOR 27 YEARS! DEPENDABLE, INEXPENSIVE -- AND COAST GUARD RECOMMENDED!
Hm?
HE SAW IT! HE'S COMING THIS WAY!
BOY --
"-- DAD CAN'T SAY I SCREWED UP THIS TIME!"
THIS WAY, GENTLEMEN.
THIS WAY TO WHAT, HEADSMAN? YOU DID US A FAVOR EARLIER --
-- BUT THAT ONLY BUYS YOU SO MUCH. WHAT'S YOUR GAME?
YOU'LL KNOW IN DUE TIME, FANCY DAN. FOR NOW, JUST --
AW, C'MON, HEADSY -- DON'T KEEP US IN THE DARK!
WHAT, YOU'RE GOING TO ROB THE PLACE FOR SOME GETAWAY CASH, OR SOMETHING? BE A PAL, SPIT IT OUT --
-- I LIKE MY BADDIES TO EXPLAIN THEIR PLANS BEFORE I MUSS 'EM UP!
SPIDER-MAN!

GET HIM, BOYS!
GIVE ME A BREAK, GUYS!
LOOK, YOU THREE MIGHT HAVE AN ADVANTAGE OUT IN THE OPEN, WHERE YOU CAN BRING YOUR ABILITIES TO BEAR --
-- AND I'M SAYING MIGHT, MIND YOU --
H-HEY!
-- BUT IN CLOSE QUARTERS, IN THE DARK, STUMBLING INTO EACH OTHER --
-- I MEAN, LET'S GET SERIOUS HERE!
WAKT
OW!!
DAD, DAD -- CAN YOU HEAR ME?
IT'S GONNA BE OKAY, DAD -- THE ENFORCERS ARE HERE, BUT I BROUGHT SPIDER-MAN IN, AND HE'LL TAKE CARE OF THEM!
NOTHING TO WORRY ABOUT, DAD!
NORM
THIS IS INFURIATING!
I BEAT HIM -- I HUMILIATED HIM -- AND HERE HE IS, LAUGHING AND MAKING JOKES, LIKE NOTHING HAPPENED!
SPIDER-MAN --

-- I'VE GOT A BONE TO PICK WITH YOU!!
YEAH? WHAT A COINCIDENCE!
SHZUKK
DO YOU HAVE ANY IDEA HOW HARD IT IS TO SEW UP A MASK LIKE MINE SO THE SEAMS DON'T SHOW? DO YOU?
Ah-ah! I'M NOT OVER THERE ANY-MORE!
I'M OVER HERE NOW! OR WAIT --
-- AM I OVER HERE?
BLAST YOU, SPIDER-MAN --
-- WHEREVER YOU JUMP -- WHEREVER YOU DODGE --
Ahh --
-- POIFECT!
ZZCHUKK
-- I'LL SLICE YOU IN TWO!!

HEADSMAN -- NO! THE SCRAP BIN --
-- YOU CUT THROUGH THE SUPPORT --!
SHRAAMMBBL
THAT TAKES CARE OF THE ENFORCERS -- AND ALL I HAD TO DO WAS WALK YOU THROUGH IT!
POK
NOW LET'S SEE WHAT HAPPENS --
"-- WHEN WE DISCONNECT THAT OVERSIZED CLEAVER OF YOURS FROM ITS POWER SOURCE!"
KRIKAK BKAKK
MY POWER PACK --!
YOU'VE SHORTED OUT MY POWER PACK!
GEE, DID I DO THAT? A "SCARED RABBIT" LIKE ME? NAW, HEADS, YOU MUST BE CONFUSED --
KIXXSKAKT
SPIDER-MAN...
Ah, I'M GOING TO HAVE TO GET BACK TO YOU, HEADS...

...GOING TO...CRUSH YOU...SPIDER-MAN...
LOOK, OX, YOU'VE HAD A ROUGH DAY -- ESPECIALLY WITH THAT LOAD OF SCRAP DUMPED ON YOU. DO US BOTH A FAVOR, WILL YOU --
KRAK
-- LIE DOWN AND GO TO SLEEP!
Oh, GREAT.
THE OX DIDN'T SLOW ME UP MUCH, BUT IT WAS ENOUGH FOR THE HEADS-MAN TO GET AWAY --
--AND AT THE SPEED THAT PLATFORM OF HIS TRAVELS, HE'LL LOSE HIMSELF IN THE BACK-ALLEYS BEFORE I COULD CATCH UP TO HIM!
Oh, WELL. AT LEAST I CAUGHT THE GUYS I WAS AFTER.
THAT'S GOTTA COUNT FOR SOMETHING, RIGHT?

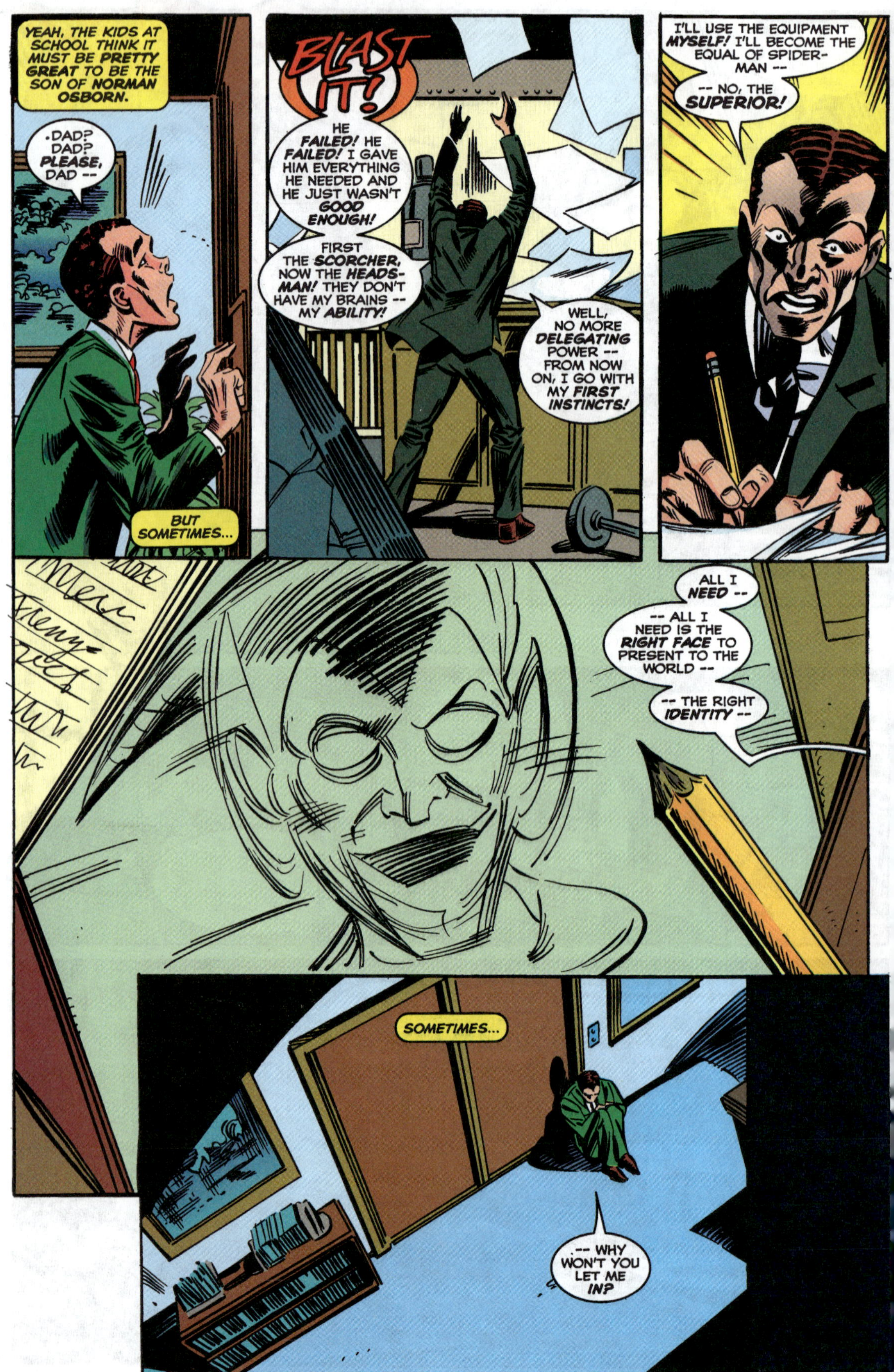
YEAH, THE KIDS AT SCHOOL THINK IT MUST BE PRETTY GREAT TO BE THE SON OF NORMAN OSBORN.
·DAD? DAD? PLEASE, DAD --
BUT SOMETIMES...
BLAST IT!
HE FAILED! HE FAILED! I GAVE HIM EVERYTHING HE NEEDED AND HE JUST WASN'T GOOD ENOUGH!
FIRST THE SCORCHER, NOW THE HEADSMAN! THEY DON'T HAVE MY BRAINS -- MY ABILITY!
WELL, NO MORE DELEGATING POWER -- FROM NOW ON, I GO WITH MY FIRST INSTINCTS!
I'LL USE THE EQUIPMENT MYSELF! I'LL BECOME THE EQUAL OF SPIDER-MAN --
-- NO, THE SUPERIOR!
ALL I NEED --
-- ALL I NEED IS THE RIGHT FACE TO PRESENT TO THE WORLD --
-- THE RIGHT IDENTITY --
SOMETIMES...
-- WHY WON'T YOU LET ME IN?